Cosmic Corks, Castles and Cat Killers

An Anna Ambleside Adventure

By Gail Meglitsch

Printed in the United States of America
First Printing: March 2016
Published by Sojourn Publishing, LLC

ISBN: 978-1-62747-188-6
Ebook ISBN: 978-1-62747-189-3

Disclaimers

Acknowledgments

Special credit goes to Rowan Tipton, plot consultant, researcher, first reader, long suffering chef, housekeeper and jack-of-all-trades extraordinaire.

Without the support of my pan-national family, Steven Meglitsch in particular, the Dragonhome family-that-chose-itself, and Tom Bird's beta group of authors this book would never have seen the light of day.

For Alison and Paul Meglitsch,

**mid-twentieth century adventurers
who traveled around the world on a shoe-string
budget with three unruly kids in tow**

Part One

On the SS Liberté in New York Harbor,
June 17, 1954

I
Day of Departure

Thursday morning at the railing on B deck
Nettie

There is something undeniably dramatic about a great ocean liner's moment of departure. Festooned with streamers, our ship towers over the quay crowded with laughing, cheering, sobbing well-wishers gathered to see family and friends off. Passengers around me lean over the railings waving, excited, eager, scared or heartbroken. Dock workers wrestle coils of rope thick as a man's leg, freeing the SS Liberté from her moorings. Tugboats tow her majestically out of her berth.

Goodbyes depress me even when I have no one to say goodbye to. My heart aches for the past or the future or both. I turn away to go to our cabin to unpack.

A haughty couple passing me on the companionway stairs gives me a disapproving look but I ignore them. The man turns to his wife saying, "Ich habe gehoert, wird's noch kaelter." *(I heard it's going to get colder.)*

Oh God! Breaking into a sweat, I grab hold of the handrail to steady myself. It's embarrassing, but even after ten years the sound of someone speaking German shakes me to the core.

"Ja, ein Sturm kommt bestimmt aus dem Norden," she answers. *(Yes, a storm is certainly coming from the North.)*

I reel, my knees buckle. In my mind it is a German soldier I hear speaking those words.

He was right. The wind did turn cold and what had been a light drizzle was quickly turning to rain. Both the officer and the soldier hurried back to the shelter of their car, leaving me standing in the rain by my bicycle, the contents of my satchel scattered on the road around me.

Numb, I lean against the wall of the Grand Salon at the foot of the stairs. Five minutes later, Anna, my recently acquired step-niece, finds me there.

"I wondered where you disappeared to," she says with barely contained excitement.

That could have been me sixteen years ago on my way to the Sorbonne, eager to set the world on fire. As it happened, two years later Hitler beat me to it. Lord, I wish I still had the innocence to share Anna's glowing exuberance, but I don't.

"We're going up to A deck to watch New York City go by. You want to come?" she asks.

"No, girl, I've seen enough of New York this week to last a lifetime. It looks like rain anyway," I sigh. "I'm going down to our cabin to unpack and grab the lower berth. Tough luck. That leaves you stuck up top."

The "we" Anna is referring to is a pretty teenager waiting at the top of the companionway anxiously eyeing a pair of little boys squealing and darting around on the deck behind her.

"It's a damn good thing most passengers are grownups," I say, shaking my head at their antics.

"Don't try to tell me you think you're a grownup, Nettie," Anna teases.

"Show some respect for your elders, child. I've invested thirty-four years 'growing up' to my current height of fifty-nine inches and attained profound wisdom in the process."

"So what? I've got five inches on you so I must be five times wiser, right, Moira?" Anna turns to her new friend but the girl is off in pursuit of her kid brothers. "Never mind," Anna says. "You can meet Moira later. She's as impressed as all get out with the gorgeous turquoise on your fingers."

I involuntarily look down at the silver rings on all seven and a half of my fingers and mutter under my breath, "The ones that are left, that is."

"Oh, well. If you want to miss all the fun, go ahead and unpack," Anna grins. "The view is better from the top bunk anyway."

I do like this bright new niece of mine. Framed in the doorway above me, she is a lovely sight, long blonde hair gently blowing in the breeze. She has the kind of beauty that will age well. She'll be more beautiful at thirty than she is at eighteen.

Still shaken by my encounter with the Germans, I reluctantly continue to our cabin. Half way there I change my mind. Here I am surrounded by doctors, lawyers, and Indian chiefs, not to mention haughty Germans, all puffed up and full of themselves with nothing to do but kill time for six-and-a-half days. What an irresistible opportunity. The irreverent trouble-maker in me spontaneously bursts out laughing. I didn't feel much like unpacking anyway.

I throw off my maudlin mood and make my way back up to the aft lounge where I find just what I'm looking for, some exceptionally stuffy school teachers from Ohio eager to talk. It doesn't take long to go through everything they have to say worth challenging. I smile to myself at their outrage when I suggest Marx at least had his heart in the right place. I give up. I know it's probably still a mistake, but I head back down to our cabin anyway.

Thursday morning on the sports deck
Anna

I can't help looking back at my beautiful, eccentric new aunt as she goes inside. She looks sort of, I don't know, out of place in a wild, wonderful way. Her bright flowing gown and all those strings of beads around her neck are so cool. So is the way her long purple scarf doesn't ever quite manage to tame that wild red hair. I've never met anyone like her. Just trying to keep up with her almost counts as an adventure.

And I'm really doing it. I'm having a real, honest-to-goodness adventure on a real ship on my way to Europe. I love it. My emergency sketch book is in my pocketbook but I'm leaving it there for now. I managed a quick sketch of the tugboats casting off but black and white just won't get it for the colors of the city and sea. Oh, well. This isn't the time to be doing watercolors.

The ocean goes on and on out there, seven days of it between me and Europe. Geez, what a strange feeling. The Great Lakes seem like an ocean but this is something different. Maybe it's the smell or something, but this is a cool new experience. I love it. I'm really, really on a ship in the ocean on the way to Europe.

I sure lucked out finding someone as cool as Moira to be friends with already. I bet she's up there at the railing at the back ...uh, stern of the boat ... I mean ship. Oh, well, whatever. I better go catch up with her up on deck.

Boy, it sure does takes a long time to get all the way out to sea. Moira's father points out all the landmarks, like the Statue of Liberty and Ellis Island. I got to say, this is a real different side of New York we're seeing, not that I've seen that many sides of New York. I just can't believe this is really happening. I really am on an ocean liner headed out to sea. Wow.

Watching the pilot boat leave is really neat. We wave but nobody waves back. Next we go over and join Moira's mother by the postage-stamp size swimming pool. I sure do like the Jacobsons. Heck, I even like Moira's awful kid brothers, the terrible twins. Wherever they are, you can bet your life there's a lot of noise and commotion.

Moira's big brother, Ted, is nowhere around. I only saw him for a minute but that was enough to see he's cute as all get out. I bite my tongue to keep from asking about him. I ask Mrs. Jacobson about the whole family instead. They come from Boston but none of the kids have seen their English grandparents, so that's where they're going.

"Your Mother is quite a character, isn't she?" Mrs. Jacobson says with an off handed smile. I'm getting used to that sneaky approach to asking about Nettie. Everybody is curious about her but she doesn't seem to care. Oh, well.

"Nettie is my great aunt, not my mother," I tell Mrs. Jacobson. "She became my great step-aunt just two weeks ago when Mom re-married and I got a new stepfather."

"Daddy is actually my stepfather, too," Moira volunteers. "I don't remember my first one. He got killed in the war when I was too little to remember."

Moira and I sure have a lot in common even if she's into the music, not art. Her English father was shot down in North Africa, mine was killed at Guadalcanal and our mothers were both nurses. Mom still is. When Moira's dad got shot down, her mom married the American pilot who was her patient. She's a housewife now, but my mom hasn't been any kind of a wife until the week before last.

It sure is easy to tell that Mr. Jacobson isn't Moira and Ted's real dad. The monster twins are blonde and blue eyed like him, not brunette. Moira is cute as all get out but Ted is just gorgeous. Marlon Brando has him beat, but not by a lot. Too bad he isn't around much. Moira says he's off pouting about missing out on baseball season and doesn't care a bit about meeting his English grandparents.

I tell Moira and Mrs. Jacobson all about Nettie's London meeting and how we're renting a car and spending the whole summer going all over England and Scotland staying in youth hostels on the way. Boy, is this summer ever a dream come true. Anna Ambleside, world traveler.

"Okay, chatterboxes," Mrs. Jacobson interrupts. "Meals are a formal affair on shipboard. We'll have to dress for dinner and at least make ourselves presentable for luncheon."

"What does it mean, dress for dinner? We're hosteling," I panic. "I don't have any fancy clothes to wear."

"I understand they wear evening attire up in first class," Mrs. Jacobson smiles. "In tourist class it's less formal. People tend to put on their Sunday best but it's not necessary."

"You look gorgeous just like you are," Moira's brother says, coming up behind me. "I'm Ted and you are?"

Oh, drat, why is it that when you need to say something clever your mind goes blank?

"Annie, my name is Annie ... Anna," I stammered. "You startled me." Brilliant, just brilliant, Annie. All you need to do now is blush or giggle.

"What you have on will do just fine for lunch as long as you put on different shoes," Mrs. Jacobson assures me. "Just remember that sportswear is frowned on and slacks or shorts of any sort are deemed completely unacceptable."

"Well, Annie Annie Anna, we're on H deck, somewhere in the middle on the port side," Ted says. "If you're going our way, I'll walk you there."

"It's just Anna but people who know me usually call me Annie. We're on G, somewhere near the back ... uh, stern, but I don't know which side," I say trying to sound cool. "It's cabin number 12 and you can see the quay out the porthole."

"Okay then, Annie, you're in the fancy cabins. Lucky you. All four of us Jacobson males are sharing a four-berth cabin down on H deck. At least it isn't third class."

"You call bunk beds, a straight-backed chair, and a dresser with four little drawers fancy?"

"Hey, anywhere away from the terrible twosome counts as the Ritz, babe."

Oh, be still my heart. This voyage just got a whole lot more interesting.

Later Thursday morning in cabin 12 on G deck
Nettie

We're traveling light. It takes only a few minutes to unpack. Alone, the memory of the German couple haunts me. I haven't been shaken like this for a long time. I know from bitter experience that I need to get the hell out of this cabin and do something, anything, but I can't seem to make myself move. I blink back tears and collapse on my bunk, still numb.

I was on the very outskirts of Paris when I came on the Germans changing a flat tire. An officer impatiently paced back and forth smoking while his driver wrestled with the jack. Since they weren't on patrol I prayed they would simply let me pass. My hopes were dashed when the officer flagged me down.

I did my best to look bashful rather than terrified as I produced my identity papers. The papers were genuine enough but they were for my landlady's granddaughter, not me. If Claudette were still alive she'd have been seventeen. I was slight. My freckles and neat red braids helped but I was, in fact, twenty-two. The real problem though was my accent. My French was good but my accent was unmistakably American.

"Where are you off to on this rainy afternoon, ma cherie?" the officer asked in such terrible French I gratefully forgave him the lecherous look on his face.

"I am on my way to Dreux to care for my grand-mere who is ill, Monsieur," I said in my best school-girl voice.

At that moment the other soldier finished with the flat and strolled over.

"You are American," he accused in flawless French.

I had rehearsed my story a hundred times, but my voice still shook. Answering him in French, I said "Mais non, Monsieur. I am French. My mother married an American when I was five years old. She died when I was eleven and my stepfather sent me back here to the family."

The officer gave my papers a suspicious look and glanced at my bulging satchel. I concentrated on finding just the right amount of innocent-but-indignant irritation as his underling unlatched my case, scattering my neatly folded clothes onto the wet pavement.

As Monsieur Jean had hoped, the officer immediately focused on the package wrapped in tissue paper and tied with a pink ribbon. Completely ignoring the all-important battered teddy bear in its convent school uniform, he handed the gift to the officer. He unwrapped the old fashioned hand-knit bed jacket and held it up in disgust. "Useless," he sneered. "No woman under sixty would wear something like this even to keep warm." Both men laughed.

The wind caught the wrapping with its attached letter and blew it across the road.

"Ja, ein Sturm kommt bestimmt aus dem Norden." (Yes, a storm is certainly coming from the North,)

The officer gave the sky an irritated look and sent his underling to chase down paper and letter. The soldier handed the officer Jean's carefully worded note.

"Best wishes for a speedy recovery, ma mere. Make sure Claudette remembers to study her German," he read.

I tried not to cringe as they tossed the teddy bear on the ground to dig out the worn German primer with Claudette's name on the fly leaf. The officer leafed through the book suspiciously, scrutinizing each page.

"Mais je suis Francais," I protested. "I have the right to circulate."

It had been drizzling all day, but mercifully it picked that moment to rain in earnest. Tossing the bed jacket and book in a puddle, the two men sprinted back to their car, leaving me weak with relief.

Unfortunately I had counted my blessings too soon. Now here in my cabin on the SS Liberté, I sit up, banging my head on the upper berth and cursing my stupidity. How could I have overlooked that fact that after all this time Germans might well be traveling on a French ship? It's a damn shame that the idea of traveling on the SS Liberté tickled me so much. The musical "French Line" was actually filmed right here on this ship. Of course I knew that Jane Russell was strutting her stuff in first class but I still couldn't resist. But then, my original booking had been for first class. When I invited Anna at the last minute, tourist class was the best they could come up with, but at least we have a porthole.

I look at my watch. I need something to keep me from thinking too much. I wash my face and make my way to the ship's library to look for something to read until I meet Anna for lunch.

Wouldn't you know, it would be my luck that the damn Ohio school teachers show up still indignant about Marx and pursue me into the library. I should never have said that it was French aristocrats' own fault that they got their heads cut off. Noblesse oblige may be a French word but the concept strictly belonged to their gentler British counterparts.

Hell, I should have followed my first impulse and gone up to the terrace lounge, had a glass of wine and simply hung out. First impulses, like first impressions should never be ignored. Damn.

Midday Thursday in the dining salon
Anna

Off with the sneakers, on with the flats. I meet Nettie outside the dining salon just as a waiter strikes a huge silver gong. Gosh, I had no idea traveling by boat would be so fancy. All this seems even more foreign than the people talking in other languages.

Nettie sure was right. The dining room looks just like the one in the Jane Russell movie. Wow. There are art deco chandeliers, linen tableclothes, china, crystal, a whole row of silverware at every place and even a waiter in a white coat behind every other chair. If this is tourist class, what must first class be like? It's a weird feeling, like I really don't belong here.

I look around for the Jacobsons but we all have assigned seats. All the other guys at the table are men but so are most of the passengers. All eight of us speak English, which is a darn good thing. Dollars to donuts, they plan it that way.

Next to me on one side there's a New York newspaper editor and a priest from Canada. The old Englishman on the other side has a red face and snorts like a donkey when he laughs.

Nettie's lucky. All the young guys are on her side of the table. The Australian brothers are from Tasmania. They aren't a whole lot older than me but they are loud and call everyone matey. I can hardly make out anything the good-looking Scotsman on her other side says because of his thick accent.

This would be kind of neat if I knew what to do. I count twelve pieces of silverware on the white tablecloth in front of me and there's a silver ring around my napkin. Nettie whispers that I should start with the outside fork first but there's an even better trick. You just spot somebody who looks like they know what they're doing and do the same thing.

I've heard of seven-course meals but I never really believed in them until now. The waiter assigned to me and the old Englishman stands behind us the whole time, serving one thing after another. He also picks up my nap ... I mean serviette, which I naturally drop. Geez, I gotta learn to say serviette. Around here napkin means a diaper or other unmentionable things like that. Oh, well.

We're sort of getting to know each other a little by the time we finish the seventh course. Alan and Andy, the Tasmanians, are a lot of fun. Even the Canadian priest takes Nettie's weirder opinions with a grain of salt. I'm pretty sure Angus, the Scotsman, is flirting with me. He's as good-looking as he can be but I can't make out half of what he says. Oh, well. He's a bit too old for me anyway.

Nettie says the after-dinner entertainment in the Grand Salon isn't very exciting so we're going to one of the lounges to have a drink with the guys from our table. That's when Ted and Moira catch up with us. The movie that's showing down in C deck salon is the "The Quiet Man" with John Wayne, which I haven't seen yet so I go with them. Nettie won't miss me much the way all the guys are flirting with her.

II

The Second Day of the Voyage

Friday morning in cabin 12 on deck G
Anna

I gotta tell you, if this narrow bunk wasn't rocking back and forth, I'd have to pinch myself to know I'm awake. I just can't get used to the idea that I'm on an honest-to-goodness adventure heading out to sea on a real ocean liner.

One thing's sure. Going anywhere with my wild new great-aunt is going to be an adventure. I absolutely adore Nettie even though she embarrasses me half to death. She is so cool and so, so beautiful. Not only that, she's invited me on the kind of adventure I daydreamed about and saved me from Mom's disastrous plan at the same time.

Poor Mom is beside herself. She's scared to death of letting me go off with Nettie but she can't say anything. Nettie is my new stepfather, Jack's aunt. I gotta say that with his Aunt Nettie, Jack scored big with me even before they tied the knot.

Mom can be a pain when she gets ahold of some really stupid idea ... like taking me along on their honeymoon. Geez ... the nice little family she always wanted. Sorry, Mom. It's a bit late for that. I'm going to be a freshman in college in the fall and won't even be living at home. Whoever heard of taking their teenaged kid along on a honeymoon anyway. For smart people, they really are dumb. Thank goodness for Nettie.

That first night Nettie showed up, Mom and I had just had another one of our fights about her stupid plan. I was out in the backyard in what I call a cosmic sandwich. That's when I lie on my back under the big oak tree and spread out my arms, imagining how I'm a little bitty speck on the face of the planet. Then I look up into outer space. I can sort of feel the Earth curving underneath me and the whole universe stretching away up above me. After a while all the chaos of my life just melts away, like Mom crying in the kitchen and my finals the next week.

The sound of a motorcycle coming up the drive brought me back to earth in a hurry. A small woman in bib overalls climbed off. Can you believe it? She had combat boots on and was wearing some kind of exotic felt cap over a wild mop of red hair. Jack came racing out of the house, swung her off the ground and carried her into the house. I knew that he was expecting his Quaker aunt to arrive for the wedding but if that was her, she didn't look like a Quaker to me. And besides that, she was a whole lot younger than he is.

I gave them a few minutes to get settled and for Mom to wipe her eyes and repair her makeup before I wandered into the house. Being a sneaky sort of person, I hung out in the kitchen eavesdropping until I got the lay of the land.

I loved it. Nettie was sitting on the floor with a beer in her hand. She's a little bitty thing but she definitely had Jack's back against the wall.

"You two are flat-ass crazy," she was insisting. "Mother of God on a bicycle, you don't take your kid on your honeymoon. Jack, you're an idiot. I can't believe you intended to put your new stepdaughter in a God-awful position like that."

"You simply don't understand, Nettie," Jack said in that infuriatingly patient and understanding way of his. "Anna and Susan have spent years dreaming and saving up for a trip to Europe. It wouldn't be fair for us to just go off and leave her behind. And after all, Susan and I aren't exactly blushing virgins."

"All the more reason to do the honeymoon up proper, moron. Don't kid yourself, three is a goddamn crowd. If you had the imagination of a codfish, you'd know Anna would hate it. Hell, it just might permanently spoil Europe for her."

Thank you, Nettie! Someone with a clue! Time to abandon eavesdropping and make myself known.

Nettie didn't wait for be introduced. "Nettie Hicks, here," she said. "Got in just in the nick of time. It may be traditional to be a bit nuts the week before a wedding but these two have carried it to extremes. Just tell me they don't plan to dress you up in pink ruffles to play flower girl sprinkling rose petals down the aisle."

"Of course not," Mom snapped. "She's going to be my maid of honor."

Nettie looked over at me and grinned. "I guess the 'she' Susan is referring to is you?"

Mom made a hasty exit to finish getting dinner ready. Jack followed, supposedly to help set the table but really to smooth Mom's ruffled feathers.

By the time dinner was over, I knew Nettie was the kid of Jack's grandfather's second wife and probably the coolest person I'd ever met. On top of that, she'd invited me to go to London with her this summer when she goes to some get-together of the American Friends Service Committee, whatever that is. After that, she wants the two of us to spend the rest of the summer touring around Europe staying in youth hostels. And would you believe it? Jack convinced Mom it was a great idea, or at least to pretend she thought it was.

So that's it. Here I am on a real ocean liner sailing for England. Wow and double wow.

Later Friday in the smoker salon
Henri

"Checkmate," my worthy opponent says, straightening in his chair and rubbing his back. "The ship's bulletin predicts rough weather tonight and my rheumatism concurs."

"Well played, Major," I say and shake his hand.

"It's been a long time since I've played a game that lasted this long," the old soldier groans. "I'm getting too old for this, Henri. I thought you had me at one point."

"So did I," I laugh. "I know the precise move that lost it for me. What say you to a return match tomorrow?"

"It would be my pleasure, sir. I note that today has become tomorrow so I assume you mean Saturday?"

"After midnight, is it?" I say glancing at my watch, "Fifteen minutes into the witching hour and apparently damn near else everyone has retired for the night. What's wrong with these people? I'll stand you to a nightcap. I predict the main lounge won't be deserted."

"You'll have to excuse me, professor. I'm not as young as you are."

"Humph," I can't resist saying. "Nonsense. Age is a secondary issue. You are inarguably better physically equipped to withstand late night rigors than I am."

Embarrassed, he nods and a hands me my cane. "Wear those scars proudly, Henri. You saved the lives of God only knows how many of my pilots and got them home right under the Nazis' noses."

I prefer to conceal those scars with my less than fashionable beard. There's little I can do about the broken nose that leaves me resembling a punch-drunk prizefighter. There once was a time when I considered appearance irrelevant. Ah, youth. Braun, brains and even beauty, we took it all for granted. We were invulnerable, me and the magical woman that made my life a joy. Even the ever-present danger in the French Resistance failed to penetrated our young psyches.

Against my better judgement I order a second brandy. Foolish. I know better than to risk relaxing the invisible walls I keep between me and my memories. I'd be hard put to say which are the more danger-ous, the good ones or the bad ones. Wisely or cowardly, I've returned to France only once since I fled to the ivory towers of the United States after the war. Not precisely after the war, I admit. Initially I was too crippled in body and mind to care if I lived or died. My exodus was necessarily delayed for eighteen months while my sister-in-law patiently convinced me to live, after all.

I heave a sigh and take a sip of the brandy. It's good, but not very good. First rate second rate or maybe second rate first rate, like me.

I must concede that the impulse to return to France even now may be an error. I was plagued by depression for months after the trip to little Henri's christening in '49. Every summer I come to Britain, I break another promise to Albert and Celeste and suffer overwhelming guilt as a consequence. My little godson must be five years old by now and it's a mere twenty-one miles across the damn channel. It's more than time now to close the door on the past and go home.

On the other hand, I can never truly go home. I wish to hell I'd never seen the heap of rubble that had once been the Lisieux Inn. That inn had been in the DuBois family for five generations. The inn, the livery, Grand-pere's big forge, two thirds of Lisieux and my childhood all blown to hell in the D-day bombardment. War-torn as it was, in my eyes France was still beautiful in 1942, but I was young and in love then. Now only ugly memories of loss and death await me there.

I know all too well that this is not a good train of thought. I empty my mind and watch the brandy tilt back and forth in the glass, a sign the rough weather predicted by the major is approaching. I steel myself, take a deep breath and get my head back where it belongs.

Looking around, I see a handful of other tables occupied by fellow night owls. I come to life around midnight and always get my best work done then. As it happens, I also like mornings, rising in the quiet, watching the sunrise while most of the world is still asleep. It's a rare day when I can do both. The prospect of those days becoming more common raises my deflated spirits. I take a sip of brandy and smile.

Blessed be sabbaticals, Fulbright Research Grants and an entire year to work wherever and whenever I please, limited only by the Bodleian and British Libraries hours. There will still be ample opportunity to start work when the sun goes down on those days when my historical research focuses on analysis or working on my book.

I pick up my cane and get to my feet. Leaving the first rate second rate brandy unfinished on the table, I make my careful way across the gently rocking deck and out into the windy night.

III

The Third Day of the Voyage

Early Saturday morning, B deck promenade
Henri

I am surprised to wake up still sitting in a deck chair with a pale sun in my eyes. The sea is rough, it's overcast but unquestionably morning. Saturday morning. I am bereft. A Saturday morning and I'm not at the farm and my forge. Fortunately, Harry's a rule follower. I hazard a guess that he'll be a hell of a lot stricter than I am. God only knows he's big enough to enforce his rules. In all likelihood the place will still be standing when I return.

Young Harry has my sympathy. He'll have to deal with the hangers on whom I've never had the heart to chase away. I warrant Jilly will be his chief headache. Accepting her as an apprentice was questionable if for no other reason that three is one too many. To some extent, I regret the decision but I do want to support the concept of women blacksmiths and blade makers.

I yawn and stretch. The breeze is sufficiently brisk to kick up whitecaps. I find it invigorating and delay going inside. Instead, I simply meditate on life in general. I can't help smiling when I think of the not quite surprise bon voyage party last Saturday. When I arrived at the farm, Alec and the Longmire boys were already making ineffectual attempts to motorize a spit for roasting a full-sized, grown pig.

I actually can't remember when I stopped pretending to be taken in by the story that the Nights of the Round Table just spontaneously happen on the first Saturday of every month. The kids "just happen" to stop by when the sun goes down, bringing guitars and drums and banjos and just about anything else that makes noise. Not to mention hot dogs, marshmallows and beer in great quantities.

Hootenannies of the Round Table? Most definitely a mixed metaphor. I don't believe Pete Seeger has a liking for kings, even ones learning the art of sword making. I'm going to miss my weekend refuge from academia.

Mon Dieu. Could I actually be feeling a touch homesick? Not possible. I'm far too French to ever be an American. Maybe I'm becoming too American to be a Frenchman as well. I rather doubt that I have much in common with the man who limped across the Atlantic seven years ago. I'm still immune to sea sickness, however. I shall grid my loins, wash my face, brush my teeth and see if I can chase down some breakfast.

Saturday morning, in cabin 12 in G deck
Nettie

I roll over and puked in the bucket the steward has so thoughtfully provided and fall back on the pillow. The Atlantic is not supposed to behave like this in June.

The door opens a crack and Anna pokes her head in. There is nothing worse than cheerful people when you feel like shit, or in this case puke.

"Go away. For God's sake get out of here and take your smiling face with you," I snarl.

"Gee, I'm sorry Nettie. I guess I have a cast-iron stomach. There was hardly anyone at breakfast. We've been on B deck watching the wake behind the ship. It's really neat and kind of hypnotizes you. We stayed there a long time but didn't see any dolphins or flying fish. Oh, well. Mr. Jacobson says you only see them closer to the shore."

"Go away. I don't want to hear about it."

"The liaison officer says that the eye of the storm passed north of us. Tomorrow will be a lot calmer and maybe you'll feel better."

"Go away." I lean over and dry heave. There is nothing left in my miserable body but my stomach hasn't gotten the message yet. Whatever possessed me to take up do-gooding? Masochism, obviously. I put the pillow back over my head and retreat to that fuzzy dream - midway between waking and sleeping. I half fear that when I close my eyes I'll be standing in the Paris hospital again. I'll see the man I love more than life itself, battered, broken and dying.

Coming to the hospital was a mistake. It was ridiculous to ever hope we could take up where we left off. He's dying a much decorated hero. I'm the fool whose dumb decision got God only knows how many men killed. Now I'll never know if he could have forgiven me for that mistake. There's no going back in any case. I came out of the Ravensbruck prison camp so broken that I hardly know who I am anymore.

I wake in a paroxysm of choking, coughing and crying. For Christ's sake, why did I book passage on the bloody French Line? I don't want to hear another French word spoken in my life – let alone German. Oh, hell. The French Line isn't to blame for this. It's the ship, any damn ship and the angry ocean. What damn good does it do to be rich enough to afford to fly if my damn conscience won't let me?

I kick off the sheet, suddenly unable to tolerate the restriction. God, I hate the sea, I hate me and ... I hate whiners. I squeeze my eyes shut and will myself back to sleep.

Shivering now from the wet and cold rather than fear, I watched the Germans drive away. It was getting late. There'd been other delays. I'd lost time avoiding the road block at Rue d'Toile and two different patrols. I was still twenty kilometers from Dreux. I might have made it before full dark but it would have been close. A school girl on the road at night in the rain certainly would have aroused suspicion but I was not far from Jacque and Viviane's farm. I weighed the pros and cons of risking going on or spending the night at the farm and delaying delivery of the money until morning. A sharp gust of icy wind decided the issue. I turned down the next country lane that would take me in the direction of a warm dry bed in their safe house and if I was lucky maybe a hot meal.

By the time I got to the farm, I was wet and cold. I stopped among the trees on the hill above the farm, according to protocol. There was an unfamiliar car parked behind the barn, not hidden but not easily visible from the road. Otherwise everything looked normal enough. The dogs were sleeping under the cover of the porch and a wisp of smoke was coming from the chimney. The car could be German but it was old. If the farm had been raided, would it look so normal? I didn't think so. The car probably belonged to some of us just passing through needing a safe place for the night like me.

I didn't think the safe house had been compromised but took the precaution of stashing the money before I went in anyway. Leaving the bike out of sight behind the hedge, I unpacked the teddy bear and made my way through the orchard to the old stone wall overlooking the pasture behind the house. I'd been to the drop site before with Jean when we picked up the desperately needed radio tubes. This section of the wall had been roughly and unnecessarily repaired making the critical loose stone undetectable unless you knew it was there. I did, but it still took me several minutes to locate it. The cavity was empty and had ample room for the teddy.

I was still a good way from the house when the dogs raised the alarm. Jacque came out; recognizing me, he called back the dogs.

"Welcome," he greeted me. "Claudette, Jean's little crack shot, as I recall."

I nodded and let him wheel my bike to the partial cover of the woodshed. If anyone were watching it would look like I was just a neighbor casually dropping by. I smelled the wonderful odor before I even opened the door. There was no sigh of Viviane but the kitchen table was set for two and a big stew pot stood on the stove promising something delicious. I took off my wet blazer and gratefully warmed my hands over the big wood stove.

Coming in behind me, Jacque called, "All clear, everyone." Viviane cautiously came from the back room followed by a man and woman I didn't recognize. What I did recognize was the telltale look of the man dressed as he was in clothes at least two sizes too big for him.

"You two can relax. This is Claudette from one of the Paris cells," Jacque reassured them. "Claudette, meet Lieutenant Billy Smith and Marie, our radio operator. His pick-up got rained out. They are trying to set up something for tomorrow or the next day."

I didn't like the sound of that. The Germans were getting too good at tracing radio transmissions. I guess Marie picked up my concern. Jean keeps telling me work on developing a poker face.

"You needn't worry. The pick-up site this time is a field seven miles from here," Marie told me. "I'll be making all my radio contacts from the loft of a dairy barn near the site, so we won't compromise Jacque and Viviane."

"Marie, you can get the dishes back out and add one for Claudette," Viviane said, taking the lid off the pot on the stove. "Here, Claudette, come slice some more bread for us."

The rabbit stew in the pot was pure luxury. With food rationed, most of us were lucky to get a taste of meat once a week. In the months ahead, I dreamed of that stew. As it was, I was on my second helping when the world as I had known it ended in horror and death.

I suppose we'll never know if someone gave us away or they followed Marie and the airman, not that it really matters. The dogs never barked. The Germans must have silently killed them somehow. A warning probably wouldn't have done much good anyway.

The rape that night was the first of more than I care to count but that first time always remains the most vivid ... lying there in a pool of Jacque's blood with Viviane screaming and

screaming, bent over the table above me under first one Ger-
man, and then another while her husband's life leaked away at
her feet.

I wake in a panic; disoriented for a moment, I look around me and sigh. The room is behaving itself in a somewhat better fashion now and so, thank God, is my stomach. I glance at the clock. Almost dinner time but I don't feel that much better. Struggling out of bed, I put on a robe and head for the bathing salon. After this awful cold, wet evening, a bath is what I need. Oh, yeah, I sigh. That was just another flashback. It's hot and stuffy and a bath is just what I need.

IV

The Fourth Day of the Voyage

Sunday morning, B deck promenade
Henri

Regardless of staying up half the night, I wake up in excellent spirits. I'm glad now that I afforded the luxury of a single-berth cabin. I'd make a poor roommate with the hours I keep. The sea is still a bit on the rough side this morning. Gingerly I stand up and test my balance. Apparently I've missed breakfast so I prevail on Raul, my most accommodating steward, to find me a croissant and a cup of coffee.

Thus fortified, I massage my bad leg and work on strength exercises before tackling my morning workout. That accomplished, I make my way to the bathing salon to dress for the day. The next order of business is to look for Major Gracer and the Swede.

The lounge is devoid of chess players. Disappointed, I investigate the ship's library but fail to find anything worth reading in either the English or French sections. Making a virtue of necessity, I go back to my cabin and retrieve my address book and stationery.

I claim a deck chair on the leeward side of deck D and pick up my pen, intending to communicate my immediate plans with Celeste and Albert. I contemplate letting Jean know that I'm back on this side of the Atlantic, too. Remembering Josette's suicide a year ago, I reject the idea. The four of us were so close before first Claudette and then

Josette were captured. Memories of good times together, those are the ones that truly hurt.

My mood is too good to spoil dwelling on Claudette, Ravensbruck and the probability that she died horribly there. I prefer to fantasize that she was the woman who came to the hospital while I was still in a coma. If she was Claudette though, she failed to leave her name or to return, not that it matters. I was a cripple at the time and none of us came through the war unchanged. Poor Josette. This is not a good train of thought. I slam the door shut on the past.

I'm coming to realize that this is emphatically not the right moment to return to France. Fortunately, the error is correctible. I booked passage to Le Havre but I can make arrangements with the purser to disembark at Plymouth. The visit to Albert and family, I can postpone until Christmas.

The decision taken, my spirits soar. To hell with research. I just acquired an entire month to myself. I take up my pen and start a letter to Dougal Macphail up in Inverness. I've been fairly itching to get back to the medieval forge he's set up. That man's forgotten more about horse armor than I ever knew. I've told Niles repeatedly that the kids reading Military and or Medieval History would benefit from a guest lecture by Dougal but Niles can't get past Macphail's lack of formal education. King College's loss.

On reflection, it occurs to me that lodging in college for an entire year may not suit me. The more I think about it, the better a flat in Oxford with a quiet pub around the corner sounds. I may not take advantage of that offer of lodgings at King's after all.

I consider writing Niles a letter to that effect. Undecided, I watch an unruly gaggle of young people troop by, mostly Americans, an Aussie or two. Their boisterous high spirits are contagious. I haven't had much luck locating a chess partner. Getting some exercise is actually a rather good idea. I put my writing materials away and stroll up to the sports deck to watch them throw quoits around and perhaps join them.

Sunday evening in the aft lounge
Anna

"Ha, we got you," Grady chortles taking the last trick. "Anna and I prove our superiority once again!"

Everybody groans as the Aussie cowboy rakes in our match sticks. I sure am liking all this. In fact, I going to buy a bunch of these decks of cards with the photo of the SS Liberté on the back. They'll make great souvenirs for everybody back home.

"Let's go back to poker. This game is stupid," Ted complains and throws his cards down. Tonight Grady is my partner and Ted is pouting about it.

I hate poker. Bridge is out, now that there are six of us, not that I like bridge that much either. I didn't even know you could play hearts with partners until tonight and I'm loving it.

"Okay, hearts may be a silly game but I'm having fun," I tell everybody. "Poker isn't even a real game as far as I can see. It's just about fooling people. In my opinion it amounts to legalized cheating. If you go back to poker, you can count me out."

It's getting late. It's been a long day and even if was cloudy, I'm going to be sorry for spending so much time sunbathing. My nose is red and my back is starting to hurt already. I'd just as soon go to bed right now.

Being a peacemaker type, Grady grins and stands up. "All right chaps, I'm ready to call it a night, take my ill-gotten gains and get out of here." He rakes in the pile of match sticks. "Do you want to divvy them up, Anna or shall I?" he asks me.

"I don't want them, I don't smoke. I hereby bequeath you my share," I say. Grady and the others head out to the promenade deck. Teddy stands in my way and offers me his arm. I hate people who pout and I'm really disgusted at how possessive he's getting. "I'm tired, Ted, and I have a headache." I ignore his hand and follow the others. He stomps after me.

Moira winks at me. "Come on, Teddy," she says. "Walk me down to my cabin."

Grady hangs back as the others go down the companionway. I'm kind of surprised at how late it is. We're the only people still around except for that surly Russian leaning on the railing in the dark. Grady gives him a funny look, then shrugs his shoulders. I don't think he likes the Russian much.

"It looks like we've been abandoned," Grady grins at me. "I'll walk you to your door."

I smile to myself. It's way out of his way. He has a whole stateroom to himself on D deck. He sure isn't a poor cowboy or I guess that would be a poor "jackaroo." When he stops in a dark spot under one of the suspended lifeboats, I figure he has a kiss in mind. He does.

His kiss is gentle and nice but his hand slips lower on my back than a nice girl allows and I am a nice girl. Darn it. Naturally I pull away. Naturally he whispers the expected declarations of undying love in my ear but doesn't force the issue. He's not as drop-dead gorgeous as Ted but very good looking in a rough sort of way. I like his laugh. In fact, I like him a lot. Gosh, I'm starting to think that it's good thing this sea voyage only lasts a week.

When I get to the cabin Nettie is asleep but she looks peaceful. The barf bucket is gone. This seasickness thing is for the birds. It's a good thing for Nettie that the storm mostly missed us.

I undress and crawl into bed without even brushing my teeth. I forgot that our steward will be coming in the morning to wake us up with cup of tea. Jeepers, there's nothing like being awakened in the middle of a dream by some strange man shoving a cup of milky tea at you. Haven't these people heard of alarm clocks? I climb back down, put on my most modest PJ's and go back to bed.

V

The Fifth Day of the Voyage

Monday morning, in cabin 12 on G deck
Anna

I manage to open one eye. Ian, our steward, is standing there, patiently holding a steaming cup of tea out at me, like I'm the Queen of England or something. I struggle up to a sitting position, take the yucky tea with milk in it and wince. Sunburn. Ouch. Nettie is already up and off somewhere. Just when I need somebody to put sunburn lotion on my back. Drat. Day five of my grand adventure is not getting off to a great start. Oh, well.

I like the way the ship rocks back and forth. It's sort of exciting and makes me think of my trusty cosmic sandwich, only now I'm a cosmic cork. I'm floating on the surface of water stretching out all around me to the empty horizon and it's two miles deep. It's still the same universe stretching off to infinity above me, though. Here I am already having my adventure and I haven't even gotten to Europe yet. Look out, day five. Here I come.

I hop out of bed and very gingerly take off my pajama top. Ouch. Whatever else happens today, I will not be sunbathing. That's the only thing wrong with adventures at sea. Lots of time and nothing to do except sun yourself, sit reading in deck chairs or play games. Oh, well.

You can always eat. I'm only half way to the dining salon when I hear the gong for the first sitting.

After breakfast, I go get my sketch pad from our cabin. I start to panic when I don't see it but it turns out that I left it under the sweater Teddy loaned me. I have a look at my drawings from yesterday. The one I did of Nettie laughing with her head thrown back really isn't too bad. I caught some of the sense of fun and energy but not her irreverence. Geez. She sure does enjoy unsettling people, attacking the status quo with outrageous ideas, what she calls nudging their complacence – but as often as not they end up smiling. You just can't help liking Nettie if you don't despise her, that is.

I look closer and know I didn't get the important stuff right. I missed that sad, distant look she sometimes gets when she thinks no one is watching. Darn and blast. I almost throw it away but close the sketch book instead. Oh, well.

Nettie is quite good at changing the subject when I ask anything about her past, what it was like when she was my age. Jack was just as bad when I asked him about her. She has what she calls her pied-à-terre in the New Orleans French Quarter but I'm pretty sure she's never been married.

I do know she was in school at the Sorbonne around the time that World War II broke out. I can't help wondering about her missing fingers. I kind of think those fingers have something to do with why she does refugee work for the American Friends Service Committee. Maybe not. With her high spirits, she might just want to have adventures same as me. That kind of job can't pay much but she must have money. She didn't even blink at the idea of paying for my trip. I can't help being curious about her.

I go to the mirror, gather up my ponytail, wad it on top of my head and sigh. Nettie is so gorgeous, like a faerie queen or maybe a mischievous pixie princess. She puts on some old rag from the Salvation Army thrift store and ends up looking great – eccentric maybe, but great. I love the way she looks but I could never pull it off. No matter how hard I try I can't make my blonde ponytail do the same things her wild red hair does without trying. I'm just not cut out to be a Nettie so I just have to make do with what I got. At least I'm not ugly and the sun is really bleaching my hair out this summer. It's also given me an ugly sunburn that hurts. Maybe I'll get lucky and it will tan. I get the sunburn lotion out of the top drawer and smear it everywhere I can reach.

"So this is where you've been hiding out," Nettie says. She comes in looking wonderfully wind-blown. "Ted and your Aussie admirer are both looking for you. What's the Aussie's name? Our Tasmanian table-mates just call him mate."

"Everybody calls him Grady but I don't know if it's his first name or last name. I like him," I tell her. I surprise myself by how much I mean it. "He's kind of quiet, not shy, he just keeps his mouth shut, sort of taking it easy. He's got a great sense of humor and isn't as ... well, I guess you'd say pushy, as Teddy is."

"You've got the makings of good taste," she nods. "Ted is full of himself. As far as he's concerned the world revolves around him. Cowboy or not, your Grady is a class act. Remember, shipboard romances are fun, honey, but keep in mind that we get to Plymouth on Wednesday."

"For crying out loud, you're the one with all the guys trailing along behind you, not me."

"Maybe, but you'll note that I'm not holding hands with any of them. I'm down here looking for a little time alone and maybe a quick nap before dinner," Nettie hesitates and frowns. "Annie, a pretty girl like you needs to learn to pay attention and watch your back. If you haven't noticed how that stout Russian stares at you, start doing so now."

"You mean that big guy who just sits around and won't talk to anyone? He was downright rude when Mrs. Jacobson tried to be friendly. Heck, it's that little old Irishman who does all the staring. I've seen him reading with his book upside down. How about putting some lotion on my back?"

I'm not exactly tall myself but Nettie is really petite. I sit down and heave a grateful sigh as she gets to work.

"Let me amend my advice," Nettie says as she adds a second coat. "Learn to read the men who stare. Shamus is a pussycat but don't you let the Russian trap you alone in a dark corner."

"Geez, auntie dear, you are paranoid. Ooo, that lotion does help. Thank you, thank you. From the bottom of my heart, thank you. Now unless I can talk you into a game of shuffleboard, I'll go away and leave you alone."

"Sorry, dearest niece, I am currently feeling decidedly antisocial and I have a good bit of reading to do before the London meeting. Not only that, there's a gaggle of school teachers constantly on the lookout for a chance to set me straight."

"Yeah, they got your number all right. You and Mrs. Jacobson are getting along like a house afire, though."

"Maureen is quite a character. Did you know she's the past president of the Boston branch of the League of Women Voters? She's also active in the Civil Liberties Union and her mother-in-law was a suffragette?"

"Gee, I didn't know all that. Did she tell you Moire and I want to have a Fourth of July party when they get to the grandparents' place in Yorkshire?"

"I don't much like visiting strangers, Annie, and we don't know the grandparents. Scarborough is a famous Victorian resort town, though. It could be fun spending a day or two on a Yorkshire beach.

We could stay in the famous Royal Hotel and pay the Jacobsons a brief call."

"Wow, that would be very, very cool. I better get out of way your now. I really just came down to take a shower before dinner and tonight's big gala. I was thinking I'd wear my good blue dress and maybe my pearls."

"Get ready for a disappointment then, two of them, in fact. From my experience shipboard galas are nothing to write home about and you'll be taking a bath, not a shower. Just be glad you're not on one of the long Pacific voyages or you'd be bathing in salt water with an attendant giving you a quick fresh-water rinse, leering at you all the while."

"That sounds really yucky," I groan. "But, heck, I'd put up with it if I could sail off to Burma or India or around the world like you do."

Nettie shakes her head. "It can be exciting, Anna, but believe me what I do is not easy and rarely pleasant."

I want to ask her more about that but she collapses on her bunk, loaded down with a pile of papers and books. Oh, well. I gather up my stuff and head for the aft bathing salon.

Monday afternoon, in cabin 45 on F deck
Henri

Rolling over in these bunks is not wise for a person my size but I can stretch and do. My watch indicates that it's five o'clock. I run yesterday through my mind trying to decide if that's a.m. or p.m. Ah, I remember now. It has to be p.m. I watched the sunset and the sunrise both, then ate a huge, decidedly not French-style breakfast before going to bed. I also remember the dining salon was essentially empty again. I roll out of bed and start my morning ablutions.

I had a fine time yesterday playing quoits and shuffleboard with the young people. They're an interesting bunch, a bit younger than my weekend apprentices but old enough to think for themselves. I have to admit it, I also enjoyed showing off. I may have a game leg but black-smithing even as an amateur does wonders for the arms and shoulders.

I suspect that my beard and scars may have given at least the girls a wrong impression though. I've been accused of looking like a thug before. Thug or not, I've been unable to beat the major at chess and I doubt I ever will. Considering what a wily old bastard he is, it's sur-prising the Nazis lasted as long as they did.

I have a sudden thought. It turns out William Fletcher was one of the Major Gracer's pilots and they still see each other occasionally. The major tells me that Willy never misses an opportunity to recount tales of the adventures I had getting him out of France, wounded as badly as he was. It seems that Willy now has a car dealership in Lon-don and I'm in the market for a car. I need to remember to get his ad-dress from the Major when we play tonight.

That brings up the subject of cars. I need one. I can't take it home with me so it doesn't need to be practical. I'm considering an MG TD.

Not that there's anything wrong with the Studebaker Champion in the garage back home or even the 1934 rust bucket of a Ford truck out at the forge, but I've coveted Laurence's MG TD for the past three years. One might not be outrageously expensive if I sell it when I leave and it holds its value well. Elated at the thought, I make five limping laps of the C deck promenade before dinner.

Monday night in the Grand Salon
Nettie

The band is atrocious. I help myself to some mediocre Champagne punch and duck behind a potted palm. I can't help smiling as I watch Anna being whirled around the dance floor first with one man and then with another. The blue of her dress matches her sparkling big eyes. She's glowingly beautiful tonight, so light hearted, so happy and so very young.

I nostalgically remember my first voyage. Like the SS Liberté the SS Normandie had a preponderance of male passengers. I had so many men lined up to dance with me I felt like a movie star. Tonight, I find the attention simply irritating. I spent enough years sowing wild oats to grow tired of reaping them. I've had my fill of dancing after the first half hour. I slip further back into the shadows, then on impulse surreptitiously make my way out on the deck and go down the companionway to deck C.

As I anticipated, I find it all but deserted. The male occupant of the single deck chair appears to be dozing. Last night's storm has moved on. The sky is clear and the sea calm. In the moonlight I lean against the railing and look out into a dark empty world. The gentle breeze on my skin brings back memories of magical moonlit evenings, of being young and in love. I stare out at the endless black waves for a long time. When the music floating down from B deck finally ceases, I sigh. They'll be giving out worthless door prizes now. I head back to my cabin before the mass of partiers can get in my way.

On the way down the midship stairway, I hear a commotion coming from the vicinity of the aft stairs on F deck. I stop and listen. It comes again. I hear raised voices and a woman's short muffled cry. That's not good. I jog along the stateroom corridor in that direction.

I see that a big man has someone backed against the wall half-way down the broad stairway ahead. Catching a glimpse of blue the color of Anna's dress, I shout her name. He backs off and turns away. It is the Russian. Anna's dress is pulled askew but I see that she's all right.

Doing a fair job of looking innocent, the Russian nods to me saying, "Dobryy vecher, ledi" *(Good Evening, lady)* and nonchalantly continues down the stairs.

"Bonsoir, monsieur," I reply pleasantly. As he passes, I fake a stumble and come down hard with my heel on his foot. There is an ominous crunch. He clenches his teeth and reaches for my ankle, but I leap back and assume a look of horror.

"Oh, my God, look what I've done. I do apologize. Are you hurt? Shall I call for help?" I give him a hard look at odds with my concerned voice. Glaring at me, he ignores the hand I solicitously offer to help him. He snarls something in Russian and limps back up the stairway.

I give Anna a grim smile, put a cautionary finger to my lips and watch him out of sight. When he doesn't reappear, I silently lead her down to our cabin and prop our chair under the knob. I consider getting our steward and having him lock our door but locked doors are a nuisance and I don't anticipate the Russian is going to be doing much walking on that foot tonight. Anna sinks down on the edge of my berth looking a bit worse for wear.

"Do you think he could have been following me, Nettie?" Anna asks wiping her eyes. "He was trying to get me kiss to him and touching my breasts. And you stepped on his foot on purpose, didn't you?"

"Yes and yes," I say impatiently. "With any luck I broke it."

"But I thought you were a Quaker," she says and looks at me accusingly.

"Yeah, which means I follow my conscience and my conscience doesn't feel a bit bad about stomping on the bastard's foot." Okay, so maybe that isn't entirely true. I may be a bad Quaker sometimes but I do try to make up for it. I can't help wincing. My conscience can be a terrible task- master.

I look at Anna and shake my head. "You, my dear, have the street smarts of a rutabaga. Why didn't you have one of your admirers walk you to the cabin, for God sake?"

"It was all because of Teddy. He was being really awful when anyone else wanted to dance with me. He tried to pick a fight with Grady. He was standing toe-to-toe with our table-mate, Angus when I got so disgusted I just stormed out. Maybe the Russian noticed and followed me. Gosh, you don't think he'll try to get you in trouble for what you did to his foot, do you?"

"Oh Annie, how can American girls be so ridiculously naive at your age? It's you who should be reporting him. Frankly, it looks like it's a good thing tomorrow is our last day."

"I'm so sorry, Nettie ... I ... I didn't mean to be ... such a moron."

She looks so woebegone, I pull her to her feet and give her a hug. "Oh, Annie, shut up, for God sake. Being over protected is a not the worst thing in the world. Now it's way past time to call it a night. I, for one am going to hit the sack."

VI

The Sixth Day of the Voyage

Tuesday morning in the Dining Salon
Anna

Gee, this is almost funny. We're all sitting here at the breakfast table staring at each other not knowing what to say. This could be our last time eating breakfast together. Tomorrow we get to England. Even people going to Le Havre will go ashore for the day. We probably won't see each other ever again. Except for maybe the Aussies. Grady is pushing for us all to get together in London.

I don't want to waste my last day but I can't make up my mind how to spend it. Out on the promenade deck I run into Grady coming the other way.

"Annie, oh, good. I was looking for you," Grady says, then lowers his voice. "Nettie told me about last night. I thought it might interest you that I saw the Russian bloke in the aft lounge drinking vodka for breakfast with a cast on his foot."

"Oh, no. Nettie must have broken his foot for real," I worry. "Gosh, do you think she's going to get in trouble?"

"Annie, he tried to molest you. I bloody well would have done more than break his foot if I'd been there. We should never have let you sneak out on us like that."

"But what if he attacks Nettie to get even?" I just can't get the incident out of my mind. It was so shocking, I can't just forget it.

"No worries, Annie, your beautiful little Aunt Nettie can take care of herself but don't you go wandering off alone again."

He's right about Nettie. It sure is a good thing for me that she came along just then. I kind of thought there might be more to her than meets the eye, now I'm sure of it. I bet she was still in France when the war broke out and whatever happened after that wasn't good. I would love to ask her but by now I know it would be a mistake. It's none of my business, but I can't help it if I'm hopelessly nosey. Oh, well.

"It might be a good thing we get there tomorrow," I say, changing the subject. "Nettie says it's going to be a long day but we'll get through customs pretty quick. We only have what we carried on with us. Most of you guys are going to have to wait for the baggage to get unloaded."

"It could be the last time we all see each other if we let it," Grady says looking pretty darned unhappy about the idea. "The Jacobsons are going straight on to the grandparents' place in Scarborough but the rest of us are all bound for London. Our Tasmanian cobbers will be staying with some cousins in Soho but the rest of us should try to book rooms in the same hotel."

"'Fraid not, Grady. We're not staying in a regular hotel, either. The Quakers have this Penn Club in Bloomsbury. It's where Nettie always stays. You wouldn't have to be a Quaker to stay there but it's not a regular hotel. You certainly wouldn't like it. I'm not too sure that I will, either."

"Well, we can at least have dinner together. Moira says you and Nettie are going to spend your Fourth of July together in Scarborough. It isn't an Aussie holiday but I might try to catch up with you there if I finish up the Guv's business in London soon enough. They say Scarborough is Churchill's favorite beach and Queen Victoria and Albert used to stay at the Grand Hotel there."

Nettie was right. Getting away from our Aussie friends is not going to be quick. Oh, well. They do keep things interesting, matey.

Grady looks at his watch. "Look, I need to get at my packing. How about meeting me in the sports deck in say, an hour?"

"Sorry. No sun for me today. My back is still red and sore. How about the aft lounge right after lunch?"

"After lunch?" he dramatically groans. "I guess I can survive the wait."

I've gotten used to this crazy life on shipboard but I really don't have anything in mind to do this morning. I'm more excited about what comes next but it leaves me feeling ... I don't know ... kind of unsettled. I keep thinking about me really setting foot in a foreign country tomorrow. Gosh, I've daydreamed about it so long it's hard to believe it's about to happen.

I can hardly wait to tell Karen and Elizabeth Ann about all this. Maybe that's what I should do, write a bunch of letters to mail when we land. I want to write a long one to Karen and at least a short aerogram to Mom and Jack at their hotel in Paris. It's funny but I haven't thought about them even once. I bet they're having the time of their lives. Mom always wanted to go to Paris and Rome, but boy, I'm I ever glad I'm not with them.

Tuesday mid-morning in cabin 45 on F deck
Henri

Missed breakfast again. I suppose it's some consolation the Dane did as well. Damn. I wish I'd run into Fredrick sooner. Last night was quite the marathon. Took five hours for me win the first game and another seven hours for him to defeat me in the rematch. Sacre Bleu, but those Scandinavians can drink.

I struggle out of bed and groan. The Dane is a dangerous man in more than just chess. I haven't had a hangover like this in years. Looking at the time, I note that I'm in danger of missing lunch as well as well as breakfast. I'm forced to choose between dining and a bath. I glance in the mirror. I look like hell. I feel like hell. The bath wins.

I find the aft bathing salon deserted which gives me an opportunity to chat with Singh while he draws my bath. An interesting man but he takes a huge risk talking to me even in the middle of the day when virtually no one is around. It would cost him his job were he observed talking to a passenger.

I must take care. Jobs like his are a precious alternative to starvation. He tells me that he is permitted to hold this job for a single year before the next man on the waiting list takes his place. He gets paid less for that year than I make in a single day. It's an unfair world but then fairness is a manmade concept rarely achieved.

I give Singh a handful of francs, luxuriate in the warm water and massage my leg. Doctors have been wrong before. Progress is almost imperceptible but I am building muscle. Despite medical opinion to the contrary, I like to believe that a knee replacement may be feasible someday. On that optimistic note, I leave the luxurious warm water and wrap up in the towel Singh holds for me.

Back in my cabin I take my time preparing to tackle the new day. Fredrik has promised me a return match. Two games out of three. I grin. Maybe three games out of five. I half regret not continuing on to Le Havre. No, that is most certainly not something I'll regret, but priority will have to be given the quest for a chess partner or two in the UK.

On deck I fail to locate Fredrik in the Grand Salon or either the terrace or aft lounges. I stroll in the direction of the promenade and a deck chair but detour instead to the stern rail to look at the ship's wake. Hypnotized, I reflect on life in the UK and the likelihood of finding chess partners there.

I've thought a lot about research and sites I plan to visit. I have letters of introduction to a dozen or so church archives and private collections from one end of Britain to the other. However, with the exception of visiting Dougal in Inverness, I haven't considered the issue of living day to day. Hell, even the Dougal visit has research implications.

A life well lived was never an issue for me in pre-war France. Starting over from scratch in the States has been something of a challenge. I've got a good life there now but it took a long time. I have made some friends during summers in Britain over the years. This time I'll be there all year, too short a time to build a life and too long not to have one.

There are times that I regret abandoning archeology. My research as a historian largely has been solitary. Working out techniques used in making medieval weaponry has been a saving grace. I'm going to miss weekends out at my forge and my damn apprentices. I complain because they expect it of me. In truth I thoroughly enjoy the hootenanny nights with their unruly friends. My British sojourn is likely to be a pretty staid existence in comparison.

I originally assumed I'd take up Niles's invitation to lodge at Kings again. Living in college can be awfully narrow but rarely lonely. London is undoubtedly full of kindred spirits but it could be damn hard to find them. I'm coming to understand that setting up housekeeping for the year will require both more thought and luck than I anticipated.

Tuesday evening in cabin 12 on G deck
Nettie

Tomorrow we get to Plymouth. Back in Britain for the first time since since March, I'm not sure whether I'm looking forward or dreading it. A bit of both, I guess. I go back to the cabin bathed, rested and ready to dress up for the last dinner on the SS Liberté. This voyage has certainly turned out to be an emotional seesaw. For once I'm not traveling alone and it's been a blessing. I adore Anna but was I ever that young? I suppose I must have been.

I wonder whatever became of Mitch Richardson? I smile, remembering a long ago, simpler time. Lordy, I was in love with that boy. It's probably just as well his family moved to California or I'd be playing momma to a brood of little Richardsons. Mother claimed our little jaunt down to the Mardi Gras had a lot to do with them moving away. Mrs. Richardson was afraid we'd actually eloped. My, but did we ever have a good time. There have been a lot of good moments in the past few years but it's hard to remember ever being so light-hearted and free.

I'm coming to realize that I've needed something like this little holiday tour with Anna for a long time. All work and no play has been my style for too long. I really am tempted to take a year off, go to Costa Rica and teach at the little school they built in Monteverde a couple of years ago. Unfortunately they're pressuring me to go to Korea and

I'm not sure I can deal with being that close to combat again. This rash of flashbacks has me feeling particularly ... breakable, I guess.

I'm not sure I can deal with kids either. Ghosts of the past lurk in the back of my mind. Imagining those little Costa Ricans in their makeshift school seems to have undone me. Damn bloody Ravensbruck. A prison camp for women means a camp with children but there weren't many there that survived. The gypsy kids were the lucky ones. They were killed when they first arrived.

Damn, damn, damn. Did I ever truly escape that Nazi hellhole? Did any of us? Yeah, a hell of a lot of us did, right into the crematorium. They say a hundred thousand of us were killed or died of overwork and starvation even before the end when they brought in the gas chamber and started killing us in earnest. I can believe it. By my count only one in five of the women I worked with survived and not one single kid under twelve did.

Stop it. Stop it. And for once I do stop it. I resolve to wash my face and put on something interesting for the farewell dinner. I mean to enjoy it. Tomorrow it's goodbye French cuisine, hello, soggy vegetables and mutton stew. Thank God for pasties, scones, and fish and chips.

Ian lightly taps on the door. "Excuse me, mam'selle. May I have a word with you, s'il vous plaît. I fear there may be a problem."

VII
Arrival in England

Plymouth Harbor

Wednesday morning in cabin 12 on G deck
Nettie

This is it. I really didn't want to get up this morning but we disembark in a few hours. After the little tête-à-tête with Ian, I didn't sleep worth a damn last night even with the door actually locked.

I almost wish we'd turned up something missing, then I'd have a "why" even if I didn't have a "who." I'd rather think it was a sneak thief than the bloody Russian. I didn't want Anna worrying so I didn't say anything about Ian glimpsing a guy ducking out of our cabin, not just once but twice. I managed to keep her from noticing that Ian locked our door, too.

Quakers don't swear vows and they don't lie or at least this one pretends to herself she doesn't. Carefully mislead, yes, out and out lie, never. I simply told Anna that it always makes sense to give a room a good search when you're packing to leave, and so it does even without the goal of seeing if anything's been stolen.

One last turn around the cabin, a fat gratuity for Ian and I head upstairs, the same stairs where the Russian accosted Anna. It's still fifteen minutes before I'm meeting her in the Grand Salon. Standing in queues is not my idea of fun, but I'll guarantee she's been biting her nails ever since the first passengers went down the gangway.

Wednesday mid-morning in the Grand Salon
Anna

Gee whiz, in just a few minutes I'll be in my first foreign county. I put my suitcases down next to the chair and wait for Nettie. I hate waiting. I check my purse for my passport for the hundredth time. My drawing pad is in there, too, but as sure as I start something, I'll have to stop. I am ready to get off this boat right this minute.

Of course I've loved this voyage, every bit of it, even the parts I hated. It's kind of like seeing how rich people live. And Nettie was right. For once in my life I was the belle of the ball but you know, it wasn't all that great. Geez. Between the lurking Russian, possessive Bostonian, and lovable Aussie this last little bit sure has been a pain. And it isn't really over yet. Chapter two could happen even on the train to London. Or maybe not if Nettie is right about beating every-body through customs. We'll be on the first train to London and there's a good chance the others won't make it.

Sitting here with nothing to do but wait sort of fits with everything else. I've spent the whole week killing time with a bunch of strangers. People are bloody interesting, as Grady would say. What different and adventurous lives some of them have lived ... are living. I want to go China and Indonesia and Algeria and the Fiji Islands. I would never get tired of world travel, as Nettie says she is. I want to go around the world. I want to see everything.

Gee, maybe art isn't such a good major after all but I don't think there's a Department of Globe Hopping, as Nettie calls it. Speaking of Nettie, where is she? Almost everyone we know is already ashore in that crowd by the customs shed. I check my watch again. Blast. She isn't due yet. For crying out loud. I sure hope it isn't a mistake to put off going ashore for so long. Here comes Grady. He isn't Nettie but at least he's someone to talk to while Nettie keeps us from getting off when we are supposed to.

"Cheerio, Annie. Mind if I join you?" He sits down next to me without waiting for an answer.

"Hi, Grady. I'm waiting for Nettie. I sure wish she'd hurry up. Most everybody else is already on shore. The ship's going on to Le Havre this afternoon. We need to get off."

"Not to worry, Annie," he grins. "They're a long way from being finished unloading the baggage hold. It's hours before new passengers are scheduled to board."

"I guess I'm just impatient. You know this is my first time in a foreign country except for Canada and that doesn't really count."

"Don't let Charlie Newman hear you say that," Grady laughs. "He's pretty sensitive about being lumped together with you USA-ians."

"Charlie? That's the tall old guy at your table. He's Canadian? I never got to know him."

"His bad luck. Anyway, being French Canadian, he's going on to Le Havre."

"I can hardly wait to set foot on this side of the Atlantic," I tell Grady. "If Nettie ever gets here, that is." I can't help drumming my fingers on the arm of the chair.

"Annie, if this is anything like the time I came over with the Guv three years ago, it's the customs shed floor you'll be setting foot on and it isn't much fun. Believe me, the waiting has just begun."

"Not for us, Grady," Nettie says walking up carrying her suitcases. "We're traveling light. We'll be carrying everything we have with us. I predict we'll have a lot more luggage going home, though. Come on, Annie. We may as well join the madhouse down there."

"Mind if I tag along and help with those not-so-light suitcases you two have?" Grady says, taking one of Nettie's suitcases and grabbing my big one.

I gotta admit I'm beginning to really like that big oaf. It should be fun doing a few things in London together, even if I never see him again after that.

I get out my passport and follow Nettie to the top of the gangway. The officer there stamps it hardly looking at it and we go down into the noisy mob waiting to collect their baggage. Grady taps me on the shoulder, says something and points back at the ship. I can't figure out what he's trying to tell me.

"Up there, Annie. There's a bloke frantically waving and shouting and it looks like he's shouting at us," Grady bellows over the noise.

I look where he's pointing but don't see anyone waving.

"He's gone. No, there he is down on B deck now pushing his way through the crowd," Grady says. "It might be that French college professor with a beard. Nettie, hold on. Wait for us."

Gee, there is some guy running along waving up there. I suppose it oould be the Frenchman but Grady must have pretty darn good ears if he can hear him shouting.

Grady gives up, shrugs his shoulders and says that it isn't us the man is shouting at. We catch up with Nettie and wade through the crowd over to the quieter tables where customs inspectors are checking luggage.

"Well, this is goodbye for now," Grady says. "I have to go back see if my baggage has been unloaded yet. If it doesn't take too long, I'll see you on the train. If not, I'll look you up at the Penn Club. I believe you said it's in Bloomsbury. I'm on the other side of Hyde Park in Kensington at Bailey's. Once I get my business taken care of, I'll treat you to dinner."

"So what were you two looking at back there?" Nettie asks.

"Somebody still onboard was shouting and trying to get someone's attention," I tell her.

"I thought the bloke was looking at us but I was wrong," Grady adds. "He wanted someone called Claudette."

"Claudette? Are you sure he said Claudette?" Nettie says. She stands on tip toes looking back at what she can see of the ship from here. "Not Annette or Babette or Josette?"

"Or Jeanette?" I can't resist adding. "You know Nettie is short for Jeanette, don't you, Grady."

Grady frowns and shakes his head. "Jeannette? Claudette? No, I have good hearing."

Nettie looks so unhappy that Grady goes on. "Nettie, the lah sound was very clear. Laudette, Blaudette, Flaunette? I can't think of any other name than Claudette with that lah sound. I promise you it was not Jeannette."

"What did this man look like?" Nettie goes on, obviously not satisfied.

"He was big and had a beard. I think it might have been that Frenchman who beat us all at quoits the other day. You remember, Annie, the one Moira calls the hit man."

"Hit man? Why does she call him a hit man? What does he look like?" Nettie asks.

"That's just a joke. He isn't a hit man, Nettie," I tell her. "He's a professor and really cool even if he does kind of look like someone you wouldn't want to meet in a dark alley."

"That beard is just how he hides some of his bigger scars," Grady adds, "He has a limp, too. I'd guess the war."

"How old? What color hair?" Nettie asks. I don't know why she is so interested in this guy.

"If it's the Frenchman you mean, I liked him," I tell her. "Older than you, maybe forty. Dark hair, actually rather attractive in a scary sort of way. Very French but with a mostly American accent. And waving at someone else, not us."

"Oh, Nettie, don't look so worried. He was just some guy looking for someone else," Grady tries to reassure her. "I tell you, he was after Claudette, not Jeannette."

"I suppose you're right and we're up next at customs," Nettie says with a final glance over her shoulder. "If we don't see you on the train, Grady, we'll hold you to that dinner invitation."

I wave goodbye and watch the Aussie walk away. Nope, this chapter is not closed yet.

Wednesday late morning in cabin 45 on F deck
Henri

"I am most sorry, sir." The voice of Raul, the steward, inexplicably echoes through the pouring rain. "But you did ask me to wake you early today."

It is the unexpected smell of coffee in the empty shell of a house that finally gives the show away. The dream dissolves and I drift back into consciousness. Reluctantly I open my eyes and groan. I knew this was going to hurt when Fredrik and I started the third game. No problem for him. He isn't disembarking until Le Havre. In fact, I'm under no time pressure, either. The crates of my books and papers are stowed with the Le Havre luggage so they'll be the last off.

Raul chuckles sympathetically. "Breakfast has come and gone, sir, but I raided the kitchen and obtained a croissant and cafe latte. If you will pardon me saying so, sir, you do rather look like you need it."

"That damn Dane sure can hold his bloody liquor. He was throwing back two to my one and still standing," I mutter gratefully, taking the proffered cup. "Merci, Raul, merci beaucoup."

On a day like this I sincerely regret the shipboard absence of showers. I struggle to my feet and look in the mirror. The scarred face staring back comes as a habitual shock. I note the sad look of resignation on his face. I also note that he needs a shave. The beard is acceptable but my mustache requires trimming. I pick up my Dopp Kit and head for the bathing salon. I want to give Singh a gratuity before I leave anyway.

It doesn't take long to pack after I get back to my stateroom. Raul appears with more coffee and another croissant before I finish. I look out the porthole and see Plymouth harbor. I resist the temptation to watch tugs maneuver the SS Liberté into her berth. I need to massage my bad leg but I can forego my morning workout. After giving the cabin a last check, I head topside, pausing to give Raul a sizable gratuity. Just how sizable, I couldn't say. I simply empty my wallet and pockets of my remaining francs.

The early birds are already queuing up by the gangway. As I have every intention of being the last man off, I climb the companionway up to C deck to look down over the railing at the queue of my fellow passengers. I have no plans for what I'll do when I get to shore. I weigh the relative merit of immediately boarding the train for London or enjoying a few days here in Cornwall. Out of the corner of my eye I catch a glimpse of wild red hair among the throng at the foot of the gangway.

After all these years my heart still skips a beat whenever I see a curly carrot top that particular shade of red. This one really does remind me strongly of Claudette. Then she steps out from behind the big Aussie they call Grady and turns her face toward me.

Sacre Bleu! It is Claudette! Unless I'm hallucinating, it's her. She's been here on the SS Liberté all along? Damn it to hell. I shout and wave, trying to get her attention, but she doesn't hear. I frantically shout again and again. As she disappears into the crowd, the Aussie looks my way. I think he may be with her. I call her name. I'm convinced that he hears me but he turns away. They keep moving deeper into the dark mouth of the customs shed.

Mon Dieu, I'm an idiot. Claudette isn't her real name. I panic and my mind goes blank. Hicks, her surname was Hicks like the Hicksite Quakers. Janet. No, Jeanette. I damn near fall down the companionway as I frantically race down to the gangway. I drop my cane in my haste to pull out my passport. A kind soul grabs it before it goes over the side and puts it in my hand.

By the time my feet hit the quay, Claudette is nowhere in sight. They must be in the mass of passengers waiting for the baggage to be unloaded. I don't see her, but then I wouldn't. She's barely five feet tall. I push my way through the mob, searching for the Aussie instead. When I see him coming back from the direction of the custom inspectors, I realize my mistake.

Hells bloody bells, they must have gone straight to customs. I very nearly knock an elderly man down in my rush to get there but they are already gone. Damn those crates of books. I'll send for them later. Fortunately the queue at customs is short. I get in line. There should be no issue with customs unless it would be my sword cane but it would take a sharp eye indeed to spot the hidden release I designed.

Out on the street, a row of taxis vie for fares. Exiting passengers are on their way as soon as they step through the doors. She's gone. Ironically we've been on the SS Liberté for a week and have never seen each other. I will find her yet. Hotel or train station? Train station. She'd go to London. I hope I'm correct, as I climb into a taxi.

"Train station and hurry," I pant.

"I'll do my best, sir," he says. "If it's the London Express you want, I don't know," he whips out his watch and shakes his head. "Six minutes. Not possible."

It may not be possible but he's game to try. Horns blare as we force our way into traffic. Roaring through alleys, knocking over dust bins and narrowly missing a collision or two, we pull into the station just in time to see the train pull away from the platform.

I want to weep or punch something. "That was one hell of a ride," I tell the cabbie. "We almost made it." I hand him twice the fare he asks with the last of my meager supply of British pounds. I square my shoulders and limp into the station to change some money and purchase a ticket on the next train.

Morosely I take a seat in the waiting room and consider the matter carefully and from all angles. Claudette ... Jeanette may have left a forwarding address with the purser. Regrettably the SS Liberté will already be on the way to Le Havre before I can get back there. The French Line offices are another possibility. I locate a phone booth and get the number from the operator. The office is already closed for the day. Damn.

I'm disconcerted to see the hand holding my ticket is trembling. I am discombobulated. It was as if I were traveling backward in time. She looks just the same, just as beautiful, just as ... alive. For years I've avoided thinking about her. That woman was my soul mate, my entire world. That world disintegrated when the Nazi's took her. I wince. Seeing Claudette has completely undone me.

Claudette hasn't changed a whit but I have. She might not be as eager to see me as I am to see her. I take a deep breath. If that was her at the hospital, she took one look at me and never came back and can I blame her? No, I was wrapped up like a mummy and the doctors didn't anticipate I'd survive yet another night. Certainly no one thought I'd walk again. After all she'd been through at Ravensbruck, seeing the wreckage of her old lover would have been an unwelcome sight. If that was her, that is.

I put my head in my hands holding tears in check. I'll never know unless I can find her.

London Express

Wednesday afternoon in the first class restaurant carriage
Anna

Boy, now I really, really feel like I'm in one of those British mysteries. I am ninety percent sure either Peter Wimsey or Hercule Poirot is sitting at the table right behind us. This restaurant car is just as high class as SS Liberté's dining salon even if there are only six courses.

"So this is what it's like traveling first class?" I say to Nettie. "Jeepers. Can you really afford this?"

"I find money a damn burden, Annie," she says with a sigh. "No matter how much or how little you have, it carries responsibilities and poses constant moral dilemmas."

"Wow. You gotta be the first person I've ever heard complain about being burdened by money. Mom and I have never had anywhere near enough."

"It's a matter of perspective, honey. You had more than you needed to survive all your life and that's more than most people in the world have. You've always had choices." She turns and looks out the window.

Gee, I suppose she's right, but I don't live in the rest of the world. I don't live in a grass hut. Of course, it might be nice to try it for a while.

"You say it's a burden," I argue, "but you haven't given it all away or we won't be sitting here deciding whether to order Roast Suckling Pig with Apple Sauce or Braised Duck Cumberland. Not that I'm complaining, you understand. I am absolutely loving this. Do we really have first-class tickets going back?"

"If it hadn't been a last-minute decision, we would have been in first class coming over. Actually you'll find first class can be pretty stuffy. We could always switch the return tickets to tourist class, but it's an experience you should have. You should have it because you need to know what it's like to be rich, what it does to people, how they see the world."

Golly, Nettie is making me a bit guilty for having enough food to eat. It's my own fault but I sure don't like the way this conversation is going. I don't know what to say so I keep my mouth shut and look out the window at the little English farmsteads going by. Eastern Iowa farms are completely different. I sure am a long way from home. In more ways than one.

The very British waiter puts the very French first course of Oyster ala Russe down in front of me. By now I've sure learned one thing. No matter how good something looks you just nibble at it or you'll never make it through all the courses. I kind of wonder how much of this seems foreign just because it's a different social class and because I'm not rich.

Nettie's giving me a strange look. By now I know better than to try to hide my feelings from that woman. I sigh.

"Thank you, Nettie, I am really enjoying playing at being rich," I say and mean it. "I think I understand what you're getting at. All this is great but I'm not too sure I'd want to live like this. It's not the kind of exciting adventures I daydream about."

Nettie gives me a lopsided grin. "Me, either. That's why we're staying in hostels when we go exploring. You're enough like me that I can say with some confidence you're going to like it."

"Yeah, and maybe I can stop worrying about getting fat. I'm going to eat these oysters and politely just nibble at the braised duck."

We are going through another little village now. I don't care. I'm loving this. This is England. I'm really in a foreign country. Every single thing I see is like a picture post card or a landscape painting. If we weren't going so fast they'd be fun to draw. I'm still looking out the window when the waiter removes my half-eaten oysters and brings the main course.

London Express

At the same time in the first class restaurant carriage
Nettie

I can't get that business at the quay out of my mind. Damn Claudette. I'm glad I thought about the restaurant carriage. Anna is obviously getting a charge out of it. It's a good four hours to Waterloo Station and it's a much-needed distraction. I ought to forget about this Claudette business. Grady might have been wrong about either the name or who they were yelling at.

No, someone on that ship recognized me, someone who searched my cabin. Someone recognized Claudette on the ship but avoided me. Good or bad, that's the question. Not a question. Bad. They avoided me until we got to shore so it sure wasn't a friend. The real question is how bad?

Someone searched my cabin. Why? Looking for something to steal and deciding my jewelry wasn't worth the risk? Some perverted impulse of the bloody Russian? Or maybe they were searching Claudette's cabin, not Jeanette Hicks's. Or maybe this worry is just a lingering habit of suspicion left over from living with fear and constant danger during the war.

No, it's the undelivered money and my guilty conscience. I failed my mission and people died because I didn't get the money to Dreux that night. I suppose there might have some bitterness about it. Maybe I shouldn't have stopped for the night but at least I did one thing right.

The damn Germans didn't get the money. They might have if I'd kept going. Jean thinks they would have but maybe he just says that to make me feel better.

All this is giving me the mother of all headaches. Yes, I came out of the war rich. I did hide the Resistance's money and I did go back for it and use it to save the death-march refugees from starving. It was a lot of money, but not that much. Anyway there was no one to give it back to after the war. It got nine of us back to France alive. It kept us almost fed in what was left of Aviva's chateau until we could get the Polish women home ... except for Gertrude and Halina and Yvon's baby. Without that money, it doesn't bear thinking about.

This idiotic guilt is just some kind of battle fatigue craziness. Not that that makes a goddamned bit of difference.

"So this is what it's like traveling first class?" Anna interrupts my thoughts. "Can you really afford this?"

What is this? Some kind of bloody synchronicity? God, I hate the damn money. I have to get myself under control before I answer that question or I'll start bawling.

"I find money a damn burden, Annie," I tell her. If she only knew how true that is. "No matter how much or how little you have, it carries responsibilities and poses constant moral dilemmas."

I'm trapped. I refuse to play games with the truth but this is a conversation I need to get out of. It's a relief when the North Wessex Downs finally diverts Anna's attention.

Dinner over, we retire to our compartment. I get out the statistics from Korea and pretend to read them while Anna watches southern England go by. I'm glad she's enjoying this so much. Every now and then, I see the world through her eyes for a moment. It's a sobering experience and keeps things in perspective.

I can't focus on Korea. I'm obsessing about the question of who might have spotted Claudette but avoided meeting me and why. It must be about the money. What else would it be?

My headache is threatening to get out of control. I came out of the war a rich woman but it's Aviva's money. None of us had any idea she was rich or would name me her heir. Hell, I'm not sure Aviva knew it herself. If she did, you can bet she'd approve of what I'm using her money for now. Could someone think that money came from the lost funds? I suppose a good dozen people may have known that I had and lost the funds but it was hardly a fortune. I made good use of it and it's gone now.

According to Grady, it was a man calling for Claudette. Not a woman from Ravensbruck, then. French, so not one of the downed pilots I helped. Another resistance worker almost certainly. Most of them were men. A beard, big and tough. None of the people I knew by name come close to the description, except the Brit. That courier who brought the money up from Marseilles was French and he was big and tough looking.

Stop it, Nettie. You are letting the past make you paranoid again. Be reasonable. Even if someone guessed that I went back for the money, would they even care? It's not like I stole it. It wasn't enough for any to be left after ten years anyway and it's not blackmail material. Yes, the lessons learned at Ravensbruck whisper in my ear. Yes, but the war left you rich and a whole lot of us came out of the war pretty damn nuts.

Plymouth

Wednesday afternoon at the railway station
Henri

The next train for London doesn't leave for an hour. I began the day tired and hung-over and my frantic attempt to reach Claudette hasn't helped much. Were it not for my survival instinct and how damn uncomfortable train-station benches are, I'd close my eyes and take a nap here in public. I look around. To judge by the steady flow of passengers arriving, the SS Liberté must have sailed for Le Havre by now. It's going to be standing-room-only soon.

I see a lot of vaguely familiar faces but no one I know well enough to chat with. I'm restless and at loose ends. I don't know what to do with myself. An idea is surfacing in the back of my mind though. Perhaps all is not lost.

The SS Liberté will sail back for New York tomorrow or next day. When she docks here from Le Havre I can ask the purser if Claudette left a forwarding address. If she didn't, I can get Raul to ask her steward about her. You can bet stewards know damn near all there is to know. So do ticketing agents.

I return to the ticket-window queue. It moves quickly, money on the counter, ticket and change returned. Next, please. When it's my turn I break the rhythm.

"I wish to postpone my trip to London, sir," I tell him. "I must retrieve an item that I left on the SS Liberté first. Can you tell me when she is expected to return, please?"

The mildly surprised agent looks over his glasses at me. "If I understand what you're after, sir, you need a ticket to Southampton. Plymouth is SS Liberté's port of call on the eastward crossing from New York. Going westward back to New York, it's Southampton." He's patient with me; if I didn't know better, I'd say he's relieved at the change of pace.

"She's not coming back here? Are you sure? Sorry, of course you're sure. You don't happen to know when she docks in Southampton, do you?"

"Friday. She be back in Southampton picking up passengers for New York the day after tomorrow. She won't call back here in Plymouth again until around sometime in the second week of July," he says, apparently unperturbed by the impatient man behind me coughing pointedly.

"I can just keep this ticket and simply break the trip at Southampton, then?" I ask trying to hurry the process.

"The London Express doesn't go to Southampton, sir. You can exchange your Express ticket for one to Southampton, then buy a second ticket from there to London."

"Then that's what I wish to do, please. When will the Southampton train board?"

"Ten past the hour. You have a twenty-minute wait. Not long enough to get a bite to eat. It will be after eight when you arrive in Southampton. I suggest that you plan to have your evening meal in the dining car."

I thank him profusely and get out of the way. Twenty minutes isn't long. I wander out to the platform and consider how to spend the unexpected day in Southampton. Molly Cotton's excavation at Clausentum immediately comes to mind. Not a battle site but it is Roman and a hell of a lot better than obsessing about Claudette.

Part Two

London, England

VIII

The First Day in London

Wednesday late afternoon in front of the Penn Club
Anna

The taxi pulls up in front of a long row of big, very British-looking buildings with stately doors and window boxes. "So this is the Penn Club? Wow."

"Yes, this is the place," Nettie smiles. "Actually it was originally three Georgian houses back when it got started a few years after World War I," she explains. "It's a real swank location. Look up the street that way and you see Russell Square. Bloomsbury Square is only a block or so in the other direction. The British Museum is just around the corner."

The taxi driver opens the big backward hinged door and helps Nettie out. As if she needs help. These London taxis are really neat. They aren't a bit like regular cars. There's this funny open place next to the driver for the suitcases. The back seats are so roomy you could have a picnic in them. Who knows, maybe they do.

I feel really dumb when it's my turn to be handed out of the car like I'm an old lady. Or I guess maybe a rich lady? Nettie pays him and we pick up our suitcases ourselves. That's not the way it's supposed to go.

"No bellboys here, Annie. This is a British club, not a hotel," Nettie says once again reading my mind. "The cabby knows the place and knows Quakers don't hold much with the idea of servants.

We open the tall main door and step into exactly what Nettie said we would. It's a British club, or maybe just what I imagined one would be like. All dark wood and big leather chairs and quiet, very quiet, a place where you feel you have to whisper. We seem loud just standing here making no noise. I expect to be thrown out at any minute when a woman comes up behind Nettie. She's somberly dressed and thin as a rail, more like what Quakers are supposed to look like than Nettie is.

Boy, am I ever wrong. That stern-looking lady breaks into a big smile and throws her arms around Nettie. She may look cold and disapproving but she sure isn't. I know right away I'm going to like her.

"Jeanette, it is so good to see thee again. Margaret got in from Hungary yesterday, completely exhausted. George won't be in from Korea until tomorrow. The situation there in Busan is even more extreme than we feared."

The lady shakes her head and looks over at me for the first time. "Oh, dear, I am rude. Please forgive me. I'm Amelia Burton and thee must be Anna Ambleside, Dr. Hicks's new stepdaughter. Please be welcome."

"I'm pleased to meet you, Miss Burton," I say, surprised she knows my name.

"Mrs. Burton," she corrects me, "albeit there hasn't been a Mr. Burton for a painfully long time. I am pleased to make your acquaintance, Anna," she says with such warmth that I really do feel welcome. "Linsey and I moved a second bed into thy usual room, Nettie, and I strongly suspect Lyda slipped in some of her African violets."

The Penn Club sure turns out to be a lot more than the hotel where Nettie stays now and then. It's easy to forget that Nettie really is a Quaker. She sure isn't much like the Quaker Oats guy but these people are obviously Nettie's Friends with a capital F even if they do call her Jeanette.

"Thee is a wonder, Amelia," Nettie says giving her a kiss on the cheek and ducking behind the reception desk to pick up a key. "Come on. Annie. Let's get these bags unpacked before it gets any later."

"Geez. You didn't tell me that you actually live here," I whisper. "I thought you lived in New Orleans."

"I do sometimes but I move around a lot, Annie. This is where I hang my hat when I'm on this side of the Atlantic."

I thought I was finally really getting to know Nettie but she has more sides than ... well, something with a whole lot of sides.

We climb a narrow staircase and Nettie stops and unlocks her door. Even though it's late in the day, pale evening summer sun streams in the big window on the row of African violets on a small table in front of it. Other than that the room is completely plain. The sparse furniture is simple and the violets are the sole splash of color. There is no phone or radio or even a clock. Nettie grins at me.

"Don't worry, Annie, the beds are exceptionally comfortable. Quakers are simple folk."

"Thee can say that again. What's with this 'thee' stuff?"

"In the old days everyone addressed their betters as 'you' and used 'thee' just for family and equals. Early Quakers went to prison for insisting that there was no such thing as their betters. Using plain speech today would be kind of pretentious and defeat the whole idea of equality so the practice died out a generation ago. Nonetheless, lot of older people still use 'thee' within the family. Dressing in plain clothes stopped long before that for the same reason though many people still choose to keep their clothing pretty simple."

"Well, no one would accuse you of dressing plain," I tease her.

"Yes, and that may seem a bit on the un-Quakerly side," she says turning serious. "Quakers have traditions, not rules, Annie. We each use the light of God within us as our guide. My conscience doesn't have a problem with how I dress. Right now I intend to undress and take a splitting headache to bed. You'll find a bathroom and water closet down the hall. If you aren't sleepy there's a library downstairs."

I'm much too excited to be sleepy. I slip out, go looking for the library and find it with no trouble. And oh, wow. It's a wonderful, wonderful room. All dark paneling and books with a big fireplace. I can just imagine what it was like when it was still someone's home. At the moment, I'm glad it's deserted and I have it all to myself.

But it isn't. Hidden in a big leather chair, a tiny old lady looks up from the book she's reading. Somehow she fits so perfectly I can imagine she did live here thirty years ago or even a hundred and thirty years ago when it was still someone's house. Any thought that she's really a ghost goes away the minute she looks at me. She may be older than old but those eyes are very, very much alive.

"Well met, well met," she says. "Thee is Jeanette's Anna and I'm Silvia Wentworth. Tell me, has thee ever wondered what it would be like to be tried for murder?" She holds up the book she's reading, the Dorothy Sayer mystery, "Strong Poison."

"Gosh, I can't say that I have," I say. The question coming out of the blue takes me by surprise. "But I have read that Peter Wimsey story."

"Absolutely my favorite detective. Very complex and full of contradictions with lingering shadows of shell shock. He reminds me of my late husband."

"I am looking for something to read, ma'am. I've read all the Wimsey books and I'm not much in the mood for a mystery anyway. What do you suggest?"

She gives me such a long and penetrating look that I actually blush.

"What is thy favorite thing to do, the thing thee would most hate to give up?"

"That's easy. Drawing and painting," I instantly say.

"Ah," she wrinkles her brow thoughtfully. "What do thee most fear being forced to do in life?"

"Giving up the freedom to decide what I do, someone else making all my choices for me," I say without thinking. "I want to ... have adventures and see the world. I don't want to be a damn housewife. Sorry. I mean darn housewife."

"No, thee meant damn housewife. Our classic dilemma, my dear. We start life as infants with no choices at all. As adults love and duty that dictate our choices and finally our failing bodies steal away the last of our choices. And sometimes we simply give away the free choices that are left, like now when thee asks me to choose a book for thee."

"That doesn't count. I freely choose to ask you to choose because there's no choice rattling around inside me."

"Oh, good. Well put" she laughs, "Thee is definitely a young woman full of choices even if they are not rattling around just now. But tonight I'll do thy choosing as thee ask. I know just the book."

She goes over and searches the book shelves for a few minute, then spots something out of reach. "Anna, my dear. Can thee please reach that orange book up there for me."

I have no trouble reaching the battered book and read the title. "Martin Johnson, Lion Hunter?" Gosh, that's a terrible choice. I can't imagine what she was thinking. "Maybe I should take my choices back, Mrs. Wentworth. I'm not particularly interested in hunting lions."

Mrs. Wentworth bursts out laughing. "Of course thee isn't but I tell thee this is exactly the right book for thee. My husband and I met Martin and Osa years ago when they were in the New Hebrides with Jack London. Thee wants to read this book whether thee knows it yet or not."

"The New Hebrides? They're in the south seas somewhere aren't they? What were you doing there?" I ask in surprise.

"Hitching a ride on a mail ship from New Caledonia to Suva. Being young and in love and incidentally being a missionary," she grins at me. "Don't look so shocked my dear. I haven't always been an elderly librarian."

Wow. I can't believe it. She looks so ordinary. I'm thinking that maybe I should go with her choice after all. "Okay, Mrs. Elderly-Librarian-with-a-Past," I grin back. "I believe I'll take this lion hunter to bed with me."

"Oh, do be careful, my dear. Thee must be very choosy about who thee takes to bed with thee."

I burst out laughing and head for our room. These Quakers sure are ... unexpected. Wait. I stop and turn. "Missionaries? I thought Nettie said Quakers don't believe in proselytizing."

"True, but I didn't discover I was Quaker until after World War I, my dear."

IX

The Second Day in London

Thursday morning at the Penn Club
Anna

"Up, up, sleepyhead." Dimly I separate Nettie's voice from a dream I am already forgetting. Drat it all. I should never have stayed up so long reading that book. I give up and open my eyes. Nettie is already dressed in something very nearly sheer and darkly flowered over black leggings and a magenta leotard.

I yawn. "How about going to breakfast without me," I ask, knowing it won't work. "I'm not hungry." I put the pillow over my head. Maybe she'll go away.

"So we'll just grab a scone on our way out. Get up. We've got places to go, things to do," Nettie says. I was right. It didn't work.

"I thought you had to go to a meeting," I complain.

"Not until one o'clock. We're gonna go car shopping."

Holy smoke. That's worth getting up for. "What kind of car?" I ask.

"Something fast, cool and probably expensive. The kind of thing I've always wanted but talked myself out of but sadly, not a drop head. That translates to convertible in American, by the way."

"Gee, what's wrong with a convertible?" I'm surprised. I'd figure her for the convertible type any day.

"It's a deal I made with your mother. No motorcycles and no convertibles. Fortunately she didn't think to forbid sports cars. I'm thinking a Jag."

Wow. I'm out of bed and getting dressed. My favorite yellow summer dress makes me feel dowdy next to Nettie. Dowdy but respectable, more like something to wear when shopping for expensive cars. I shrug my shoulders. I sure hope Nettie knows what she's doing. Oh, well. She usually does.

An hour later, I'm not so sure when our taxi pulls up to the very swank H R Owen dealership. It takes a while before a young man dressed to the nines finally comes over with one of those polite but not exactly friendly smiles on his face.

"Is there something I can do for you young ladies?" he asks. He may be polite but I know that he's really hoping to get rid of us before any high-class customers show up.

"Possibly," Nettie coolly tells him. "We will be visiting Britain for a few months and need a car. Something fast, reliable and not more than three years old. I would prefer to hire one and avoid the hassle of reselling it when I leave but will purchase one if that's what it takes to get what I want."

"I'm not entirely sure we are the dealership to best meet your needs, Miss. You might also consider contacting HHS Hire."

"Is Mr. Swain available?" Nettie sighs and gives him a withering look. I have no idea who Mr. Swain is, but it sure gets a rise out of the guy.

"Mr. Swain is not currently present. Perhaps I can help you." He hands Nettie his card and actually smiles.

Nettie glances at it impatiently. "Very well, Mr. Smyth. I have a Jaguar or Daimler in mind," she says.

"A Daimler is a bit pricey but we do have several other roasters available for less two thousand pounds, miss."

Geez, two thousand pounds? You can buy a house for that, at least a small one. I can't believe Nettie is that rich. I know Jack had to put himself through med school waiting tables. What kind of game is she playing with this guy?

"That's Miss Hicks, if you please. No, I do not want a roadster. I'm thinking more along the lines of a fixed head coupe."

"I do have a 1950 Mark V coupe for just under 1300 pounds."

"Too old, and I told you that I want something fast. The XK120 FHC maybe."

"Three years old or less I believe you said? We should be able to obtain such a vehicle but it will take some time," he says in a some-what changed tone.

"I plan to leave London the first of the week. If you cannot ac-commodate me we shall look elsewhere."

"I feel confident we can find several suitable vehicles by Monday, Miss Hicks. I must ask you for a substantial deposit, however."

"Contact Mr. Albright at Barclays. He handles my affairs in Britain. I will require a complete mechanical inspection of prospective vehicles conducted by a professional. That will be satisfactory, I presume?"

"That will be highly satisfactory, Miss Hicks," he practically purrs.

"Albright will screen the prospective cars prior to my final decision on Monday morning at, shall we say 9 a.m.?" Before the man can reply, Nettie is striding toward the door. I wonder if it's as obvious to him as it is to me that she dislikes the guy.

Boy, Nettie really must be rich. Either that or she's a darned fine con man ... uh, woman. If this comes off, we're going to be going to youth hostels in style.

X

The Third Day in London

Friday afternoon at Paddington Station
Henri

Southampton is several hours closer to London than Plymouth, which may be responsible for Paddington Station seeming so much more welcoming than Waterloo usually does. I'm in high spirits at the prospect of seeing Claudette, even if nothing comes of it. The woman has floated around in my dreams for so long that I'd almost forgotten she was real. It won't be easy but with luck and determination I will find her.

My leg is a bit sore for walking any distance today but I thoroughly enjoyed myself at the Clausentum dig yesterday and I don't regret it. I'm hungry as Hell and remember a pleasant pub nearby on Straithearne Street. A ten-minute walk and I can be sitting in the pub with a Bass in front of me and a ploughman's lunch on the way.

By rights I should be discouraged. Realistically I recognize that finding Claudette will be difficult but now I have something to work with.

The ploughman's lunch arrives and it's a good one and big. I smile at the waitress, "That bread smells like it just came out of the oven, and Stilton cheese?" I ask hopefully.

"It is and that's York ham," She says putting the plate down in front of me.

I take a swallow of Bass and pop a pickled onion in my mouth. I do love London, it is so hopelessly British. Paris will always lay claim to a Frenchman's heart but London is ... well, London. Among other things it has both the British Museum and the British Library. It looks like I'll be revisiting a lot of landmarks in my search for that red-headed sprite.

It is very like Claudette not to have left a forwarding address but Raul proved to be an invaluable resource. I now know she goes by Nettie, not Jeanette. I can't see her as a Jeanette but Nettie fits her. I know she's traveling with that pretty blonde girl whose name turns out to be Anna Ambleside and is her niece. I know the big Aussie is Grady MacFarland and he's paying court to the girl.

I know Claud ... Nettie. Her name is Nettie. I need to start thinking of her as Nettie. She's planning to spend the summer taking her niece on a tour of Britain staying in youth hostels and at some point is going to visit friends on the Yorkshire coast. The friends' surname is Jacob-son but it won't be much help. They are visiting the parents of Mrs. Jacobson's first husband. I now have a general idea of the places she'll be, just not when. Tricky. I need to give this some serious thought.

I had intended to look for a flat but I can afford to delay house hunting for a week or so to look for Nettie. She'll tour London first.

The kid will want to see the Tower of London, Buckingham palace and this is Claudette ... Nettie we're talking about, Hyde Park for sure.

I'm feeling expansive. I decide to splurge on a room at the Russell Hotel for a few nights. It's a bit pricy on a teacher's salary but it's in the heart of Bloomsbury adjacent to the museum, making it worth the occasional splurge. I have a second Bass, finish the most excellent lunch and take the tube to Russell Square.

London

Friday afternoon on Bedford Street
Anna

Boy, what an exciting morning this has been. First the car and then shopping in a foreign country. Nettie says that hostels are really set up for hikers, not for people driving, so she bought us both backpacks to use instead of suitcases. She also bought me a pair of cool hiking boots. Her paying for the trip is one thing, but buying things for me doesn't seem right. That wasn't the time or place to argue about it, but we're going to have to talk about this.

Anyway, I just love the hiking boots. The plan is to do some hiking now and then and I could never afford such high class boots. The Tasmanian boys are going to hike all hundred miles of the way the pilgrims took from Winchester to Canterbury in Chaucer's Canterbury Tales. We may hike a bit of it too, but we sure aren't going on a pilgrimage.

Right now Nettie is at her meeting. Here I am in a foreign country and I'm on my own. How cool is that. I have three days to do anything I want. Right this minute I have six hours before I meet Nettie back at the Penn Club. This is exciting.

I'd be a bit on the scared side if people were speaking a foreign language, but they aren't except maybe Angus. I gotta smile. After a week together it was getting so every now and then I sort of understood what he said.

Golly, what do I want to do first? Nettie bought us a travel guide yesterday. I walk up the street to Russell Square, sit down on a bench by the fountain and turn to the section on London. There's an insert about Queen Elizabeth's coronation left over from last year with a map of the procession route. She turned at Hyde Park and never got this far north, so this map isn't much good to me. I almost throw it away but it would make a good souvenir so I tuck it in the pocket at the back of the book.

I want to see the Tower of London and the Crown Jewels and Saint Paul's. Madame Tussaud's is over by Hyde Park and so is the zoo. I want to see Buckingham palace for sure. Gosh, I can't even begin to see all this in three days. Oh, well. Nettie can't wait to try out the new car she's getting Monday but there's no reason we can't come back later.

I kind of like Nettie's suggestion that I just get on one of these wild red double-decker buses and ride around looking at things. This guidebook has maps of all the bus and tube routes if I can just manage to understand them. This sure isn't going to be as easy as Nettie made it sound. Everything I want to see is in a different direction and the maps look like so much spaghetti.

Getting to Buckingham Palace doesn't look too hard. I could walk by Bloomsbury Square to Bloomsbury Way and the bus stops a few blocks away on Museum Street. This other red route starts near the palace, goes by St Paul's Cathedral and the City before it gets to the tower and you can see the Tower Bridge from there. I was a Girl Scout. I should be able to do this.

London

Friday afternoon in Penn Club conference room
Nettie

God, I can't do this. I simply can't do this. Not with all that shooting. I hope no one notices my hand tremble when I pick up my tea. I can barely make myself sit here listening to George talk about the desperate plight of refugees in Busan. It's bad, really bad. No crematorium, no fatal morning roll calls but the terrible suffering is just the same. The hopelessness, the weak and old and the heartbreakingly young slowly dying around you. It was the sadistic roll calls with their random executions that destroyed my soul. I can't. I just can't.

I look around the table. Everyone here has suffered. Amelia was widowed during the riots in the India relief effort after the partitioning.

Gentle little Lyda Wilson-Smythe was an Algerian harem slave for six years, for God sake. I've proved I can take a lot. I thought I could go to Busan until George started talking about the snipers and midnight raids, but I can't.

Beatrix de Jonge is putting down her tea, standing up and coming my way. She sits down beside me. I admire that woman. I wish I were more like her.

"I couldn't go there either," she whispers. Her own hand is trembling when she takes mine. She knows. Of course she knows. I've heard about what the Japanese did in Indonesia to the European women and children during the war. The same inhuman nightmare as Ravensbruck.

That tips the scale. This is one time when I'm going to take the easy way out. I'll call New York and transfer some funds to Barclays. At least I can throw money at the problem, as Aviva Belanger would say. I can still see her standing there at our camp in the ruins of what had been her home, sobbing, "Oh, Claudette, why couldn't we have gotten the money in time to save Yvon's baby? Why? Why? Why?"

I don't suppose deep down inside any of us will ever stop asking why. I hear myself mutter under my breath, "Too late. Oh, Yvon. I'm so sorry. I found it, but it was such a long, long way."

I'm finding it very hard to hold back tears. My guts are seething. I have a familiar ache in my chest that I don't know what to do with.

Beatrix squeezes my hand. She is a very special woman. Her eyes are glistening with my tears.

I keep wondering how many of these people have figured out it's my own money I managed to raise. It's not something I want known but it's hard to sit here looking like a coward. Never lie to yourself, woman. You are a coward. But at least you can throw Aviva's money at this problem.

XI

The Fourth Day in London

Saturday morning in the Russell Hotel
Henri

The lack of a view from the window of my expensive, Russell Hotel room not withstanding, I assume the sun has risen on yet another Saturday. I'm as wide awake and eager to get the day started as I am on most Saturdays. I anticipate my London search, however, will be less enjoyable than my weekend efforts at the forge. I sincerely hope the success of the search exceeds that of my usual Saturday efforts.

Deciding how the search should proceed is an issue of dependencies. On reflection I conclude the need for automobiles is the primary issue. Based on the intelligence report from Raul, it would seem that Claudette... Nettie, resides in the States as do I. That almost certainly means she will require a car for touring Britain with her niece. I, too need a car, but her need is likely to be short term as opposed to mine. Buying a car to resell when I leave will be by far the least expensive alternative for me, but there is a high probability Nettie and the niece will rent one.

I conclude that my number one priority of the day is to ring up Fletcher. If it's true that he's in the automotive business, he may be able to help me out both with an MG and a list of places where Nettie might hire a car. With a list of those in hand, I'll be in a position to

101

investigate. If Nettie's rented a car, I'll find out the model and conceivably her destination. At the minimum I can determine the date when she's scheduled to return it. If she hasn't rented one yet, a small gratuity will almost certainly buy me a notification when and if she shows up.

I don't recall whether car dealers are open on Saturdays in this country and they certainly won't be open this early. I go down to the hotel dining room and indulge in a huge English breakfast for a change. Once that's over with, I'll ring up Willy Fletcher at home. It may be a bit awkward. Ten years is a long time but if Major Gracer is to be believed Willy remembers me well.

Success. This may work out better than I could have hoped. Willy not only remembers me, he's determined to take me under his wing. He may even have an old car I can use temporarily while he looks out for a MG TD for me. Now let's hope he recognizes me with this damn beard when he comes to pick me up tomorrow.

In the meantime, what course of action should I undertake? Nettie and … Anna ... her name is Anna. Nettie and Anna will be visiting major tourist attractions and there are literally hundreds of them in London. Randomly taking my search to the most likely places without a plan will be an exercise in futility. My quarry undoubtedly will be zigging when I am zagging.

A couple of alternative approaches come to mind. I could make the rounds asking ticket takers and guards if they've seen them. People tend to notice pretty girls like Nettie and her niece. Nettie's red hair is distinctive even at a distance. In addition I might leave notes addressed to Nettie to be delivered should she show up later. It might work or it might not. Those notes will take a bit of thought, more than I feel up to giving at the moment. Letters make good late-night projects.

Since nothing else immediately suggests itself, I have an excellent excuse to pop around the corner to the British Museum. I can't remember when I just wandered around the place as a tourist. I can't think of a better way to spend the afternoon.

You can't get much closer to the museum than Russell Hotel but I've given my leg quite a workout the past few days. I'll cut through Russell Square and spend a few minutes resting the leg and feeding the pigeons. I forgo lunch and pocket a few pieces of bread for the pigeons and a scone for myself, then head for the park.

London

Saturday afternoon in the British Museum
Anna

Geez. These Quakers really don't get what weekends are all about. Nettie sure does needs one, though. Yesterday she was on top of the world about the car and all. Then her stupid meeting spoiled everything. She was really grumpy the whole rest of the day. It's supposed to be shorter today and we are going over to the British Museum as soon as it's over. I don't care if she's still in a bad mood, she can't stop me from having fun. I'm really going to love seeing some of the stuff they got there.

Anyway I've got time for the next chapter of the lion hunter while I wait for her. I cheated last night and sneaked a peek at the photos of Martin's adventures in the South Seas. That's the place where I am now. He's all alone surrounded by cannibals. Uh, oh. They aren't happy about having their souls captured on the photos he took. And that's when Nettie sneaks up on me. Well, she doesn't really sneak, but I still just about jump out of my skin.

Oh, good. Nettie is back to her old self but I play it safe and don't tell her about the blister I got yesterday. I'm not going risk her changing her mind about the museum.

Oh, blast. I didn't think I was limping enough for anyone to notice. I forgot about that eagle eye of hers. She doesn't say anything but heads back upstairs. I'm thinking the museum is off. Darn, darn, darn. Oh, well. At least I can find out how Martin talked the cannibals out of eating him.

"Stop pouting," Nettie says. "I've got some mole skin."

"I wasn't pouting," I tell her. "And what do ugly furry little moles have to do with anything?"

"A little moleskin over your blisters will take care of those blisters, honey," she says and starts rummaging around in her suitcase.

I don't think even Nettie carries dead moles around but I'm not putting dead animal skin on my blisters, not even to go to the museum.

Out comes her little first-aid kit. Oh, good. The stuff she pulls out is too pink and square to have ever belonged to a mole. She cuts a neat patch. The back is just sticky enough for it stay put.

I put my shoes back on and try walking around the room. Golly, this mole-skin stuff really works. I can hardly feel the blister on my left heel and it's the real bad one. As Nettie would put it, goodbye, cannibals, hello museum. We're out the door and on our way.

There sure are a lot more people in Russell Square today than there were yesterday. It's still a cool place to walk. I gotta make some drawings to remember it by. Nettie is back to her crazy self. We're both laughing our heads off when we get to the museum's main entrance around on the Great Russell Street side.

We walk in and wow. Without even getting to the Seven Wonders of the World, the forecourt is really something, almost as neat as Buckingham Palace ... well, maybe not quite. And jeepers, is this place ever big. Nettie and I each get a map. I'll keep mine as another souvenir.

"So Annie, mole skin isn't magic," Nettie warns me. "We need to pick and choose our exhibits carefully to avoid long hikes. We can only see a fraction of what's here anyway and we have the whole summer ahead of us. Me, I want to see Egypt and Persia which aren't too far apart. What about you?"

"I want to see the South Seas Room and maybe the Greeks. I love Greek vases."

We study our maps. Not good. Egypt and the South Seas are about as far apart as you can get. Oh, well. Maybe we should go our separate ways. Nettie is thinking the same thing.

"There's nothing for it but to split up," she says. "Let's meet over there in the Reading Room in, say two hours. It's where Marx sat and wrote his manifesto and is worth seeing. It's a good place to sit down if one of us gets back first."

Cool. The primitive artifacts I'm looking for are on the ground floor just a short walk away. There are a bunch of rooms with everything from African drums to Maori treasure boxes. It doesn't take too long to figure out that the idea of going to the places is more exciting than the things they make there. Drat it anyway. The map shows a Greek room just on the other side of the forecourt.

This is more like it. Everywhere I look, everything I see is gorgeous and that's even before I find the vases. I love Greek vases. The old Greeks painted cool scenes of all kinds of things using pure black against the warm natural tones of the clay. They are really wonderful. They are more than wonderful. They tell all kinds of things about the times when they lived. I hated history in school but this is really ... well, really, real. I love it.

There are even more on the upper level. I still have a little time left so up the stairs I go. Ouch. The mole skin Nettie put on my blister gives up the ghost just as I get to the top of the stairs. Darn it all. My hiking boots would have looked ridiculous with this dress, but I wish

I'd worn them anyway. Oh, well. I limp in to the room with the vases and look for a bench where I can sit for a minute. I'm in trouble now. This is for the birds. I better start back to the Reading Room but it's going to hurt. Blast, blast and double blast.

"Annie, Annie, you're here, too. This is amazing," Grady calls from the medieval and Roman stuff down at the end of the hall. Rotten timing. Oh, well, it can't be helped. He jogs up, grinning like an idiot. Blister or not, I'm glad to see him.

"It's great to see you, Grady, but not what I'd call amazing," I manage to smile. "We're both in London and both have this place on our list of sights to see."

"Did you get the message I left with your receptionist?" he blurts out. "I want to make a date to take you and Nettie out to dinner."

"You'll have to be quick, then. We start for Canterbury and all points east as soon as we get a car Monday morning."

"How about tonight, then? I've already invited Alan and Andy."

"Oh, Grady, I am afraid not. I got a blister yesterday that just decided to get out of control," I groan. "I won't be going anywhere tonight. As it is, I'm meeting Nettie down in the Reading Room in a few minutes and getting there is going to hurt like blazes."

"Well, the Reading Room is the perfect place to nurse your blister. Don't think I'm going to let you wiggle out of your promise that easily, love. If I get you to the Reading Room the very quickest way, will you come to dinner with us?"

"The Reading Room is not exactly inconspicuous, Grady," I laugh half-heartedly. "I can find it on my own without being blackmailed. You just leave these exhibition rooms, go down the forecourt stairs and it's on the right, when you get to the bottom."

"But this sneaky Aussie is a resourceful bloke. I know where to find the freight elevator we aren't supposed to know exists. Also being a gentleman, I'll take you to it for free."

Gosh, leave it to the Aussies to come up with something like that. I limp along after Grady over to a dark corner. Grady puts his finger to his lips, looks around, opens a small door and pulls me after him into the narrow hallway.

"This is it," he says leading the way to a somewhat battered metal door. "This is the tricky part."

I don't quite see what Grady does but the elevator door opens. Yay. I limp in and Reading Room chairs, here we come. Nettie is waiting when we get there and double yay, she has more moleskin in her purse.

Saturday afternoon in the British Museum
Henri

I walk into the museum through the front door like a tourist. It's an odd sensation but I have no desire to visit my ex-colleagues there. I proceed directly to the upper level to learn what they've done with the Roman Britain Exhibition since I was last here.

"Monsieur, le Doctor," a familiar voice greets me from the far wall. I should have known odds were against me escaping notice.

"Mr. Pinkerton. Still keeping the bad guys in line, I see." The guard's name isn't Pinkerton and I'm not a doctor, at least in the sense he means. I can't remember how the nicknames got started but they've stuck. I join him at the back of the big room.

"What are you doing up here with the tourists, Doc? I didn't know you were back again."

"I arrived just a few days ago," I tell him. "I'm not planning on announcing my presence on this side of the Atlantic for a week or so. Will you keep my secret, Pinky?"

"If you want to lie low, you better keep out of the pub, then. And it's only fair to warn you, my game has improved."

"I'm quaking in my boots. You keeping busy?"

"Well, Doc, it's been a long day and bloody boring one."

"Boring is good. How's the family?"

"I'm a granddad twice over, now. Me being on duty is the only thing saving you from admiring my portable photo gallery ..." He hesitates and looks past me. "Uh, excuse me, Doc. I need to relocate."

Pinky has his eyes riveted on two men over by the display of two-handed swords. One, an American judging by his buzz cut, has his nose against the glass. His companion, a virtual caricature of an upper-class Brit, politely looks on, clearly not sharing the American's fascination.

The intensity of the American's interest is odd. His tall, skinny frame remains hunched over the display as the minutes pass, his fixed stare never wavering. Small wonder Pinky has his eye on him.

"That American is absolutely fascinated by something," I quietly mutter.

"Haircut or not, he's no American, Doc. Pure Saville Row. I've had my eye on him off and on for the past two hours. He spent twenty minutes staring at the Reguibat daggers from Morocco."

"His companion must have the patience of Job," I say looking at the man stoically watching and waiting.

"A man in his position doesn't have much choice. Take a professional's opinion, he's either the bodyguard or the watchdog."

I re-examine the pair with a new eye and suspect Pinky is right.

"Well, you're the expert in this field. You think he's going to try to steal something?"

Pinky shrugs his shoulders. "With someone like young evil eye over there, anything could happen or nothing at all."

At that moment, what Evil Eye abruptly does is to straighten up and look toward the next room. He takes a step or two in that direction and freezes, his companion at his elbow. He's staring at something over in the Greek section but it's unclear just what. Vases don't generally have sharp edges.

When Pinky casually walks in his direction, I decide it's time for me to leave him to his work. As I walk by, I idly look into the next room to see what the guy found so interesting and abruptly halt as well. The couple standing on the far side of the room are unmistakable even at this distance. It's Nettie's niece and the Aussie. Eureka. What exceptionally good luck.

A mob of school kids surges into view as I limp in their direction as quickly as I can. As I wade through the small bodies, I momentarily lose sight of the pair. I am mildly surprised when I fail to see them again but this is basically a one-way set up. There's nowhere for them to go.

I make a circuit of both that room and the adjoining one. They aren't there. They haven't passed me. Now I am both surprised and puzzled. I retrace my steps, almost colliding with Evil Eye's companion. I surmise he must be looking for his charge, too. I scan the faces around the room and see no sign of either of our quarries. It's as if they vaporized.

They aren't here, they didn't pass me and people don't vaporize. I search for an explanation and come up with one. It's a bit of a long shot but they must have found their way into the maintenance hallway, maybe for a quick kiss?

There is, in fact, a maintenance door not far from where I last saw them. I limp over and pull open the inconspicuous door more than half expecting to embarrass the pair. What I see is an empty hall with the freight elevator at the far end. What I see is disaster. They're gone but fortunately no farther than the ground floor. The freight elevator is notoriously slow and I'm in a hurry. I take the forecourt stairs at a racing limp.

Downstairs the forecourt is crowded. A group of Asian tourists streams through the entrance. To complicate matters, a museum tour group has just returned. I hastily make my way to the exit. I don't recognize the guard there but when I describe the niece and Aussie he assures me no one matching their description has left. I scribble a note and when I mention Pinky, he reluctantly agrees to give it to them if he sees them. I am confident I will find them but it still never hurts to enlist a bit of backup help.

When the museum closes two hours later, I am in despair. Pinky and I stand beside the guard until every straggler has left. The two must have used the Montague entrance before I thought to alert the guard there.

The day that started out so well has gone to hell. I console myself with the fact that this was just a fortuitous opportunity missed. Tomorrow Willy and I will either find the place where Nettie has rented a car or the place where she will rent one.

Instead of going to the pub as planned, I go back to my hotel room, stopping to pick up a travel guide in the gift shop. I spend the next half hour making a list of the most popular tourist attractions. As the evening wears on, I proceed to fill the wastebasket with unsuccessful attempts to write a letter to Nettie. It may be an excellent strategy to contact the elusive lady but it emphatically does not rate high as the first words I say to her since I kissed her goodbye the day she was arrested in 1943.

When I finally go to bed, I still haven't managed to pen a single letter or even a brief message.

Later Saturday afternoon in the Penn Club
Anna

Ugh, even under the new moleskin my blister is still hurting and my feet are killing me. We go out the smaller entrance on Montague Street which turns out to be closer to the Penn Club. Nettie immediately abandons me to run an errand by herself. Even limping at a snail's pace I beat her home.

Home? Stepping into the Penn Club is like stepping into a Peter Wimsey mystery, but it's starting to feel sort of homey. Speaking of Wimsey, Mrs. Wentworth is over there curled up in a chair reading again. Dollars to donuts, it's a Peter Wimsey mystery. It sure was fun talking to her the other night. That lion hunter book is so, so cool. I love it. I sure would like to do a drawing of her. She has the most amazing wrinkles and I love the twinkle in her eyes.

I limp over to Mrs. Wentworth, meaning to ask her if she minds me drawing her. Before I get a chance to ask, she looks up and smiles. "Anna, my dear. What sort of mischief have thee and Jeanette been getting into today?"

"Hi, Mrs. Wentworth," I say, sitting down in the nearby chair. "I absolutely love 'Martin Johnson, Lion Hunter'. Gee, he sure was a lot more than a lion hunter and so was his wife. Those photos he took of primitive people are a really amazing record of something that is already disappearing. I have a new ambition now. Not hunting lions, of course, but traveling to wild places and taking photographs like he did. I'm going to finish the book before we leave no matter what. I'll stay up all night if I have to."

Mrs. Wentworth looks up at me, a sly smile on her face. "If I'm not mistaken, we have two copies of that book and there isn't much call for it. In fact, thee may well be the first person to check it out in the last ten years. I do hereby donate the copy thee has as career advice for the adventurous."

"Can you just do that?" I ask her.

"I dare say I can, I'm the librarian, aren't I?" she shrugs. "In any case half the books here originally came from our family library in Sussex."

"Oh, wow. Thank you, thank you, Mrs. Wentworth. I'll treasure it." I love this old lady. I bet she could tell some stories herself.

"I'll expect a photograph from the cannibal isles in, say, about ten years," she says.

"You can count on it. I'll even try for five years. Where are the cannibal isles, by the way?"

"The Fiji's are out in the Pacific somewhere between Hawaii and New Zealand. Don't be disappointed. I got the impression the islanders don't eat long pig anymore. Maybe they did in 1920 but if the islanders still do, they weren't admitting it the last time I was there. If you don't send me at least a small watercolor of a jungle, I'll regret giving Mr. Johnson the chance to posthumously lead you astray."

I want to ask her more about her adventures but I've learned to tread carefully around here. Nettie isn't the only who has sore spots, places you just don't touch. Oh, well.

"I was going to ask you, Mrs. Wentworth. Would you mind if I make a quick sketch of you reading here?" I ask. Believe it or not, for once I'd almost rather have a story.

I can't believe the rest of the afternoon has slipped by when Nettie finally gets back from wherever she went. The sketch is coming out better than I hoped but I'm afraid we're going to have to hurry to be ready when Grady's taxi gets here. I have a feeling Bailey's restaurant is going to be both classy and expensive so I need to put on something nice and do something with my hair. Grady really wants to see more of us and Nettie's random itinerary is driving him around the bend. Boy, oh, boy. This thing with him sure could get complicated.

I'll never know if I was right or not about Bailey's hotel restaurant in Kensington. I don't know exactly where Rules is but it is one classy restaurant. Even Nettie is impressed and the Tasmanian brothers are practically paralyzed.

Grady laughs. "I thought you'd like this place. The Guv took me here three years ago. It's swank all right but the food is more my style than the French grub on the ship."

The food is really something and so is the wine. We have a great time comparing our various plans. I'm a bit tipsy by the end of the dessert course.

Grady is going to be stuck here in London handling business for his father for another day or so. When he finishes, Andy and Alan want him to join up with them hiking in Wales and then exploring the Lake District. They spotted a village on the map in the Lake District named Ambleside. I love it. I don't think my ancestors came from there but the guys enjoy the heck out of teasing me about it. Anna, the Duchess of Ambleside.

Grady is more interested in where Nettie and I are going by car than where the Tasmanian boys are going by train but I still think he'll meet them in Wales. And I wouldn't be surprised if he shows up in Scarborough on the Fourth of July even if he is an Aussie.

Nettie and I are thinking about going to the Lake District ourselves and looking for Ambleside village when we leave Scarborough. I don't know where my father's side of the family came from but it might have been there. Even if they didn't, it's on a big lake and I'm going to paint a picture of it. I can't imagine a cooler souvenir of this trip than a painting of Ambleside by A. Ambleside.

I had a darn a good time tonight but this is really, really not good. I'm starting to like Grady a bit too much. He's heir to some monster Australian sheep station and even a few woolen mills over here, for pity sake. Things could never work out between us. Golly, listen to me talk. A few kisses and I'm looking at him as potential husband material. Really, really, really not good. I want go on adventures, not get married and for sure, not to an Australian. We'll go our separate ways in just a matter of weeks and that's the end of that.

XII
The Fifth Day in London

Sunday afternoon in Russell Square
Anna

It's already our last day in London. It sure did go by fast. Tomorrow Nettie gets her car and we take off on day one of our grand tour. Today we take a taxi to get to Hyde Park. We take a taxi because my darn blister is a nuisance. Oh, well. Nettie says the guys speaking at the Speaker's Corner today have no brains except for the bald one and he's crazy. Boy, she's got that right. If some famous guys did debate stuff here they sure aren't around today.

By the time we get back to the Penn Club Nettie is already late for another meeting. As for me, I have too much time to waste and not enough time to do much. Oh, well. At least my blasted blisters are healed enough to walk up to Russell Square. I love Russell Square. A drawing of it is one souvenir I can afford.

Most of the trees aren't very big but I bet the cherry trees were something a month ago. There's this one really big tree that's doesn't look like any kind we have at home. I can't decide whether to sit under it or draw it, so I don't do either. The fountain isn't very exciting but I like all the pigeons and the benches there are comfortable. I sit down, get out my sketch pad and go to work.

A real old couple with a lazy yellow dog on a nearby bench are just what I need. I'm working on the dog when naturally somebody stops to talk to them. Darn, darn, darn. He's right in the way. Then I see his helmet. Wow. He's a real live English bobby. I turn the page and try to capture him quick before he moves, so naturally he does.

Uh, oh. He's coming this way. I hope drawing bobbies isn't rude or something. Gosh, maybe calling them bobbies is insulting. It sounds nicer than calling them cops but then they are nicer. I'm not being fair. The British are so well behaved the bobbies don't even have to carry guns. I could probably take a walk here in Russell Square alone at night without worrying. The bobbies can afford to be nicer.

"Good afternoon, miss. An artist, I see," he says, breaking into a friendly smile. "My missus fancied herself an artist before we got married and the boys were born."

I stop trying to hide my drawing and relax. This guy has a cool smile and a twinkle in his eye. Who says the British aren't friendly. "I guess I'm a bit like your wife," I say. "I'm not an artist but I'm hoping to be one some day."

He turns his head sideways to look at my sketch. "Nice," he says. "It's amazing how much you manage to show with just a few lines. Amazing. You're a Yank, aren't you?"

"Well, I am an American but not a New England yankee," I say. That face of his is just full of character. "Your face would be fun to draw, lots of interesting lines ...." Oops, I didn't mean to say that out loud. Oh, well.

"Wrinkles. I am getting more and more of them, I'm afraid. I'm glad they have some use."

I'm drawing as fast as I can while he's talking. "Gee. I don't suppose I could get you to pose for me, could I?" I ask.

"I'm afraid not. I'm not just strolling through the park for fun, you knows. I'm at work." He gives me a sly grin. "I do have to admit it is kind of fun, but one should never push at the limits so I'd best get back to it."

I memorize every line and plane of his face and keep working as fast as I can. I'm still working on his portrait when a shadow falls across the page. It's the bobby back again and craning his neck to see what I'm drawing.

"Oh, gracious me," he says in hushed tones. "That's me. That really is me." He reaches out and gently touches it.

"Annie. I thought I might find you here," Nettie calls from the street. What bad timing.

"You better look alive," she yells, "We're going to have to hurry if we're going to get any shopping done before dinner."

Blast. Shopping is the last thing I want to do ... wait a minute. "Hey, it's Sunday, Nettie. Shops are all closed."

"Not the kind we're going to. Come on. There's stuff we need for the trip tomorrow."

Blast and darn. I tear off the page and hold it out to the bobby. "Here, take it," I say. "If you like it that much, I want you to have it."

"Thank you for the kind thought," he says wistfully. "An officer can't accept gifts."

I nod. "Of course, even something without value is a kind of a bribe, isn't it? It's too bad this is no good." I sigh and carefully deposit it in the dust bin and give him a big grin.

"Get a move on, Annie," Nettie calls. "We better get out of here before you get us in trouble."

"Getting us in trouble," I say, "is typically your job." I gather up my stuff and wave goodbye to the bobby. He grins and reaches into the dust bin.

Sunday evening at the Penn Club
Anna

Well, that sure counts as an adventure. We must have been the only English-speaking people anywhere around there. Gosh, I wouldn't have guessed there were exotic places like that in London.

I never really thought about trying to fit everything in those back-packs. At least now I have some cool silk clothes that will pack small and dry quickly if we have to wash stuff by hand. I'm really excited about getting the car and starting the tour tomorrow, but I almost hate to leave.

Back at the Penn Club I unlock our door and pick up the folded piece of paper lying on the floor. Nettie dumps our parcels on the desk and collapses on the bed and I kick off my shoes. Boy, it sure has been a long day. We're both pretty darn tired. I go sit down by the window. I don't know if the note slipped under the door is meant for me or Nettie, but I unfold it to see. Wow. Double wow. Triple wow. I'm so shocked I almost drop it.

Jeepers. An obscene drawing of a naked woman fills most of the page. Her legs are spread wide apart. She's holding a man's you-know-what in one hand and a toy in the other. A ghastly looking knife is stuck in her throat. The whole drawing is done in stark black and white with three bright splashes of red, the woman's privates, her braids, and all the blood dripping from her throat. It's sickening. It's embarrassing. It's awful but I still can't help noticing that it's practically a work of art.

I quickly fold it back up and look over at Nettie. "Somebody sure has a dirty mind and doesn't like us much," I say making a face. Nettie holds out her hand for it. I look over her shoulder as she unfolds it.

There's a thing about Jack the Ripper pasted in the top corner above the naked woman. Or I guess she must be a little girl. She's got bows on her braids and a teddy bear. Nettie reads the block letters neatly printed over the naked girl's head out loud.

The first line says "They say Jack only killed five female whores." The letters in the second line are bigger and say, "How many male souls died at your hands, Slut?"

Geez, the thing is really awful. It's scary. We used to laugh at the dirty notes Crazy Craig put in all the girls' desks back in fifth grade but there is nothing funny about this dirty note. It sends chills up my back.

Nettie crumples the page and hurls it across the room at the waste basket but misses. I can't help going over and picking the nasty thing up. I hate to say it but the dirty drawing is very well done. The splashes of red are perfectly balanced against the black and white. Someone put a lot of time and effort into the shading that gives it such a horribly lifelike look.

"Throw it away," Nettie snaps. "Somewhere out there there's a sicko jacking off imagining women looking at his art work. Don't oblige him."

"No, I think we should show it to Mrs. Burton. It's evidence, Nettie," I argue. "Other people probably got them, too. If no one speaks up he'll go on getting away with it."

"You do whatever you need to," she growls. "Me, I'm going to take a long hot bath and a nap. Wake me up at seven."

Mrs. Burton is as shocked as we were when I show it to her. If anybody else got one, they haven't reported it. Geez. I kind of wish I'd never mentioned it. Miss Wilson-Smythe insists on sending a boy out to look for Sergeant Walsh, the bobby I met in Russell Square.

The sergeant's eyes lose their warm twinkle when he looks at the drawing. "I do apologize," he says disapprovingly. "A nice girl like you should never have seen a piece of filth like this, Miss."

"You know Jeannette Hicks, Sergeant Walsh," Mrs. Burton says. "This is her niece, Anna Ambleside."

"Oh, Miss Ambleside and I are old acquaintances," he winks at me. "And I can testify that she is a better artist than the man who sent this. Miss Ambleside, I'm giving the portrait of me that you happened to throw away to my granddaughter. I intend to get it framed."

I'm embarrassed and don't know what to say. It was just a quick pen-and-ink drawing. Fortunately I don't have to say anything.

"I can understand something like this happening in one of the big tourist hotels but not here at the Penn Club. You Quakers are gentle, quiet sorts but I guess some non-members do stay here. It will be interesting to see if more of these ugly letters start showing up. I hope you two weren't singled out. Did you list this as your forwarding address anywhere?"

I shake my head.

"Nettie and Anna are the only two unaccompanied women in residence at the moment," Mrs. Burton says thoughtfully. "That might make them a target for a disturbed person."

"Except, they aren't," Miss Wilson-Smyth contradicts her. "There are the Newman sisters and the missionaries from Kenya."

The sergeant smiles gently. "Considering the ages of the other women in question, I'm inclined to think Mrs. Burton's observation is valid. Nettie and Miss Anna here are exceptionally attractive young women. Has anyone inquired about their room number, Miss Wilson-Smythe?"

"No, but someone might have noticed when they left their keys before going out," Mrs. Burton signed. "Or been watching when Anna's nice Aussie friend left that message for them yesterday."

"Has there been anyone suspicious hanging around the lobby today?" he asks.

"No, no one but that young American sitting in the corner reading this afternoon. I believe he was waiting for the party from Philadelphia. He left when they did."

"Well, make an effort to watch for anything or anyone unusual and we'll see if any more incidents occur."

Nettie comes down the stairs and gives Sergeant Walsh a peck on the cheek.

"If I were your father I'd turn you over my knee," he bristles. "Or send you to your room with no supper, young lady. You are entirely too forward. I don't wonder that you brought this on yourself."

I can't help smiling. Sergeant Walsh is another one under Nettie's spell. People love that woman or hate her but they rarely ignore her.

"Then I take it we are the sole recipients of this guy's art work?" Nettie frowns. "I was kind of afraid of that. And for your information, I am not forward. No one gets kisses from me but you, Ian Walsh and I've been home early every night since we got here."

The sergeant shakes his head resignedly. "I know, I know, but you have to admit that you do tend to attract attention and turn heads. Suppose someone followed you back here from a restaurant ..."

"Not likely. I still have the habit of paying attention to things like that. Come on, Annie. Let's go try that Portuguese place for dinner tonight. Just for fun we'll keep an eye out for anyone following us home. If we're lucky maybe the asshole will just move on to another victim."

Part Three

The Grand Tour

XIII
The Sixth Day in London

Monday morning in the Penn Club
Anna

Blast and darn. I've been trying to pack for the last half an hour. Nettie may be used to traveling light on a motorcycle, but I'm not. There is no darn way I'll get everything I can't do without in this stupid backpack. Even with that new silk stuff, it doesn't come close.

I don't see why we can't just wait until we get the car. We don't know that there won't be room for our suitcases until we know what kind of car she buys. Oh, well.

"Geez, Nettie, is this necessary?" I ask. "Aren't we sort of jumping the gun here? If we take this stuff with us and they don't have a car you want, we'll be stuck lugging all this darn stuff around with us."

"Playing it safe can save your ass in life and death situations. This, dear heart, isn't one of those times." She sets her neatly packed backpack by the door and stows her suitcase in the closet. "There are also times when it gets in the way of the important stuff. And that is why I intend to trust fate and karma today and see where it leads us."

That's a scary philosophy. Maybe you have to be someone like Nettie to pull it off. Or maybe it's why Nettie is Nettie and Mom is Mom.

Oh, well. I shrug my shoulders and start stuffing things into my pack. Here's hoping karma doesn't leave me short on socks and underwear.

Someone taps on our door. It's Miss Wilson-Smythe telling us that our ride is here. I put my sketch pad and lion hunter book in my pack. It won't buckle. I sigh and take out my new sweater.

It's no surprise to find a cluster of people in the lobby waiting to see us off but the uniformed chauffeur standing at attention by the door does surprise me. I bet he's just as surprised when he sees backpacks instead of suitcases. He takes them out to the car anyway while we say our goodbyes. He holds the front door for us and wow. I can't believe my eyes.

Nettie grins at me. "Haven't you ever seen a Rolls Silver Cloud before?"

"Don't be silly and stop smirking. You know I haven't. I guess your Mr. Albright isn't hurting for money. Where is he?"

"We don't need him. By now the business end of this endeavor is all taken care of."

"Geez, Nettie. It must be nice to be burdened with money," I say. I'm wondering if she's emptied her bank account blowing money on stuff like cars and taking me to Europe. I could sure see her doing something like that. Karma, fate and all that. Still I can't keep from wondering just how much money Nettie really has.

There are four shiny sports cars lined up in front the dealership. Mr. Smyth comes out to the Rolls and holds the shop door open for us. Nettie ignores him and walks straight to the long, low white car at the end of the row. It's flat-out gorgeous. The white is sure eye-catching but I figured her first choice would be red. Sports cars are supposed to be red aren't they? Or is that just Italian ones?

Mr. Smyth practically knocks me over in his hurry to open the car door for Nettie, the right one which is the wrong one, of course. They drive on the wrong side of road here. She gets right in anyway and starts examining the controls. I go over to the passenger's side on the left. Gosh, it is small inside, very fancy, all leather and shiny wood, but just two bucket seats.

"Get in and close the door," Nettie orders. "Let's give this baby a test drive."

Without a word, Mr. Smyth hands her the keys and we're off. Holy smoke, are we ever off. All I can do is squeeze my eyes shut and pray. When we get back to the dealership, we're still alive. I practically fall out of the car.

"The Jag will do nicely," Nettie tell the man. "I'll take it."

"Don't you want to look at the other cars," he asks. "Or inquire about the price?" He gives Nettie a shocked look.

"No, this is my car. Do I need to sign anything?"

"Just a couple of forms. The bank has taken care of everything else. If you'll follow me, please." He opens the door for her with a big smile on his face.

"Annie, please tell the chauffeur to put our backpacks in the boot of the Jag and then let him go," she calls over her shoulder. "This won't take long."

I can't believe how small the trunk is. The blasted spare tire takes up almost all the space. Our packs barely fit on the leather shelf above it. The chauffeur takes off as Nettie comes out beaming.

"Get in, Annie dear. We'll have lunch in Canterbury. Sixty-five miles, two hours? Bah, we'll make it in one."

Okay, we are off on day one of our tour. I just hope we live long enough to get to day two.

Monday morning in the Penn Club
Nettie

I'm as eager as a kid on Christmas morning. I was worried that nightmare might spoil things but mercifully it dissipated almost before I opened my eyes. Damn that awful obscene note. He would have to give her red pigtails and a teddy bear, a coincidence no doubt. I don't go around killing men's souls, whatever that means.

I suppose I could have bought a sports car anytime I wanted to. Bless Anna for finally giving me an excuse. The whole trouble is I want a sports car but I don't want to be the kind of person who buys one, a person like Albright. I can see him pulling up in a Rolls to order a bespoke Ferrari like it's his God-given right or sending his gentleman's gentleman to do it.

I detest the man and he detests me but we put up with each other. He's damn good at what he does and I'm the kind of client men like him dream of. I want a car right now and he's the kind of person who has the pull to make it happen. You can be damn certain he's put a knowledgeable peon on the project.

I have to smile at Anna's reaction to his bloody Rolls. I can hardly breathe when the Rolls turns on the street in front of the dealership. At the end of a long block, I see a glint of shiny red in front of the place. Seen head-on I can't make out the make of that one or the British racing green one behind it. Then there's something big and black ... and oh, my. Something long and lean and low and dazzling white at the end of the row. An XK120, my XK120 FHC. In my mind I always saw my dream car as red. That's because I never saw that sleek white vision parked up the street.

Keep cool, old girl. I patiently wait like a good little rich girl for Albright's chauffeur to open my door. I get out and stroll, not run, but stroll past an array of the most beautiful cars I can imagine and go straight for the unimaginably magnificent Jag.

I feel my calm demeanor start to slip as I sit down behind the wheel. I hear the purr of the engine as I start the car and almost cry.

This is my car. Please don't let me find anything wrong when I drive it, as if anything would dare be less than perfect here.

I pull out into traffic and put the Jag through her paces. Poor Anna is terrified. She shouldn't be. After over a year on the racing circuit with old lover boy, I'm a damn good driver if I do say so myself, and a passable mechanic in the bargain. I guess there's no way for Anna to know that. She's as white as a sheet by the time we get back.

That was bloody exhilarating. This summer is going to be a hell of a lot of fun and you know, I think I earned some fun after Djakarta last winter. Calm, cool and collected, I tear myself out of the seat and follow the man inside to make the Jag mine.

Monday morning in the Jaguar XK120 on the Great Dover Road
Anna

Wow, I've fallen in love with this car even though it terrifies me – or Nettie's driving terrifies me. She drives like she thinks she's on a motorcycle, for pity's sake. Maybe I should try to think of it as an adventure. To tell the truth, it's exciting sitting in this little cockpit racing along just inches off the ground. That long sleek hood in front of us does kind of remind me of a big cat. Jaguar is a good name for it even if it doesn't have spots.

Blast. Adventure or not, I can't help squeezing my eyes shut when Nettie takes a sharp left without slowing down. She just looks over at me and grins.

"Maybe you should keep your eyes shut until we get out of London," she says. "It will be easier on your fragile nerves once we get out of the metropolitan area."

Yeah, maybe I should take her suggestion. The outskirts of big cities are all alike. They're dirty and ugly, London included. Oh, no. I catch my breath as the rear end of the bus in front of us looms closer at an alarming speed. I stifle a scream as Nettie smoothly darts around it.

Believe it or not, every now and then, I manage to relax and almost have fun, like rides at the fair. But there's a king-sized difference. At the fair you know you aren't about to die. Mom would have a fit if she could see me now. She'd have a fit but Karen and Elizabeth Ann would be jealous as all get out.

As we get farther out of town, I can spend more and more time with my eyes open. I see fewer buildings, more green and less traffic. I sure do like that.

"You will find that the scenery gets a lot more interesting when we get to the Kent downs," Nettie tells me. "The most interesting thing along here is Watling Street."

"When will we see that?" I ask.

"We won't. We're on top of it. Don't tell me you've never heard of Watling Street. Don't they teach you anything in school these days?"

"Well, they don't offer courses in Watling Street in Des Moines," I tell her.

"What about history? Watling Street is the road the Romans built across England a couple of thousand years ago and it's still here though they paved over most of it in the 1800's. They renamed this section the Great Dover Road."

I'm really beginning to enjoy myself once we leave London behind. It's like on the train but a lot cooler except it doesn't have a restaurant car. Nettie must be just as tired of sipping lukewarm water from her Army surplus canteen as I am and we need gas, I mean petrol, so we stop at Rochester.

Golly, it looks just like an English town is supposed to, with a castle and everything. Nettie vetoes climbing up to see the castle. She says I'll be sick of the sight of castles in a week. Fat lot she knows. We buy a couple of bottles of ginger beer at the market and leave the castle behind.

English villages and farms fly by for close to an hour when I see two massive towers high above the roofs in the distance. Cool. It has to be Canterbury Cathedral. Nettie should be happy. She got her wish. It's only a few minutes after eleven when we pull into Canterbury.

XIV

The Grand Tour, Day One

Canterbury

Monday morning coming into Canterbury
Nettie

"Ha, we're here," I say, feeling rather pleased with myself. "Made it before noon. You are going to absolutely love Canterbury, Anna."

Reluctantly, I slow down to a more decorous sped as we pull into town. I smile at the rapt look on Anna's face. Sure, London is impressive, but it has none of the compelling intimacy of England's small cities.

"Wow. That must be the cathedral," Anna says excitedly. "Mrs. Burton says we should look up, not down, and be sure to go down into the undercroft and look at the arches in the colonnade outside."

"Okay, but first things first," I tell her. "It's approaching noon and I don't recall having breakfast. This town is choker-block full of historic pubs but I'll take you to the Parrott Tavern. It claims to be the oldest of the lot."

We cross the Great Stour river at the Westgate towers and pull into the oldest part of town.

"Golly, Nettie, you never told me there were canals and a castle, too," Anna says, sticking her head out the window to get a better view.

"That's the west gate through the old town walls, not a castle. Wait till we get to Dover. Now that's a castle."

I turn on Pound Lane, which will take us right to the Parrott. Anna seems very taken by the houses along the Stour. I, on the other hand, am taken aback by the white Vespa we picked up in Rochester turning in behind us.

"I think I want to live in that little one with the window boxes," Anna mutters happily. "No, I take it back. It's that half-timbered one hanging out over the water, I want."

I do get a charge watching Anna. "Trust me you don't," I laugh. "Picturesque, sure, but if I don't miss my guess, old and damp. There's the Parrott up ahead. Picturesque, old and definitely not damp. If I re-member rightly we just may find a parking place down that alley."

I'm right. I park and we start walking to the Parrott. I relax as the Vespa disappears in the distance. I'm surprised at myself. I generally reserve my paranoia for times and places where it's appropriate.

"I'm glad you wore your hiking boots," I tell Anna and dismiss the Vespa from my mind. "I imagine we'll need them today. Good thinking."

"No, just blind luck. I wore them because they were too big to fit in my darn backpack."

"Annie, my dear, never ever, ever turn down a compliment. There may not be one around when you need one most."

Anna is as impressed with the Parrott as I thought she would.

Monday mid-morning in the historic
town center of Canterbury
Anna

I love it. Maybe if I'd grown up around here I'd have like history class more. Everything I see has been here since peasants were scurrying out of the path of medieval knights in shining armor. It's kind of eerie. The buildings are just the same but the world around them has totally changed.

When we get to the Cathedral there's a line of people waiting to get in. Way up at the front of the line, I see two familiar figures, Alan and Andy, the Tasmanians. They're doing the same thing we are, exploring Britain and staying in hostels but then they are doing it the hard way – on foot and by train. They planned to leave for Canterbury first thing Sunday morning. I'm surprised they haven't gotten farther but they were talking about hiking from Winchester like the pilgrims in the Canterbury Tales.

At the cathedral door, Nettie hands me a handkerchief to cover my head with. I'd forgotten about needing to do that. Andy and Alan are over by the place where Thomas a Becket got murdered. They say the old blood stains are still there even after eight hundred years. I gotta see that.

"Annie," Alan shouts. "Over here." Heads turn and Andy claps his hand over Alan's mouth. You don't yell in Cathedrals, you whisper.

I'm surprised at how glad I am to see them. It turns out they really did hike the entire length of Chaucer's Pilgrim's Way. No wonder they only got this far. Being on my own in London was cool but it's fun to sightsee with company.

This is the first medieval cathedral I've been in, not counting Saint Paul's, which has a dome. All these great soaring spaces and big stained-glass windows make me feel very small and insignificant. Even the boys get quiet. I love it. Think what it must have been like for the peasants living in their wattle-and-daub huts. Or even the knights living in their grim stone castles.

The tomb of the Black Prince is really moving. I keep staring at his face wondering what he must have been like five hundred years ago. This place sure is beautiful ... scary beautiful.

Mrs. Burton was right. The undercroft and colonnade are very, very cool but after almost two hours exploring the cathedral, I'm a bit dazed. I think we all are.

We're going to the white cliffs of Dover next and so are our Tasmanian friends. If the Jag wasn't a two-seater we'd offer them a ride. Their train doesn't leave for a couple of hours, so we'll probably miss them there. Oh, well. I'm looking forward to hiking along the white cliffs but if we intend to get to Winchester tonight, we probably won't hike very far.

I sure was right. Hiking along the white cliffs of Dover is really cool, better than cool even. We miss Alan and Andy, but not by much.

We spot them at the top of the cliffs as we walk along the water's edge. Too bad. We wave at each other but we are on our way back to the car by then.

Even the way Nettie drives, Winchester is a couple of hours away, but we stop for dinner at Folkstone, a really cool fishing village right at the foot of the cliffs. Golly, we keep coming to places I want to come back to.

The youth hostel in Winchester is the old city mill on the river so there's no place to park. We leave the Jag around the corner by the old guildhall. This is my first time in a youth hostel. Boy, this is so, so cool. The mill was built in the 1700's and you can actually see the river between the floor boards.

We arrive just before the 9 p.m. check-in deadline but it doesn't matter. The women's dormitory is half empty. I'm beginning to get the hang of this hosteling thing. It's really neat. You can rent the sleep sacks but Nettie goes ahead and buys us each one. In the morning everyone has a chore to do before they leave. I now know what Nettie meant about it being a lot more fun staying in hostels. People come from all over and get to know each other. There's a kitchen with a bunch of stoves and pots and pans. We don't have anything to cook but I get to know a couple a girls from Denmark there anyway.

XV

Second Day of the Grand Tour

Tuesday morning in Winchester YHA Hostel
Nettie

Anna is up bright and early. I keep my eyes closed and play possum. I don't know why I should be so tired. Probably all the excitement. Thinking about the Jag eventually wakes me up, though. Today we'll hit Stonehenge and then head back to Oxford. Anna is going to love Oxford.

I haven't gotten organized yet to cook in the big communal hostel kitchen so we make do with a breakfast of toast and jelly. I've already finished my morning chore, which today meant sweeping out the dorm. I wash the few dishes we used, gather our packs and head back to the guildhall and car. The minute I see the Jag I know something is wrong.

"What the hell?" I drop the packs and sprint over to the car. The driver's door handle is smeared with what looks like blood with great red globs trailing down the door. I feel a scream trying to escape but manage to hold it in as I gawk at the car.

I touch the thick wet liquid. Not blood. I've seen far too much blood to be fooled by it. Oh, please God, let it be washable. People are beginning to gather as I cautiously sniff my fingertip, then touch it to my tongue. Poster paint. Plain old fashioned water-based poster paint. Several people stop to see what the fuss is about.

"Same over here on the passenger's door, lady," a gentleman calls from the far side of the car.

A man I recognize as another hostel guest pushes his way through the onlookers. "What the hell is this?" He angrily circles the car. "Vandalizing a car like this one is an offense to the gods. Thankfully it isn't blood or real paint."

Anna looks to be on the edge of tears which actually calms me down a bit. She leans on the hood of the car, reaching for something stuck under the windshield wiper.

"No!" the big man behind me shouts. Grabbing her hand, he roughly yanks it back. "Don't touch that."

Anna gives him a dumbfounded look. "What is it? It doesn't look like a bomb or anything."

The man looks over and meets my eye. It's a condom and it looks used.

"I think I'll go get Donald. He probably ought to see this," he mutters, heading back to find the hostel host.

Anna looks confused. Eighteen and she's never seen a condom before? Yeah, I remember. Ninth-grade health class in the U.S. Boy's in one room to learn about VD. Girls in the other learn about ways to fold diapers and potty-train babies. It would be hilarious if it weren't true. "It's a male contraceptive, Annie." I quietly explain.

"Oh," she says, "Oh, my. But what's it doing ... Oh." Noticing the looks on the faces of the bystanders, she turns beet red. The first man jogs back bringing the hostel host with him.

"Damn!" The host growls, making his way to the Jag. "How many other cars have been vandalized?"

The group of onlookers breaks up to check other parked cars. None of the others appear to have been touched.

I stand there paralyzed, wondering why us. Someone tempted to ruin something both expensive and beautiful, maybe? Anna comes and stands next to me. Quietly she voices the question in my own mind. "Nettie, do you think this could be related to the pornographic note slipped under our door last night?"

I sure hope not. That would imply that we're being pursued. Our cabin on the ship being searched and then the Claudette incident have left me a bit on the paranoid side.

"Highly unlikely," I tell her, hoping it's true.

"But doesn't being singled out for nasty ... pranks twice seems just as unlikely?"

A couple of young hikers come out of the hostel lugging buckets of hot soapy water. "Is it okay if we clean this mess up for these ladies?" the taller of the two asks. "Or do you need to get the constable first?"

Donald, the host, looks at the group around the Jag and scratches his head. "I'll put it in the log, of course, but when you get down to it, there was no real damage done."

He gives us an embarrassed look. "I, uh, hate to ask but are there any jilted boyfriends or divorced husbands in the picture?"

"No," I tell him. "We've only been in England a week and before you ask, no, we haven't done any pub crawling, either."

"This sort of thing should never be allowed to happen," the man who fetched Donald says angrily. "Hold off with the water for a minute, boys. At least let's take some Polaroid pictures of this to put in your log, Donald."

Anna gives me an unhappy look. I know she thinks I should tell him about the dirty London note. Why? What good would it do? Like the man said, there's been no damage done. Except to my nerves, maybe.

"Why don't you take these ladies in and make them some tea while we take care of this," Donald asks the man who'd fetched him.

I hesitate. I'm not at all sure I want to leave my pristine car in the hands of incompetent strangers.

"Go on, lady," one of the young men says. "Me and my old man are car buffs. I know exactly what a gem you have here and how to treat it. Frankly you and your friend both look like you could use a cuppa."

It's well after ten before we finally get back on the road. It's not much more than a hundred miles to Oxford, even detouring to see Stonehenge.

I spend the entire trip and even the tour of Stonehenge looking over my shoulder for the follower I feel sure must to be there. I see a suspicious Vespa but it's pale yellow, not white and drops out of the picture at Stonehenge. A Ford Anglia shows up every now and then but leaves us in a residential area of Marlborough. The suspicious Triumph Mayflower turns out to be a young couple with an infant.

To be on the safe side, Anna and I unanimously decide to stay out of hostels for a day or two. When we get to Oxford, we book into the Kings Arms on Holywell Street and park the Jag out of sight in a quiet alley behind the building.

London

Tuesday morning in young Henry Fletcher's bedroom
Henri

"Wake up, old man, I've found her."

I jerk awake, and sitting up, hit my somewhat hung-over head on little Henry's Model B52 and set it swinging. "What? Where? Oh, my aching head," I manage to say, as I struggle out of bed.

"Don't complain. You're not the one catching the bus for work in fifteen minutes. And you owe me a bottle of Gentleman Jack. I've found her, or at least I've found the car and know where she's going."

"Hell, I'll buy you a whole case. How? What? Where?"

"What, is a 1953 XK120. Where, is Canterbury. How I found out is classified."

"A Jag XK120? Where would Nettie get a Jag XK120?"

"H G Owens, where else? White, pristine, low mileage, fixed head. Bloody gorgeous."

"I find it exceptionally difficult to believe Nettie would have that kind of money. I suspect it must have been a different red head."

"Named Jeanette Hicks? No, you don't weasel out of my fifth that easy," he grins at me.

"That does indeed sound definitive but I'm hard put to understand where Nettie could get that kind of money."

"The usual place a beautiful red head does, I imagine. She married it. There's undoubtedly a rich husband back in the States. Prepare to get your heart broken."

"Don't be absurd, William. I told you nothing of that sort is involved. I haven't seen her since the war. It never occurred to me that she'd still be single."

Willy raises an eyebrow and grins. "Nettie aka Claudette? The girlfriend you were fretting about the whole time in that bloody damp cellar way back when? Come now."

I'd forgotten about that. We put away a lot of wine hiding out under the inn.

"I have to get a move on or miss my bus, old man. I assume you're off for Canterbury. It's a good thing we went ahead and tuned up old Winston and changed the oil yesterday. I rechecked the air in the tires this morning and the boys are out there polishing him up for you."

"I'll be on my way as soon as I find my other shoe. I can't begin to thank you enough, Willy."

"Yes, you can. I'm expecting that bourbon."

I am out the door in under twenty minutes, clean, fed, hung-over and excited. The 1939 Morris, aka Winston, and I are going to get along famously. Winston, for crying out loud? Crazy damn Brits. I've mastered Winston's idiosyncrasies before I get to the highway. Winny and I are going to have a fine relationship whether or not Claudette ... Nettie and I ever do. I'm not entirely sure I can deal with calling Claudette Nettie, or this thing, Winston.

As I recall, YHA hostel rules call for check-in at 5 p.m., checkout by 10 a.m. I check my watch. In theory the Morris should have a top speed of sixty but fifty is the best I can hope for. With luck I may just make it to Canterbury before they close up for the day.

It's 9:45 when I arrive. I stop at the post office and get directions to the hostel. The host is just running the last stragglers out when I find a parking place on the street. He checks the log for me. Nettie and ... Anna did not spend the night here. They might well have stayed in a hotel or inn but if they did they'd probably have checked out by now.

I take a quick turn around the old section of Canterbury looking for a white Jag and don't see one. So where would they go next? South along the coast or west to Winchester and the other end of the Pilgrims Way or maybe Stonehenge? I could just toss a coin but decide instead to gamble that Nettie isn't the Brighton sort and head for Winchester.

I get to the Winchester by mid-afternoon, long before check-in time. I park the Morris and wander over to Bridge Street and the old city mill that houses the hostel. There are several young people with backpacks lounging on the bridge, probably waiting for the hostel to open.

There's little option but to wait. There's a pub on the corner. I've recovered from my hangover and would dearly love a Bass but unfortunately we're into the afternoon closing time so I settle for a ginger ale. The place is virtually empty during this dry time of day. I take my ginger ale and retire to a corner table. An old duffer at the bar turns and eyes me.

"You a hiker waiting for the mill to open?" he asks.

I'm not feeling particularly sociable but I take the opportunity to ask about white Jags.

The handful of other patrons all turn and stare at me. When the publican demands to know why I'm asking, I get the distinct impression that there must be some issue related to white Jags.

"I'm trying to catch up with some friends of mine but I'm so far behind them I fear that I may have missed them," I say, doing my best to sound casual.

"You say you're friends of Mary and Linda?" he challenges. "You a husband or boyfriend?" There's no missing the suspicion in his voice.

"No, Nettie and ... Anna. Don't tell me there are two white Jags in the area."

"You probably want to talk to Donald, then," he says in a slightly friendlier tone.

My heart skips a beat. Something is definitely amiss. Evidently I've won their grudging trust and they take pity on me. Everyone there is eager to relate a different version of the incident. The details don't matter. I've learned what I needed to know. Nettie and Anna left for Oxford via Stonehenge this morning. They'll be in Oxford by now.

I arrive Oxford in just under three hours, completely exhausted. Oxford is one city I know well. There is no sign of a white Jag within walking distance of the hostel. I can well imagine Nettie and Anna might choose to avoid hostels after the experience in Winchester. Apparently Nettie can afford to stay anywhere she chooses. Oxford has no shortage of inns and pubs. On the other hand there probably aren't that many white XK120's in Oxford. The search is on.

After spending the next four hours in search of a white Jag, the situation strikes me as ridiculous. Perhaps I'm just tired and out of sorts but I'm starting to suspect that I've been making a fool of myself. I've spent an entire week obsessively looking for a woman I lost touch with ten years ago, a woman who probably has no interest in seeing me again and must have a jealous husband somewhere in the background.

I drive to the Owl and Fox Tavern out on the Banbury Road. I stayed there for nearly six weeks back when I was here two years ago. I liked the place and the people and I'm in luck. They have several vacancies and the congenial publican remembers me. I suppose that's to be expected in view of the many hours I spent playing chess at the corner table by the fireplace. I impulsively book a room for a week. Whether I abandon my search for Nettie or not, I can do a bit of house hunting. I am seriously considering Oxford as my home base for the year.

Part Four

Hot Pursuit

XVI

The Third Touring Day, Stratford-upon-Avon

Oxford

Wednesday morning in the Owl and Fox Tavern
Henri

I wake up this morning in a much improved state of mind. I unload the Morris, unpack and shake the wrinkles out of my few remaining clean clothes. The publican's wife, Molly is quite the character. I spend half an hour in the pub kitchen sharing a cup of tea with her as if my stay hadn't been interrupted for two years. Then I wander out to the garden to sit in the sun and ruminate on my search for Nettie.

I've had a week since sighting her to adjust to the idea that she survived her two years in Ravensbruck. We were passionately in love on that long ago morning when she kissed me goodbye, climbed on her bike and rode away into the hands of the Nazi SS. Ten years later we're strangers. The people we were that morning have changed, in my case almost beyond recognition. Nettie is almost certainly wealthy now and judging by the Winchester incident may be dealing with a complicated relationship of some variety. Reestablishing contact could conceivably be disappointing.

If the information I got in Winchester is accurate, she will have spent the night here in Oxford. She and Anna may be a mile or so away exploring Oxford or they may be on their way elsewhere. I might actually find her today, I might not. I have no idea what I'll say to her when and if I do. I weigh the merit of calling it quits versus continuing to search today while it is still an option.

Undecided, I procrastinate and call Dougal Macphail up in Inverness. He's been waiting for a call since he got my letter. He's a Gaelic speaker and understanding his heavily accented English is a bit of a challenge, particularly over the telephone. Nonetheless I successfully alert him to expect a visit sometime during the next month. I'll kill two birds with one stone and stop off at the Scottish Historical Society in Edinburgh on the way.

Regardless of the outcome of my search for Nettie, I ought to take some steps to deal with the housing issue before I go north. I have three crates of books still stored down at the waterfront that need a home. Oxford, Cambridge or London all commend themselves as home bases for this year. Oxford currently is the favored candidate and there are several letting agencies on Banbury Road. I may as well fire up the Morris and do a bit of house-hunting while procrastinating about the Nettie search. I can drop my mounting laundry off at the same time.

A quarter of an hour later I stop at the first estate agent I come to on Banbury Road. I delay going in and idly look at photos of fancy houses posted in the window. It's too nice a day to waste. To hell with house hunting. It's becoming increasingly clear that I'm not quite ready to give up on Claudette despite that she's now Nettie and essentially a stranger. I get back in the car.

I hazard a guess that the logical next stop on the women's tour will be Stratford-upon-Avon and I haven't visited the place in years. Of course there's a reason I haven't been there. Every damn tourist that comes to Britain has Shakespeare at the top of their list. It's the height of tourist season and I generally avoid wading through crowds.

On the other hand, I would pass through the Cotswolds en route. I haven't done my morning exercises in two days. A short walk in the hills on a lovely day appeals to me and I can still be in Shakespeare country by early afternoon. I get on the A40 and take it west to Chipping Campden in the Cotswolds. It's a place with some history as a medieval wool trading center and as I recall, there's a superior fish and chips shop there.

Stratford-upon-Avon

Wednesday afternoon in the
Anne Hathaway Cottage car park
Nettie

When Anna points out the piece of paper under the windshield wiper, I know everything. I know everything except who he is. He's been following us ever since we left London. No, longer than that. Ever since he recognized me on the SS Liberté, then searched our cabin for confirmation. A bone-deep dread threatens to overwhelm me. For just a second I think the old familiar numbness will paralyze me. I start to feel faint, then anger saves me. Anger and the passage of time.

I know what I'm going to see, but my hand still trembles as I unfold the new drawing. It's the same girl, me, spread-eagled on the ground but this time the man has dragged me up by one red pigtail and plunged a knife into my throat with the other. Vivid red blood, my blood, spurts out and drips all over the black and white page. It shows me clutching the accusing teddy stuffed with the lost funds and a grinning skull looks out where my face should be. The words "Alas, poor killer bitch, I knew you well. Now you die" are neatly printed in a cartoon bubble over the murderer's head.

That sick drawing confirms what I suspected. Whoever he is, he's broken, locked in the past waging war against ghosts. Oh, I understand him. The ghosts still haunt me but I'm not the woman he thinks I am. The woman who failed her mission and lost the Resistance funds died ten years ago in Ravensbruck.

He's a deluded fool, whoever he is. Men fight and fail and die in war. So do women and children. I'm not a killer bitch and never was. I'm the cold, hard woman who found the rage to overpower our sadist guard, flee the death-march and get the others back to France alive – or some of them. I'm the one who hid the money from the Germans, escaped, went back to find it and use it to keep us all alive.

I tear the drawing in half. Anna takes it from me and forcefully stuffs it into the trash bin. I can see she's scared. She's angry, too.

That's good. I wish to Hell she wasn't caught in this, but she is. She's such an innocent, but she's strong. Anger is a good antidote to fear.

Neither of us say anything as we get back in the car. What is there to say? Except that maybe we should go to the police. Maybe I shouldn't have thrown the drawing away. I can tell Anna is thinking the same thing.

"There's nothing the police can do, Annie," I say. "It's no different than Winchester, no actual damage has been done. We don't live here. We're already on our way out of town," I sigh as I pull out into traffic.

"Gosh, isn't there a law against making threats?" she asks. "This time it really is a threat. It's beginning to really scare me."

"You think that we should stay here for a month or so while they investigate, then? Ten to one they wouldn't catch him anyway. We have to deal with this on our own, Annie."

"How do you propose we do that, for crying out loud? We don't know who he is or where he is and even why he's doing this. Geez, we wouldn't know what do with him if we did catch him."

"I expect we'd think of something." My harsh tone of voice shocks poor Anna. I'm glad. It means she's lived in a safe, tame world and that's as it should be.

"What we do, Annie, is identify him," I tell her more calmly. "Once we do that, then we go to the police. Whether they throw him in jail or not, losing his anonymity will spoil his fun and get us off his radar."

"Fun? Some fun. He's crazy, that's what he is."

"Yes, he is. But unfortunately he's also crazy like a fox. He's managed to follow us since Sunday and that took some doing. He's smart and obsessed and that makes this whole setup seem a bit odd." I probably should explain what's going on to Anna but I'm a coward. Maybe later.

"What if he was back there in the car park watching us? Will he follow us up to Scarborough and the Lake District next?"

"Of course he was there. He needs to enjoy seeing his power to terrorize us. He won't be following us to Scarborough though. We're heading to Gloucester. If you aren't hungry, let's hit the road."

"I've lost my blasted appetite, Nettie. What's in Gloucester?"

"The A48 to Cornwall, Wales and all points southwest but we'll pick up A38 instead," I say making a plan on the fly. "We'll go south by the road less traveled. If he's still following us he'll be easier to spot with less traffic. If he's not, he won't know where to look for us. Meanwhile why don't you get out your sketch pad and start listing cars behind us who may turn out to be him tailing us."

A bit earlier in the Anne Hathaway Cottage car park
Anna

I think I like cottages better than I'm going to like castles. Even with all the tourists you can just imagine what it was like living there. Shakespeare really sat on the rickety bench by the fireplace with his girl. I kind of drag my heels on the way back to the car. The thatched roof is so cool and I love the garden. Gosh, I hate to leave.

When we get close to the car, Nettie points out the piece of paper stuck under the windshield wiper and my heart sinks. Darn, darn, darn, I know before we ever get to the car that it's going to be something else nasty.

Boy, I called that one. It's another bit of dirty artwork and this one is even worse than the one at the Penn Club. It makes me very, very mad, so mad that my hand is shaking. If that sicko was in front of me right now I'd bash in his head, smash his face, poke out his eyes. I'd kick the crazy bastard where it really hurts a guy. Wow. It's scary how angry I am. I grab the blasted note and toss it in a trash can.

The darn parking lot is one solid traffic jam. We sit in the queue waiting to get out and I worry that we made a mistake. I tell Nettie that we should have kept the nasty thing to show the police but she disagrees. The grim look on her face when she says we have to deal with this guy ourselves sure scares me. Some fearless adventurer I'll make. For crying out loud, a little thing like a threatening drawing wouldn't phase Martin and Osa Johnson.

Earlier near Shakespeare's birthplace
Henri

I arrive in Stratford-upon-Avon shortly after one, making Shakespeare's birthplace my first stop. I realize my mistake when I see a wide street leading in that direction clogged with cars and buses. It takes me fifteen minutes to go two blocks and my good mood is rapidly deteriorating. I'm not in the least bit tempted to brave the car park in search of white Jags. I turn off on the first side street I come to.

Ann Hathaway's cottage is located in a residential neighborhood. I speculate that it may be less crowded. The several entrances into the car park are hidden behind hedges but encouraged by the light traffic, I pull in. Too late, I discover that the hedges hide the mass of cars circling around looking for parking places. There's no possibility of escape now, I'm committed.

Trapped and immobilized, I stand on the running board to scan the car park for the white Jag. This would be a more successful strategy were Jaguars not lower than most cars. The driver behind me toots his horn. I share his frustration but neither of us will be going anywhere soon. I get back in, move three car lengths forward and get out again.

I don't really expect to see the Jag. I'm just getting back in the car when I do see an unmistakable Jag grill and headlamp and possibly a minuscule bit of white fender in the next section of the car park. I hold my breath as the Jag rolls forward. The nose is now visible and is clearly white. A green driving cap appears over the taller cars as Nettie steps out.

Success! Anna's blonde head joins the red hair and green cap at the front of the Jag. The two women study a piece of paper left on the windscreen. Whatever it is, they aren't pleased. Nettie tears it in half and wads it up. Anna takes it over and violently stuffs it in the trash.

Only a suspicion that the drivers behind me would lynch me keeps me from abandoning Winny and racing over. I'm within a mere car length of the main drive to the exit when the Jag slowly goes by, stopping just two cars back from the exit. I get in the rapidly growing queue three cars behind her. I'm stuck waiting near the trash bin and being unforgivably nosey, hop out and retrieve the pieces of paper that Anna threw away with such feeling.

When it's my turn to pull out of the car park, I see the white Jag up ahead, pulling on to the Eversham Road. They must be going to either Cornwall or Wales. It doesn't matter much which one. I'll follow and overtake them before they reach their destination. I'm only a few cars behind them as we leave town. I am now faced with the question of what comes next. I suppose I just wait until they stop, go over and hope Nettie recognizes me under the beard.

As we approach Tewkesbury Nettie abruptly turns into a residential neighborhood without signaling. I'm just far enough back to manage the unexpected turn. I can't spot Jag and fear I may have lost her again. I glance in the rearview mirror just in time to see her pulling back on the highway. I suppose she might have simply made a wrong turn but it occurs to me that she suspects she's being followed. I am about to confirm her suspicion. Perhaps an examination of that note they angrily threw away is in order.

I fumble around and find the wadded-up note on the floor. Back on the road, I spread the two halves on the steering wheel in front of me. Whoa! Small wonder they tossed it. Whoever left this is not their friend and is probably the same vandal that left another nasty item on their windscreen in Winchester.

In Nettie's place I would be on the lookout for a follower. Damn. They probably think I'm the one who left it. Damn, damn, damn it to hell. I don't see any viable alternative to following them until they stop. I have to hope they don't start screaming before I get a chance to explain.

Wednesday afternoon on the road west out of Stratford-upon-Avon
Anna

I really like the idea of escaping to Wales. It's where the Tasmanians are going to meet Grady. We might run into them again, but probably not. Oh, well. I count up days on my fingers. Are we still going to be able to get to Yorkshire by the Fourth of July? I have to keep reminding myself how small Britain is. The guide book says you can drive from the farthest place in the south of England to the farthest place north in Scotland in less than three days on the new motorways. Geez.

Ah ha! Daring adventurer on duty. I just got assigned lookout duty for cars tailing us though I kind of doubt it's necessary. Oh, well. I wrestle my sketchpad out of my purse and dig out a drawing pencil. Nettie reaches up and tilts the rearview mirror so I can see the road behind us. The road is straight and flat for the most part so this should be pretty easy. I can see a green car way back and some sort of tan car behind that.

There's quite a lot of traffic, but Nettie leaves those first cars behind. We pick up a red car around Alcester but I can see it's a family with at least two kids. This is not exactly exciting. I start thinking about the things Nettie said earlier.

"Nettie, what did you mean back there when you said the whole setup is a bit odd?" I ask. "You mean because he's so crazy?"

"People don't do things without a reason even if they're crazy, Annie. Their reasons may be crazy but that doesn't mean they don't have them. Some victims are unlucky enough to be in the wrong place at the wrong time. More often they know their stalker and there's some kind of obsession involved."

I gotta think about that for a minute. I know what Nettie is saying. This guy has gone to a whole lot of trouble to follow us. That does sound a whole lot like an obsession.

"So this creep is obsessed, but why us? That's what I don't get," I think out loud.

"My point exactly," Nettie says grimly. "Guys like this creep don't just randomly get obsessed with some woman. If it isn't someone they know, it's someone they have regular contact with or someone famous.

You saw how the Winchester hostel host immediately asked about jilted boyfriends and ex-husbands. There was a reason for that. We, however, are sadly lacking in boyfriends or husbands. Obsessions take time to get going and we just got here. I'm thinking that this guy must have latched on to us before we ever got to London."

"Like someone from the past or someone on the ship?" I ask.

Nettie shrugs her shoulders and keeps on driving. I find myself wondering about her past, then I remember the Russian.

"What about that crazy Russian?" I ask. "He might want to get even with you for breaking his foot."

"No, Annie. I've met his kind a dozen times over. He's just a dirty old man with a lecherous nature, not crazy. Getting his foot broken is the kind of risk a man like him is used to taking. He may hate our guts but it's no big deal in the scheme of things."

Geez, that says something about the scheme of things Nettie must be used to herself. Dealing with disaster relief and refugees has to be dangerous sometimes but I can't see why she would make any big-time enemies.

"We're going to need petrol before we make Gloucester," Nettie tells me. "Anybody behind us that's been there long?"

"Well, since we got stuck behind that lorry, there's quite a line back there. We picked up the first red one about ten miles ago. The black one is new. I can't see well enough to say about the others."

"If he's there, I'll try to lose him. Brace yourself." Nettie whips into a side road, her driving style terrorizing me for the first time all day. We drive around for a few minutes, then pull back on the highway.

"I'm not sure, Nettie, but the tan car back there for waiting for a break in traffic looks like the same one I saw a while ago. I bet it followed us into that neighborhood."

"If it's him behind us, we'll have to take our chances," she says looking at the gas gauge. "He'll have to pass us or stop at a busy petrol station, which won't please him. We're coming to Tewkesbury. We'll stop there."

"Even if it is him, I bet he doesn't stop. If he's been following us since London, he hasn't ever stopped yet."

"If he's really smart he'll give us credit for having figured he's back there and won't be showing himself until the final chapter he's working up to. At least if he's smart he won't. I'd just love to get my hands on that asshole right now."

"Don't tell me that, Nettie. I'm scared enough as it is."

"Trust me, whatever he has in mind, it isn't something he plans to do at a busy Tewkesbury petrol station in the middle of the day."

XVII
Confrontation

Tewkesbury

Wednesday afternoon in search of a petrol station
Nettie

That settles it, I was right. No question, that tan Morris is following us. We have him but what in the hell do we do with him? I didn't expect to spot him this fast. I guess we stop at a busy petrol station and see what he does. First guess, he'll want to avoid a confrontation. He'll keep going and get ahead of us at least until we come to another choice point.

What do I do if he does stop? He won't try anything serious in a crowded place. I confront him, find out who he is, and threaten him with the cops. Then what? Once he's no longer anonymous he'll have to give up or what? Stop trying to scare me and make a run at me? Not there, but somewhere? I'm getting ahead of myself. First things first. We start by pinning down his identity.

On the edge of Tewkesbury we come to just the busy station I'm hoping to find. I stop and pull up to the last pump. Behind me I see the tan Morris pull in and park on the far side of the building. So much for guesswork. Things are about to escalate. Let's go see just who the bastard is.

An attendant comes over to pump the petrol. I'm pleased to see he's a burly guy who looks like he can take care of himself. I warn Anna to stay with the car. Another car pulls in. Ha. The Morris is cornered. I've got the bastard now. He gets out of the car...

Oh, dear God. It can't be. I'm hallucinating. Please, let me be wrong. I'm not. He may look a bit worse for wear but I'd know my Henri anywhere. My heart beats faster and my head spins. I want to run and throw myself in his arms but I guess he hates me now. Please God, don't let this be happening. Henri can't hate me, he simply can't. I think I'm going to be sick to my stomach. I can't deal with this. I turn and run.

At the same time Wednesday at the petrol station near Tewkesbury
Anna

I cross my fingers and close my eyes as Nettie cuts across oncoming traffic and pulls into the crowded service station on the other side of the highway. Just as the service attendant starts pumping our petrol, the tan car pulls in and parks next to the building.

"Nettie, did you see that?" I blurt out. "That's the guy. Anyway, that's the tan car I keep seeing."

Nettie nods and looking like a thundercloud, gets out. She tells me to stay in the car and starts in the direction of the parked car. Geez! What is she going to do? I'm scared but I get out and start after her.

The tan car's door opens and a figure slowly gets out of the car. A big man. Gosh, I hope Nettie knows what she's doing.

Nettie freezes dead in her tracks as the man turns to face us. Me, I'm surprised and relieved. It's the Frenchman from the ship, the one Grady calls the professor. That's when I hear Nettie's stifled scream. I turn and see she's wild-eyed and shaking like a leaf. I think she's going to faint and try to take her arm. She shakes me off.

"No, no, no, anything but that," Nettie sobs hysterically. "Not you, Henri, I can't bear it. No, no, no. I knew you were disappointed in me, but I never thought you'd hate me. Not like this. Oh, God, please don't let this be happening."

Nettie staggers, then turns and runs back to the Jag where she collapses over the fender crying. Golly, what now? I look from her to the professor and back again. He throws his hands up and gives me a helpless look. I don't know what to think. Is he the maniac chasing us or isn't he? Nettie seems to think so, but he never seemed weird or mean to me. We all liked him. It's hard to picture him as crazy and he looks as upset as Nettie.

I look over at Nettie. The worried attendant is hovering by her but she waves him away. Frantically beckoning me, she climbs back into the driving seat.

"Anna," the professor holds his hands out pleading. "Anna, please don't go. You have to help me. I've been searching for the two of you since I recognized Nettie disembarking in Plymouth. I spotted you just today at Ann Hathaway's Cottage. I don't know who Nettie mistakes me for. I'm an old friend."

Oh great, just great. Now what does this intrepid adventurer do?

At the same time Wednesday at the petrol station near Tewkesbury
Henri

Mon Dieu, mon Dieu. Nettie is terrified of me. Anna at least is hesitating. I pray she'll listen for a minute even if she fails give me time for explanations.

"Anna, please. You'll never know who I really am, unless you listen," I say, striving to sound harmless and professorial.

"Okay," she says, "I'll listen but you better talk fast before I get left behind. Just who in blazes are you and what do you have against us?"

Hostile, but she's listening.

"Someone may well be harassing you, Anna, but it isn't me. I'm Dr. Henri DuBois," I say talking fast and using my title as a shield. "Nettie and I were friends during the war. We were more than friends, much more. I haven't seen her since she went to prison. Until I saw her disembarking in Plymouth, I believed her to be dead. Now that I've at last found the two of you I've been simply trying catch up. If someone else is following you, believe me, my motivation is not the same as theirs."

I pause to take a breath. Anna's still listening, which gives me a modicum of hope. Judging by her reaction to my reference to prison, I suspect she knows nothing of Nettie's past. I take advantage of her momentary confusion and frantically attempt to win her trust. When in a tight place, lay down a barrage of credentials.

"I teach military history at Duke University, Anna. I'm on sabbatical this year with a Fulbright Grant to do research in Britain and France. It is unfortunate that my addiction to chess kept me out of circulation on the SS Liberté. It was only by chance that I spotted Nettie as the two of you were disembarking. You were so quick to get to the London Express I failed to intercept you."

"I'd like to believe you, professor, but how come you know all about someone chasing us if it isn't you?"

Good. She called me professor and she is listening. Unfortunately the explanation she asks for may not work in my favor. Telling her that I retrieved the pornographic threats from the trash will suggest that I've been spying on them. In fact, that is not wholly untrue.

"I stumbled on the possibility when my search took me to the hostel in Winchester yesterday," I tell her. "The vandalism to Nettie's Jag was the talk of the nearby pub. By the time I left Winchester, I knew about the red paint and the souvenir left on your windscreen. I also knew your next destination was Oxford. I failed to spot you or the Jag there and guessed you'd go the Stafford-upon-Avon next."

Anna apprehensively looks over her shoulder at Nettie who's urgently beckoning her to return to the car. I grit my teeth and talk faster.

"Anna, you will remember the car park at Anne Hathaway's Cottage was a madhouse. I spotted Nettie from a distance when the two of you were angrily examining the note on the windscreen and watched you throw it in the trash. I speculated that the Winchester culprit was responsible. When I found myself trapped next to the trash can, I couldn't resist the impulse to retrieve the note. I admit the ethics were questionable but it proved most helpful. I could never have understood Nettie reaction without knowledge of her pornographic artist friend's existence."

A car honks at us and I realize we are standing in the middle of the drive. I start to take Anna's arm to guide her out of the way. She cringes so I drop my hand but at least she follows me to stand over by the building.

"What made you think we went to Winchester in the first place?" Anna asks narrowing her eyes suspiciously.

Like Nettie, this girl has a good head on her shoulders. She's not one to be taken in by the first con man who comes along. It's damn unfortunate she has me in that category.

"I didn't," I tell her. "All I knew was that you were headed for Canterbury. After that it was just trial and error checking out popular tourist places. When I didn't see any sign of you in Oxford last night, I was on the verge of giving it up as hopeless. If I hadn't found you today, Stratford-upon-Avon would probably have been my last throw of the dice."

Anna falls silent for a moment before launching her next challenge.

"Why should I believe you when you're only giving me half the story?" Anna impatiently glances back at Nettie. "You said you knew we were going to Canterbury. How could you possibly know that?"

"I apologize for omitting details, Anna. It is a rather long story and I assumed that your patience is limited," I explain. "When I missed you in Plymouth I waited for the SS Liberté to come back to Southampton so I could question the purser. You didn't leave a forwarding address but I learned from your steward that you planned to spend the summer touring Britain and staying in hostels. I tried every car-rental agency and left letters addressed to Nettie with ticket agents at tourist attractions all over London. The first breakthrough was when Nettie purchased the Jag. When she took possession she mentioned that she was immediately leaving for Canterbury."

"That doesn't mean you aren't the maniac who's been following us." Anna glances over to the car where Nettie is impatiently giving us the evil eye. "That sure sounds obsessive to me."

"I admit it probably is a bit obsessive. Hell, Anna, Nettie once meant everything to me. I could hardly just walk away knowing that she is still alive. The last thing I want to do is harm her."

I'm starting to lose my voice. When I pause to clear my throat, Anna hesitates and looks back and forth between me and the Jag. I heave a tentative sigh of relief. I think she's starting to believe me.

"Anna, you know Nettie won't give me a chance to explain. You have to do my talking for me. Please. If this guy is really crazy, you're going to need all the help you can get and I'm more than willing to help."

"All right, professor. I don't know if it will do any good, but I'll see if I can get her to listen to you. But this is a rotten place to talk."

"I suppose it's too much to hope for, but there's a pub just across the bridge in Tewkesbury. The name escapes me but it's an old Tudor building on the corner of Brendon Road. Perhaps you could talk her into meeting me there. It's at least as public place as this petrol station and a lot more comfortable."

Anna gives me a long look. "I'll see what I can do, professor. I sure hope you don't turn out to be the monster. I'm tired and thirsty and ready to be done with all this."

Tewkesbury

Later Wednesday afternoon in Olde Black Bear Pub
Nettie

I don't know what I feel as I follow Anna into the pub. I want to believe her so much that I can't trust my own judgement. Regardless of the story he tells Anna, I can't get around the fact that Henri fits awfully well and coincidences have to be suspect. How likely is it that two of the handful of men who know about my horrific failure would both just happen to be traveling on the same ship as me ten years later?

I sit down, my head spinning. It almost has to be Henri. Love can turn to hate. He probably thinks that I abandoned him. Well, I did, but he'd been in a coma for weeks. They told me he was dying. I couldn't bear to watch it happen, but he doesn't know that. It has to be him. Who else would still remember my mess-up? Someone who lost someone who might have been saved if I'd gotten the money to Dreux that night? Maybe, but a long shot. It breaks my heart, but I'm betting on Henri.

We sit at a table in the far corner near the window. I catch my breath as I see Henri park across the street. Tears start in my eyes as I watch him awkwardly get out of the Morris. He's no longer the athlete he once was. It makes no difference and neither does the beard. I'd recognized him anywhere. I swallow the lump in my throat. Scars and all, he still has the power to make my heart race.

He stands by the table and grins down at me. "Bonjour, Claudette. I've been practicing calling you Nettie in my head but I'm afraid it's still Claudette I see sitting there looking at me like I'm the devil incarnate. May this incarnate devil join you ladies?"

"Bonjour, Henri. I guess you aren't dead after all." Devil or not, that was an utterly inane first thing to say after ten years. Embarrassed, I feel myself blushing.

179

"I was as good as dead, Nettie. I spent over a year in a wheelchair not caring if I lived or died. If I'd had the energy to care just a little bit more I probably would have killed myself. I'm glad I didn't. I've made a new life for myself in the States and I'm enjoying the hell out of it."

"In the States?" Nettie says. "That surprises me, you always said Americans were self-centered asses oblivious to everything and everybody but themselves."

"Life is certainly unpredictable, isn't it? When I was tentatively coming back to life, an old colleague now at Duke University History Department offered me a job teaching military history based on the research I did at Bibracte. I'm more of an American historian than a French archeologist now. What about you? Judging by the gorgeous Jag out there you've done well for yourself."

Damn, that's the last thing I want to try to explain here.

"That is an extravagance made possible by an inheritance," I tell him. Actually it is the truth, just not the whole truth. "I mostly work with the American Friends Service Committee doing disaster and refugee relief."

Henri nods thoughtfully. "I'm not unduly surprised. You're still a woman with the strength of your convictions, I take it."

I'm not happy about how this conversation is going. Time to get down to business.

"Henri, all this is very interesting but kind of skirts the issue we have here," I tell him. "Someone has been harassing me since I got off the ship. That someone pictures me with red braids and a teddy bear like the one I lost on the way to Dreux. That someone doesn't like me a whole lot. You are the number one candidate for the role."

Henri sighs and runs his fingers through his hair. "'If drafted I will not run, if elected I will not serve' ... it isn't me, Nettie," he smiles. That takes me back. He always wisecracks and throws quotes around when he's most serious.

"I'm the last person in the world to want to hurt you, ma cherie," he says so earnestly I want to believe him. Dangerous, very dangerous, I have to watch myself.

"I guess the best defense I can offer is that I'm no artist," he continues. "You know me well enough to know I lack to talent and expertise to produce that masterpiece of pornography. Your nemesis is an artist, not a scholar or even a blacksmith."

That's a point I hadn't considered. But then Henri might have taken up drawing sometime in the last ten years. He's always been good at everything he tries. If he started drawing he'd be bloody good at it. I don't know what to say. We all sit in an uncomfortable silence.

"Hey, I'm hungry," Anna says breaking the tension. "It's way, way passed lunch time. Let's order something to eat before I waste away to nothing."

Henri quirks an eyebrow in a disconcertingly familiar way. "A most superior way to deal with an impasse," he says. "I haven't indulged in steak and kidney pie since I was here back in '52 and it goes exceptionally well with Bass."

Henri is right and I find that exceptionally annoying. I don't want to sit here breaking bread together as if ... as if it were all okay. As if everything Henri says is true ... as if maybe I can't help loving him anymore than I can exorcise all the Nazi ghosts. Damn him. In spite of what he says, I know he must be our bad guy.

Wednesday late afternoon on the road south to Wales
Anna

We are really, really making a mistake. That professor is not the crazy creep. He is a cool guy who is still in love with Nettie. It was really, really stupid to turn down his offer to watch our back. Geez. It would be a way we could have caught the bad guy before he can do whatever he's got planned next. It might really be the only way to catch him short of going to the police. Darn, darn, darn. There's no guarantee the police would be more help. I bet they wouldn't take crazy creep's threats seriously and if they did, they'd never catch him. For crying out loud, one sign of the cops and all he has to do is lie low until they get tired and go home.

I look out the window. We haven't even been on Nettie's so called highway-less-traveled since Breadstone. If the one-lane cow path we're on now has a name, I bet not even Nettie knows it. At least we don't meet many cars and Nettie is driving a lot slower. It's a good thing she is or we'd picking wool out of the Jag's grill. Gosh, if I wasn't so scared, this would be the coolest thing we've done yet. I bet this area looked just the same a hundred years ago … or two hundred, or five hundred. Too bad I can't enjoy it more.

"Hey, Nettie, will this road really take us to Cardiff?" I ask, as we inch around a tractor going five miles an hour. The farmer gives us an unfriendly stare.

"All roads lead to roads that lead to roads that lead to Rome, honey. But we aren't going to Cardiff, at least not tonight."

"But you told Henri that we were going to Cardiff ... Oh." I sigh and try again. "Nettie, the professor isn't our bad guy. He can't draw and he has an alibi. Besides, he's very cool and is still in love with you, for pity's sake."

"In ten years you can learn to draw and he can get his buddy, this Willy, to lie for him. All con men are cool, Annie. Never forget that."

"Geez, give him a break. You can learn to draw but you can't learn to be a genius. Did you really look at those nasty drawings? Our bad guy is a real honest-to-goodness artist. I'd give anything if I could be even half as good."

Nettie doesn't have anything to say to that. I concentrate on looking at the scenery as we continue in silence for a while. Finally Nettie clears her throat.

"Annie, I have no intention of being victimized. As of today the hunter becomes the hunted. We're going to catch this bastard doing his dirty work and bring him down. Whether he's Henri or not, there are details in those drawing that tell me he's someone from my past. I may know him or he may be someone who simply knows of me and blames me for something I did in the war. Either way, that gives us something to work with."

"Cool. So where do we start?" I ask. "I mean besides losing him here in the wilds of Wales."

"Losing him is today's plan. I afraid I haven't quite figured out tomorrow's plan but this will give us some breathing space. How long it takes the creep to find us again is going to tell us something. Also I'm hoping to eliminate Henri as the bad guy if we can. If we establish that Henri is definitely in Oxford when something happens here, it's an argument in his favor."

"I get it. That's why you turned down his help."

"One reason, certainly. God help us if he's the bad guy. We won't beat that consummate chess player unless it's by blind luck. We gotta hope creep's a different story. First off, we discover his pattern. Then we use it to trap him."

"Nettie, you've done things like this before," I say. "Henri said something about you actually going to prison." Oops. The look on Nettie's face warns me I really goofed. I think she's going to ignore the question but then she sighs and looks over at me.

"Yes, Annie. I've been in several very unpleasant prisons and a concentration camp as well. Henri and I were active in the underground in Occupied France. After I was arrested he joined the maquis resistance fighters in Normandy. That is absolutely all I have to say on the subject, okay?"

"I'm so sorry, Nettie. I had no right to trespass on your privacy." I feel terrible. But the French Resistance, wow. I think I read about maquis resistance fighters. Henri must have been as tough as he looks before he got hurt.

"You have every right, Annie. You're stuck dealing with the fallout from my past, but it's a past I avoid thinking about. I promise you, if a piece of that past turns out to be relevant to the present, I'll tell you."

"Around here it's hard to tell the past from the present," I say, glad of an excuse to change the subject. "The village ahead looks like it came right out of a museum landscape painting."

"Berkeley, I believe," Nettie says. "Ah yes, there's the castle. We're only about twenty miles from Chepstow and even at twenty miles an hour we'll be there before the shops close."

"And he won't bother going to Chepstow. Good."

"Wrong. Chepstow isn't large but is the crossroads into Wales. He'll certainly go there but he won't find us. Two years ago I worked with some Welsh Quakers who have an automobile repair shop on the north edge of Chepstow out near the racecourse. We'll ditch the Jag there and have them put it under cover and out of sight. Then we'll hike to the youth hostel unobserved. The only tricky part will be getting across the bridge. There's no help for it. We'll be visible for a few minutes crossing it. If we are unlucky enough that he's watching the bridge, we'll find it out when we get to the back streets and he follows us."

When we get to Chepstow I see what Nettie means about crossroads. The A4 from London and the A48 from Gloucester meet at the bridge and there's a lot of traffic. But Nettie is right, there are enough other white cars and lorries so that we don't stick out like a sore thumb.

XVIII
Wales

Chepstow, Wales

Late Wednesday afternoon at the Cadigan's auto repair shop
Anna

This is more like it. Wales is really cool. The quaint stone houses and steep streets have a different look from the English villages I've seen so far. The Cadigan's garage is right in the middle of a wonderful garden and not a bit what I expected a car-repair shop to be like. Believe it or not, both the Cadigans are car mechanics but it's the husband, Meurig who's the better cook. I sure do like them and their garage. I sure do like all of Chepstow that I've seen so far.

Drat, stuffing myself at the Black Bear at lunch time was not smart. The dinner here is something called Welsh Cawl, which is wonderful even if is some kind of lamb stew. And wow. The Welsh cakes and speckled bread that they call bara brith are really, really good. We have a whole bag of it to snack on while we hike to the hostel where we're going to spend the night. And this time, we'll be using the hostel kitchen. Meurig's wife, Angharad has stuffed our backpacks with the makings of a real Welsh style breakfast including laverbread and cockles.

The youth hostel is in a wonderful big white mansion that's only a bit over a mile away. A busy street runs right beside it but it really faces a narrow lane and backs up on farm land. And here's the big thing. Guess who is there. All three of the Aussies! Grady has rented a big British car I've never heard of called a Humber Super Snipe and they're on their way to go hiking in Snowden.

Golly, it sure is good to see them. They're all in high spirits and naturally ask about the Jag. Of course they don't know anything about our trouble with the crazy creep so we tell them it's in the shop getting a tune-up which they seem to believe. I forget all about the creep when the Aussies invite me and two girls from Liverpool to an insane game of croquet. Surprisingly, even Nettie joins in. The day is ending up a whole lot better than it started.

Wednesday evening near the Chepstow youth hostel
Anna

This last watercolor of the hostel isn't too bad and it pays to stop when you're ahead. A gentle breeze stirs the leaves along the overgrown lane bordering the green fields surrounding the lovely old house. It's a great evening for a walk. I put up my paints and start down the lane.

The half-light of the sunset is magical. Grady falls into step beside me. We walk along in a comfortable silence but I can tell he has something on his mind. "Okay, out with it," I finally say.

"Annie, I don't know if I should say anything, but I'm a spot worried."

"Worried? Geez, I'd be worried, too if I was traveling with those two devils from Tasmania," I tease.

"No, I mean seriously. Is there a reason why some guy might be following you?"

Blast. So much for forgetting about crazy creep. Oh, well. This could be important if he's not talking about the professor.

"If you mean a guy with a beard driving an old Morris, he's that professor from the ship," I tell him. "It turns out that he's an old friend of Nettie's."

"The professor? No, this is some chap I've never seen before. This bloke I'm talking about was hanging around watching you in the car park when you were out sketching earlier. I caught a glimpse of him again just now behind that wall watching us. He does have binoculars around his neck so I guess he might just be a bird watcher."

I catch my breath. Blast and double blast. I can't believe that crazy creep could have caught up with us that fast. I really don't want to get Grady involved in all this but I need more details.

"Actually it's probably nothing," I say casually. "But Nettie and I have had the uncomfortable feeling someone beside the professor was following us. You didn't happen to see what kind of car he was driving did you?"

"That's just it. I didn't. He just suddenly appeared, stood in the shadows and then hightailed it when he saw me. If he's a hiker staying here in the hostel, I sure haven't seen him. It's probably nothing but it just seems wrong to me."

"I don't much like the sound of that either, Grady. What did he look like?" I ask. I really, really need to get a description.

"Well, I'd say he's fairly young. He's tall and slim and wears a blue windbreaker. That's all I know." Grady takes a deep breath and give me a worried look. "Sound like anyone you know?"

Gosh, I wish Nettie was here. I don't know if I should tell him what's going on or not, so I just shake my head.

"I don't want to worry you so probably shouldn't mention this," Grady continues. "Alan and Andy tell me there was a bloke on the cliffs at Dover watching you through binoculars when you and Nettie were walking down along the water. It bothered them enough that they mentioned it to me when I picked them up yesterday. They thought that he was acting suspiciously but you two were gone before they got a chance to warn you. I didn't take it seriously but they described him wearing a blue windbreaker. Now I see this bloke with binoculars in a blue windbreaker and I start to worry."

This is really scary but it's also darn awkward. I don't know how much to tell Grady so I keep my mouth shut and keep on walking. He gives me a long unhappy look.

"Look, maybe I've seen too many movies. He could have been a bird watcher but I sure don't like the sound of it. I can't help it but I find myself wondering about Nettie again."

I pretend I didn't hear that last part and sigh. "I guess I'm worried too, Grady," I say trying not to sound as worried as I feel. "I think I'd better tell Nellie about this."

"Anna," he hesitates, then says in a rush, "Annie, what does Nettie do when she isn't on holiday? No, don't answer that. It's none of my bloody business. It's just that I ...."

Grady stops, pulls me close and kisses me. I start to push him away but ... well, it was a very nice kiss. He runs his fingers down my cheek, kisses my eyes.

"Annie, Annie, you're the most wonderful woman I ever met or can even imagine," he whispers, then kisses me again. It is a very, very nice kiss.

"No, Grady, please ..." He shuts me up with another kiss.

"Grady, stop," I gasp. "This is a bad idea. I like you, I like you a lot but my mother warned me about giving my heart to a passing stranger. Our paths may have crossed but we are headed in different directions."

Slowly he lets me go and looks away.

"You are right, damn it," he groans. "Why does the first really wonderful girl I ever meet turn out to be a bloody Yank?"

"And why did you have to turn out being a blasted Aussie. I don't even like loud, obnoxious Aussies," I can't help adding, as the Tasmanians descend on us looking for a game of cards now that it's too dark for croquet.

I beg off and go to the dormitory upstairs, my mind full of guys with binoculars and Grady. Drat. It's ridiculously early but Nettie is already asleep. The guy with the binoculars is kind of a big deal but it's been a rough day for her. Oh, well. I start for the showers, then change my mind. This really is a big deal.

"Nettie," I whisper softly, "Wake up. It's possible we were followed here after all."

She sits up so fast she hits her head on the upper bunk. "What?" she blurts out. The woman with the kid in the next row over glares at her. Nettie apologizes and follows me out into the hall in her purple and red PJ's. She listens while I carefully repeat everything Grady told me.

"It sure could be him," she says frowning. "He could have been on the bridge on the lookout for us with those binoculars. That would be a clever ploy. It would tell him if we were going to Cornwall or Wales even if we didn't stop here." She grits her teeth and shakes her head. "Or he could have been a bird watcher who enjoys watching pretty girls when the opportunity presents itself."

"There's one of those red phone booths by the back door. Henri will be back in Oxford by now. You could call him and ask him what he thinks," I suggest. "It would be good to get a second opinion."

Nettie sighs. "Yeah, and if he's in Oxford, he isn't here. He gave me the number for the Owl and Fox. Let's find out."

Nettie looks disappointed when she gets back from making the call. "He wasn't there," she tells me. "Mrs. Wood bent my ear for ten minutes and cost me a handful of coins. She says he and her husband left half an hour ago to check out a flat that's coming up vacant. Evidently they think pretty highly of him at the Owl and Fox.

"Actually so I do I," I smile. "Even if you didn't get to talk to him, it sounds like a pretty good alibi to me. Not to mention the fact he's neither young nor skinny."

Oxford

Wednesday night at the Owl and Fox Tavern
Henri

I'm tired and discouraged when I arrive back at the Owl and Fox. I've come to an unfortunate and most inconvenient realization. I am as in love with Claudette as I ever was. Damn. It remains to be seen if that means I'm in love with the Nettie Hicks she is now or if it simply seems as if I am. I know nothing of the woman she is now. I'm not convinced that I truly understand who I am now, either. I do know I'm not the man Claudette was in love with ten years ago.

I also know that I rather like my life as it is and unrequited love is exceedingly unpleasant. So why can't I manage to forget about Nettie and get on with my life? Because the twenty-year-old Claudette and the thirty-year-old Henri were true soulmates, desperately in love in an insane world. Damn it all. That's not something that often occurs in life and not easily forgotten when it does.

I settle down in my usual corner of the pub feeling sorry for myself. Mrs. Wood appears with a Bass and a glass. She grins and puts her hands on her hips.

"You, my dear Henri, look like you just lost your best friend and your dog died, too." She hasn't changed a whit since the summer I stayed here. She's still quite the character and damn difficult to ignore.

"Worse than that, Molly. I found the onetime love of my life with a maniac chasing her, intent on hurting or perhaps killing her. And to make things really interesting she thinks I'm him." I'm surprised to find myself whining to my old landlady. I really must be feeling sorry for myself.

The pub is empty except for a few regulars. Molly draws a Guinness and sits down across from me. "You can't get away with dangling a teaser like that in front of me, Henri DuBois. I haven't heard a good, real-life soap opera in weeks. An old flame, a maniac and obviously a delicious misunderstanding."

"I never learn to hold my tongue, do I, Molly? It's just old history left over from the war. You don't want to hear about it and I don't want to talk about it."

"All right then, I'll tell you the story. Let's see. We all know or at least guess that you were wounded in the war. Your French sweetheart thought you were dead and married someone else who turned out to be a bad penny. She's trying to hide from him on this side of the channel and runs into you. How am I doing?"

"So-so," I can't help laughing. "She's not French and she's not married and she has no idea who the bad penny chasing her might be."

"But like a bad penny you've turned up so she's jumped to conclusions. Now you have to save her and keep out of sight while you do it."

"You clearly are an undercover member of MI5 weaseling secrets out of your clientele." I manage a rueful smile.

"Don't complain. This MI5 agent has been on duty looking for a flat for you. My sister-in-law's neighbor has a flat that looks like it may be vacant soon. The student renting it thinks he's about to be sent down. It's within walking distance of everything that counts and has off-street parking. Interested?"

"Most definitely. I'd like to arrange to see it when it falls vacant."

"Talk to Duncan. He's planning to drop off some things for his mum this evening or tomorrow."

This cheers me up considerably. Unasked, Molly brings me a couple of pickled eggs and another Bass, then disappears into their living quarters down the hall.

An hour later, Duncan and I are on our way back from the center of Oxford and it's just possible I've found my flat. I feel a touch guilty for wishing the present occupant bad luck but it certainly will be convenient if he does get sent down.

Molly meets me at the door. "Your old flame called, Henri. I take that as a hopeful sign."

"I told you, she is not my old flame," I say trying to hide my elation. "What did she want?"

"I, Molly Wood, say she is your old flame and she just called to hear your voice and make sure you weren't out with some blonde. I assured her you weren't and told her she was crazy if she lets you get away."

"I hope to hell you are joking, Molly. Did she leave a message for me?"

"No, just that you can't return the call after 10 p.m. which hardly matters. She didn't leave her number."

I go upstairs to consider the news. I don't know whether to hope nothing has happened or hope that something has, thus exonerating me. Speculation is pointless but I agree with Molly. It is a hopeful sign. I'm ridiculously elated. That elation, however, is also a sign and a most inconvenient one.

I know damn good and well that this is a situation to leave alone. That thirty-year-old lecturer at the Sorbonne had little in common with this forty-year-old historian. A more unsettling insight comes to mind. The Henri who fell in love with Claudette has even less in common with the Resistance maquisard I became after Claudette was arrested. The bottom line is, Nettie and I no longer have anything in common.

I realize that none of this matters. An unbalanced madman is threatening Nettie and there's too much of maquisard left in me to turn my back on the situation. It's as inconvenient as hell that she suspects me that but that makes no difference. I have no choice but to go after the bastard.

I retrieve the torn-up drawing from my briefcase and look at it critically. The red braids and the teddy bear might not have anything to do with the failed Dreux mission but they might. It's a place to start. I can collect names of people who were directly involved in the funds transfer either at the sending or receiving end. I know a few names and I can make some shrewd guesses about some others. Jean will be able to fill in most of the blanks or know who can. I'll trace the ones still alive and eliminate any that I can establish are somewhere else.

It's too late to do anything tonight but I have an agenda for tomorrow.

Part Five

Foul Play

XIX

Blood and Guts
The Fourth Touring Day

Chepstow

Thursday morning in the YHA youth hostel
Anna

It seems as if I just fell asleep when I wake up to the sound of the Liverpool girls noisily deciding what to wear. Nettie is up and finished with her chores and by the time I get to the kitchen, she's already cooking the Welsh breakfast including eggs, cockles and what they call bacon here. Cool. Very cool. The Dutch bicyclist is the only other person still eating and she's at the other end of the kitchen so Nettie and I can talk about stuff and there sure is stuff that needs talking about.

"Tell me again what the guy looked like," she says as she sits down.

Yeah, the sneaky birdwatcher. He snuck around in my bad dreams all night. I bore Nettie with the details of my dreams until she throws up her hands.

"How sure was Grady that the man was young?" she finally asks. "If I'm right about what's going on he has to be at least forty."

"I think it was just an impression he had," I tell her. "You'll have to ask him."

"I will. We can't ignore the possibility that this guy with the binoculars is our crazy creep which blows all the plans I had to hell. I'm seriously considering going along with Grady's suggestion that we all go to Cardiff together. The Aussies already know we're concerned about the guy with the binoculars and are excited about watching our back."

"Or we could go back to Oxford and take Henri up on his invitation for dinner now that he has an alibi," I suggest. "I sure am sick of fish and chips and our own cooking. Heck, Nettie, I like Henri and even with a bad leg the guy is mighty big and sure looks like he knows how to take care of himself."

Of course what I don't say is that traveling with the blasted Aussies just might be too much fun. It would really be a disaster if I fell for that jackaroo.

Nettie shakes her head and frowns. "Maybe Henri has an alibi and maybe he doesn't, Annie. We are only two hours from Oxford by the main highway. I'm not ready to trust him. He is entirely too good at taking care of himself."

Alan and Andy would pick now to show up in the kitchen. Darn. So much for making our plans.

"Okay, Ladies, "Alan says. "We are packed up and ready to go. Grady has gone looking for petrol. Whether we all go to Cardiff or not, we can crowd in and take you as far as the repair shop."

"You're on," Nettie tells him. "A ride to the garage will be greatly appreciated and maybe I can talk Angharad into parting with some Welsh cakes and tea while we hash out plans."

Blast and double blast. It doesn't matter whether I like the idea or not. We have our things packed and ready to go by the time Grady gets back. The Humber's back seat is really big and Nettie is small so three of us easily fit. But Heaven help us, the Tasmanians break out singing Waltzing Matilda at the top of their lungs. It's a really, really good thing we're not going all the way to Cardiff.

We get a few blocks from the garage and traffic comes to a screeching halt. Grady is tallest so he gets out and cranes his neck trying to see what's going on.

"It must be a pileup," he informs us. "There are a couple of police cars and some kind of lorry blocking the street. Ah, they are waving people down that side street. We're on the move."

The lorry in front of us pulls around the corner out of the way and so we can see ahead.

"Holy smoke," I gasp. "That's the Cadigan's Garage up there where everything is happening. Gosh, I wonder what's going on up there."

Grady rolls down the window. "We're here to see the Cadigans, officer. What's going on? Are they all right?" he politely asks.

"There's been a break-in, sir. Nothing to worry about. I suggest you come back in an hour or so."

"Actually, Mr. MacFarland is just dropping us off to pick up my car," Nettie leans forward and tells him. "We'll go up to the house on foot and wait there."

"Your car, Miss?" The man frowns. "That wouldn't be a white XK120, would it?"

Nettie turns white as her jag. "Yes, as a matter of fact it would," she tells him "Please don't tell me something has happened to it."

"Nothing serious, Miss, but yes, you do need to come up to the garage. The rest of your party will have to wait. They can park on next street."

Thursday morning at Cadigan's Garage
Nettie

Damn it to hell. What has that bastard done to my Jag? The cop said it wasn't serious but his idea of serious and mine are probably damn different. I'm just sick about this. I never dreamed we'd be bringing our trouble to Angharad's door. The officer conducts us to the garden where Meurig and Angharad are sitting in lawn chairs, drinking tea and looking dazed. We join them.

"Oh, Nettie," Angharad says and pours us some tea. "It is just awful. The only damage is to the overhead door. It's insured and nothing seems to be missing. The Jag can be cleaned up but the neighbor's poor cat is dead."

"What do you mean, clean up the Jag?" I ask, holding my breath. "What's happened?"

"It's all on the outside and blood washes off," Meurig assures me.

"Blood?" Anna and I gasp in unison. "What do you mean blood?"

"It's Tomas, the neighbor's cat and it isn't pretty," Angharad says grimly.

"The cat? I'm so, so sorry," I say and mean it with all my heart. "This is our fault. I wouldn't have come here if I knew our troubles would follow us."

Anna is strangely silent and I feel her tremble. I am so, so sorry I got her into this mess.

The white shirt, tie and silver buttons on his uniform identify the tall man who strolls up as the boss. "Inspector Jones," he politely introduces himself. "You are Miss Hicks, the owner of the vehicle?"

"Yes, and this is my niece, Anna Ambleside," I tell him. "Can you tell us what happened or better yet let us see for ourselves?"

"I don't think you really want to see, Miss Hicks. I understand that this isn't the first act of vandalism you've been subjected to recently."

"It sounds like this is more serious. On Tuesday night in Winchester, someone smeared red poster paint on the car door and the handles. They, uh, left a soiled prophylactic under the windscreen wiper. The manager of the youth hostel put the details in his log and I believe someone took a few Polaroid pictures."

"Do you have any idea who might wish you ill?" he asks, looking back and forth at Anna and me. I'm of two minds whether to tell him about the drawings, so I procrastinate.

"Please, may we see just what was done?" I ask.

"Yes, but I don't recommend it. I don't believe that it will tell you much and it's quite unpleasant."

"Nonetheless, I wish to understand exactly what was done." I put my tea down and stand up. Anna starts to get up too but she's moving very slowly. "Annie, you really don't need to come with me for this," I tell her.

"I think I do," she whispers. I take her arm and we follow Inspector Jones around the corner. Activity stops when they see us. The photographer puts up his camera and the other men step back.

A once white cat lies cut open on the Jag's bonnet. His intestines are stretched out around him artfully draped in symmetric swirls. Our artist friend must have collected the blood somehow and used it to paint death threats here and there on the car.

Anna cries out, her knees buckle, and she goes down. I wish I had realized how bad it was going to be. I'm pushed to the side and the police take over.

Anna is in alarmingly bad shape. Angharad puts her to bed upstairs. The cops run off the Aussies who have slipped in over the back wall and politely give me the second degree. I do my best to remain calm but I've had bad experiences being questioned in the past. My eyes keep straying to my missing fingers.

It may be a mistake, but I force myself to tell the inspector everything, only keeping my suspicions about who might be behind it to myself. Of course he asks to see the drawings. Either Sergeant Walsh or Mrs. Burton will still have that first one. Henri had the other one and I'm sure he didn't throw it away. I give Jones the telephone numbers for the Owl and Fox and the Penn Club. One of his men goes off, presumably to make a few phone calls.

The inspector finally finishes with me. Thank God. I'm exhausted and it's clear we aren't going to be going anywhere for a while. I go in and find Meurig and the Aussies with their heads together in the kitchen. Evidently the police found them harder to run off than they thought. I try to tell them to go on to Cardiff without us, but they aren't listening.

Anna is my chief concern now. I go upstairs and find her tucked up in the guest room, red-eyed and dazed. The cat was a nasty sight but I'm a bit surprised at how hard Anna is taking it. I sit down beside her and pour myself a cup of lukewarm tea from the pot next to the bed. I don't say anything. She'll talk when she's ready.

Anna opens her mouth to say something and bursts into tears again. "It's Snowball all over again," she manages to sob. "It's just the same as poor Snowball."

There's a story behind this. I sit back and close my eyes prepared to wait while Anna continues to sob.

"I had Snowball ever since she was a kitten," Anna eventually whispers. "I was in seventh grade when it all happened and I know exactly who did it but no one did anything about it. Craig, the untouchable rich weirdo. I hate him. I hate him. I hate him. I hope he's locked up somewhere but of course he isn't. His father owns half of Des Moines and is probably going to be the next governor."

I let her cry for a while and then encourage her to talk more. She needs to get this out of her system.

"Craig Stewart Dawson, the third. He was in my class from first grade until sometime in our junior year. He was always a monster, even when he was a little kid. He liked hurting things and was really good at getting away with it," she says between tears. "He was rich, the smartest kid in school and was even better in art class than me but none of that made any difference. He was weird as all get out. I mean really, really weird. I mean by the time we were in junior high, he was scary crazy. We were all afraid of him."

I took Anna's hand. "I've had to deal with a few monsters, too. Annie. There are evil sadists in the world. When they get in positions of power, they do horrible things, like killing six million Jews. That doesn't make it any easier when someone you love becomes their victim. I'm so sorry about Snowball."

I can't let myself think about all the people I'm so sorry about. Henri is one of them. I wish ... never mind what I wish. He's probably on his way here now if the inspector got in touch with him about the Stratford-upon-Avon drawing. I don't suppose there's any way we could leave for Cardiff before he gets here. This emotional roller coaster is just about more than I can stand. I yield to an impulse, lie down beside Anna and close my eyes.

Oxford

Midday Thursday in the Owl and Fox Tavern
Henri

Molly is waiting for me when I come in the pub door.

"You picked a hell of a time to pick up your laundry, Henri, my boy," she says with her hands on her hips. "I've had the Welsh police on the phone looking for you and no less than two telegrams came for you from France."

"The Welsh police? That is alarming," I say. It takes a concerted effort to remain calm. "Did they give any indication of what it is about?"

"Inspector Jones was not in a talkative mood but he did say it was urgent but not an emergency. No one is hurt or dead. He left two numbers, one for the constabulary and the other for Cadigan Garage in Chepstow."

Sacre Bleu. Whatever has happened is bad, maybe exceedingly bad for Nettie to have given them my number.

"May I use your phone to make a trunk call to Wales, Molly? I'll pay you or you can put it on my tab."

"I thought you'd never ask. I'll put the kettle on for some tea and bring it to you in the hall."

Inspector Jones is not in the office but he left a message for me. Could I please drop the threatening message Nettie received in Stratford-upon-Avon off at the Oxford Police Station as soon as possible? Hell no, I'll deliver it to him in Wales in person.

I call the garage number and get a Meurig Cadigan on the phone. Neither the inspector nor Nettie is available. He puts his wife on the line. She explains that they've had a break-in and the Jag's been vandalized. I get directions to the garage and ask her to tell Nettie and the police that I'm leaving for Chepstow now.

Molly hands me a cup of tea. "Drink this, you need it if you're driving to Wales. Duncan is packing sandwiches and a thermos for you to take with you."

"Thanks, Molly. I'll just get my briefcase and be on my way to Wales."

"Pack some spare socks and underwear just in case. You want these telegrams?"

"I'll take them with me and read them on the way."

Duncan gives me a thermos and big basket of food which I doubt I'll eat. Molly hands me the telegrams and I'm out the door.

"Say hello to your old flame from me," Molly calls after me.

I'm half way to Gloucester before I calm down enough to remember the telegrams. I expected one from Jean but not this soon. He's sent addresses for both Armand and Victoria and promises more later. The other wire is a surprise. Jean has enlisted Claude's help in Calais. He thinks he can get addresses for Benoit and Auguste. Gaston has emigrated to Canada, possibly Quebec City. Five of us are deceased. I never met Bruno. I knew about Josette and Paul but not William or Marie.

Jean is a true friend. I've missed him more than I realized. If I'd read these telegrams before the Welsh phone call I'd be elated by what he's accomplished in so short a time. As it is, my mind is on Chepstow. I push the Morris as hard as I can, but it takes another hour and a half to reach Wales.

Chepstow

Thursday evening Cadigan's guest room
Nettie

When I wake up from my impromptu nap, Anna is next to me reading the true life adventure book Silvia Wentworth gave her. I hear the unmistakable voices of the Australian boys coming through the window. I get up and look out. There's a small mob of people around the big round table under the maple tree. One of them is Henri. I'm not entirely sure how I feel about that but there are tempting smells in the air as well. How Quakerly. Meurig and Angharad are turning this into a community picnic. I look over at Anna.

"I guess I'd better go down and see what I can do to help Meurig in the kitchen. You feel up to coming down, too?" I ask Anna.

She looks up from her book. "I feel good enough, I just don't want to. I'm tired of dealing with the blasted Aussies."

"I hazard a guess that it's more like you are tired of dealing with your feelings toward Grady. Am I right?"

"Geez, you do have an annoying way of reading my mind, Nettie, but you're right. I'll never see him again after this summer and really hate it that I like him so much. But how about you? I heard Henri's voice a while ago. I suppose the fact you're up here has nothing to do with being tired of dealing with your feelings about him?"

"Touché, you got me. At least it's a short–term problem for both of us. The only difference is that Grady is going home about ten months sooner." Only difference? Man, is that ever a lie.

"Okay, I'll face the music if you will," Anna says and closes her book.

We make our way out to the garden together and join the noisy group around the big table under the tree. I do my best to make conversation with Henri but I'm simply not ready for this. Before long I slip away into the dark garden to quietly watch from afar.

At the same time in Cadigan's garden
Henri

When I get to the Cadigan's Garage, I'm surprised to find a Welsh feast in progress under the maple tree in the garden. An animated group around the big table is reminiscent of Nights of the Round Table at the farm. The Aussies greet me with considerable enthusiasm. It's close to an hour before Anna and Nettie put in an appearance. Clearly shaken, Anna is silent. Nettie is aloof.

The high-spirited Australians would fit right in the kids who haunt my forge. The older one who has his eye on Anna is just the sort of rock solid youngster I look for in an apprentice. They are all good lads.

As for Meurig and Angharad, what can I say? They're a lot like Nettie, something rare and special. As the evening wears on, their acceptance of me goes some way towards getting Nettie to let her guard down. The friendly scene actually makes it possible for us to make a start at getting reacquainted.

All in all, this is working out better than I could have hoped. Breaking and entering is a crime regardless of whether anything was stolen or not. I'm pleased that the police are alert to the problem and apparently take it seriously. It's unclear how much help they can offer but everyone, including Nettie, knows I can't be the bad guy. What's more, Jean and I've have made a start at figuring who he is or at least who he's not.

At the table, three animated conversations are going on simultaneously.

"Hey, professor," Andy says, raising his voice to be heard. "Tell me again about turning an old cast-iron sink into a forge. Do you have a recipe for that home-make refractory you line it with?"

"When you two return from hiking Snowdonia, stop off in Oxford and I'll give you some references and a pointer or two."

"Fair dinkum? That would be absolutely beaut."

I've only seen pictures of Welsh crwths but Angharad comes out of the house carrying one of the primitive violins. Shortly something rather on the order of a Celtic hootenanny gets under way.

Currently I'm not in the mood for hootenannies, even Celtic ones. I quietly slip away into the shadows by the grape arbor and practically step on Nettie sitting there with her back against the wall.

"I'm sorry, Nettie. I didn't see you. What are you doing back here?"

"Nothing. Just sitting and thinking. My question is what are you doing out here? Following me?"

"Damn it, Nettie, do you have to turn everything into a battle? I'll leave you to your thinking and find somewhere else to vegetate."

"Wait, Henri, don't go. I'm sorry, that was totally uncalled for. There's room enough for both of us to vegetate here."

I sit down next to her, but not too close. We sit in silence for a while. Then Nettie clears her throat.

"Henri, I'm so sorry. I'm sorry about everything. I'm glad I've had the chance to get to meet the man you are now. I enjoyed your account of your apprentices's pig roast that went wrong."

"Pretty tame compared to your hair-raising time in Djakarta last winter." We fall back into silence watching the occasional faint glimmer of a few garden glowworms.

"Nettie, none of us came out of the war unchanged. I'd really like to get to know the woman you are now. From what little I've seen you are well worth knowing."

"Worth knowing? That's generous considering how quickly I jumped to the conclusion you were the author of these nasty incidents."

"You were justified, Nettie. Jean and I are now investigating who else knew about you and the teddy bear. He's worried as hell about you and eager to help for Josette's sake if nothing else."

"Yeah. I heard about Josette, of course. I assume you heard about Paul."

"According to Claude, Paul lost both legs and was blinded. In his place I would have done the same."

"Henri, you know at the hospital they told me that you were dying and would never regain consciousness, don't you? I felt like a ghoul standing there waiting for you to die, so I left. There were people from Ravensbruck whose lives depended on me getting back to Boulogne as fast as I could."

"Boulogne? That's a long way from either Ravensbruck or Paris."

"Longer than you can imagine. I can't talk much about Ravensbruck, not yet. Maybe never. When the Nazis knew they were losing, they went into overdrive, killing political prisoners as fast as they could, never mind the Geneva Convention. They even set up a gas chamber at the end. Shooting us was too inefficient, I guess."

"I understand very few prisoners remained when the camp was liberated. Two years had passed since you were deported, I assumed you would be among the dead. But I wasn't doing much thinking by then."

"I was one of the twenty-four-thousand prisoners on the death-march to Mecklenburg during those final days."

"Mon Dieu, mon Dieu. You were on that horrendous march? Oh, Nettie, I heard descriptions of places where bodies were piled up along the road like cord-wood. I thank God you survived."

Nettie looks down and doesn't say anything for a while. I regret bringing up the subject. I, of all people, should have known better.

"It was not unlike Ravensbruck. If we collapsed or even looked like we might, they shot us and left us for the crows. There was one male guard who was particularly sadistic. He was fond of raping women before he shot them or sometimes while they were dying. One dark night, he was the only one guarding our part of the line. I seduced him and Greta bashed in his head with a big rock. We all went on hitting him over and over again, then fled into the fields. They came after us before long. Twenty or maybe closer to thirty of us were still alive when they eventually gave up. I guess by then they didn't really give a damn."

"And you managed get back to France from there? Surely not. That has to be a good five hundred miles."

"It took weeks, how many I couldn't say. At some point I stopped counting. A lot of us died in the first few days. Between starvation, cold and the hostile villagers, less than half of us made it as far as Hanover. Four of us were killed there but the rest of us got as far as the Netherlands. A few of the Dutch people actually shared their food with us. One man gave us his coat for Yvon, who had pneumonia and was eight months pregnant. With their aid, nine of us made it alive to what was left of Aviva's chateau in Boulogne. We couldn't save the baby, though."

The lump in my throat threatens to choke me. The war was a nightmare for so many of us. So many of us are gone.

"You know it's ironic, Nettie. Around that same time I was an invalid feeling sorry for myself in Harfleur less than fifty miles down the coast from Boulogne."

"You weren't even supposed to get out of the hospital alive. We are both survivors, Henri."

"I was as good as dead and hospital space was at a premium. Albert and Celeste came for me. The DuBois place in Lisieux was lost in the D-day bombardment so they took me to Harfleur where her parents

217

live. They all assumed I would die. In fact, Celeste's father and mother very nearly came to blows over the issue of whether I should be buried in the family plot. I didn't give a damn whether I lived or died, let alone where I was buried."

"I wish I'd known, but it's probably a mercy that I didn't. As I said, there were people in Boulogne depending on me. Boulogne and Harfleur aren't that far apart. Later things might have come out differently if I'd known."

"Maybe, maybe not. I was a cripple with enough pride to have sent you away. I was hardly human at that point, Claud ... Nettie. Celeste was a saint. She made a bed for me in the garden where I could see the river. Actually, it was probably the river and the birds singing in the treetops that called me back. I spent over a year sitting in a wheelchair by the Seine before I decided to survive."

"I'm glad you did. Oh, Henri, life can really be the pits sometimes. You're right, there might not have been anything I could have done."

I'm of two minds whether to tell her about the role she did play in my struggle to learn to walk again. It is a bittersweet memory but embarrassingly maudlin. Every damn thing about finding Claudette is bittersweet.

"You remember that night we were walking along the Loire?" I tentatively ask.

"I definitely remember a certain weeping willow tree. I hardly noticed how rough the bare ground under it was. Or cared."

We both smile and fall silent for a while. I start to reach out to her but don't.

"A big tree hung out over the Seine about a hundred yards away from where I sat. It wasn't a willow tree but I spent a lot of time staring at it, remembering. I realized eventually that the doctor was mistaken. If I could take that one step from the chair to the bed I should be able to take another. It took me nine days to achieve that second step but I stubbornly kept at it. I had nothing else to occupy me. It took me only seven months to get to that tree and a week after that I was out at that Roman site in Harfleur."

Nettie and I look at each other. Neither of us quite knows where we go from here. The rambunctious attempt at music over by the table abruptly dissolves into laughter.

Nettie stands up and brushes off her velvet Navajo skirt. "It sounds like they're having fun over there. Maybe if we join them they'll quit singing songs they don't know, off key."

XX

Yang and Yin

Chepstow

Later Thursday evening in Cadigan's garden
Anna

I watch Nettie and Henri coming back from a walk. Gosh, they look like they are really together, not just walking side by side. Cool. Really cool. Those two sure belong together. They have too much history not to. Or maybe it's the other way. There's more history than they can deal with. Grady is watching them, too.

"It's a night meant for walking," he leans over and whispers in my ear. "What do you think about getting some exercise, Annie?"

I still feel so torn up about Snowball that I could use a hug, but that would be a major mistake.

"Better not. Don't you guys have to leave soon?"

"No, first thing in the morning. Angharad organized us with air mattresses on the back porch. We need to talk about this, Annie. I have to go up to Glasgow after I drop the boys off at Caernarfon tomorrow. When am I going to see you again?"

"You're not. Grady, this has to stop and you know it."

"Maybe, but it doesn't have to stop yet. I'll be in Glasgow until Monday afternoon. That's the fifth. Aren't you going to be in Yorkshire with Moira and Ted on the fourth? If I got on the road Monday night I could be in Scarborough the morning of the sixth."

"I don't even know where we'll be on the sixth, Grady. You're just making things harder."

"Are you going to be staying at the hostel there? Maybe I can call you."

"No, I think we're supposed to be staying in some historic hotel. I forget the name of it."

"Better yet. I'll get the hotel name from Nettie."

"Grady, stop it." I think I'm going to start crying again. Why does everything have to be so blasted difficult?

"Hey, Grady," Alan interrupts. "If you two love birds would shut up, Henri just told me that John Laundry beat Bannister's four-minute mile while we were on the ship."

"We've got the world record," Andy says. "Can you believe it, Grady? An Aussie holds the world record for the four-minute mile. That makes Landry a national hero."

"Temporarily, just temporarily," Henri laughs. "They're going to have a showdown at the Commonwealth Games in Vancouver this August. Bannister will win it back. Wait and see."

They sure do get a kick out of arguing back and forth. Men. They all have hero complexes.

"You men are all hero worshippers," I tease. "It doesn't matter what you do to get it, just as long as you have a medal to show off."

"Yeah, how many men did you have to kill to win that Croix de Guerre, Henri?" Nettie blurts out. With a horrified look she claps her hand over her mouth.

Silence falls over the group as Henri slowly gets up from his chair.

"I threw it into the Loire, Nettie and sent the Medal de Resistance after it," he says coldly. "I'd have thrown them in De Gaulle's face if I'd had the use of my arms."

Without another word, he turns and walks away. Nettie looks like she's going to cry. She starts to get up but Meurig puts a restraining hand on her arm.

Alan and Andy looked confused. "Why's he mad? The Croix de Guerre? He is a fair dinkum hero, someone I'm proud as hell to have the honor of knowing," Andy says, giving Nettie a puzzled look.

We hear the Morris start up out front, then pull out on to the St. Laurence Road.

"I just proved I'm a flippant fool," Nettie whispers. "I'm too fuck-ing stupid to be allowed to live."

She runs back into the house. A minute later we hear the Jag start up and drive away.

It looks like I've been abandoned.

"You don't have any more air mattress around do you?" I ask Meurig.

"The guest room is all thine, honey," Angharad says. "Don't worry, I happen to know everything will be all right. I come from a long line of pagan hedge witches."

Late Thursday night on the road to Oxford
Henri

This kind of anger has been known to get me in trouble and this just may be one of those times. Whether I have enough petrol to get back to Oxford is questionable and no stations are open at this hour. I might still be able to find a room at an inn or pub even this late but my desire to get on the road is overwhelming. If I get stranded somewhere, the Morris isn't the worst place I've ever slept.

I'm the sole car on the road once I get out of town. Anger fades to disappointment and then depression. I hadn't understood that Nettie had become so important to me, how much I still saw her as Claudette. How many times have I told myself that we aren't the same people we were? Nettie just proved that she isn't Claudette. Now that I've been laid low by reality maybe I'll start to believe it.

The trip back to Oxford is endless. A numbness sets in as I pass through Gloucester. I hardly care that the petrol is holding out better than I thought. Sanity finally begins to reassert itself and I find a new inner calm. I chastise myself for blaming Nettie for being Nettie. What else could she be after what she's been through? If she can talk about the death-march, Ravensbruck must have been soul-shattering. My poor, brave Claudette. If only I could turn the clock back and smuggle you out of France along with some of those airmen.

As Gloucestershire rolls by hypnotically, I feel a qualm of guilt. I brought it on myself. Nettie wanted no part of any of this. Disappointment not withstanding, I'll deal with this crazy, cat-killing bastard for her. I'd do the same for any old friend and Nettie certainly qualifies. I almost have myself back under control when I get to Oxford. Nonetheless, when I spy a white car parked in front of the Owl and Fox, I have to fight an impulse to turn back.

I get close enough to identify the Jag but then I never doubted identity. As I pull in behind it, Nettie puts her head out the window. I resent being forced to deal with this but there's little alternative.

"Get in," Nettie says pushing the passenger door a jar.

I stand in the street paralyzed. There is no chance that I'll get in that car but I can't just walk away.

"Get in," Nettie repeats impatiently. "Get in, damn it."

I sigh and walk over. "Nettie, I really don't want to talk about this. You probably shouldn't have said what you did. It probably shouldn't have bothered me as much as it did. Call me tomorrow evening. I'll have heard from Jean and know a bit more about potential suspects by then."

"So don't talk. Get in." There is no compromise in her voice. Damn. The last thing I want is for this to degenerate into a scene. Molly has probably been at the window ever since Nettie got here. I shrug my shoulders and get into the Jag.

Nettie doesn't say a word as she pulls out on to Banbury road. It's just as well that it's the middle of the night. Driving faster than she could get away with during the day, she heads north out of Oxford in the direction of Milton Keynes. Neither of us says a word.

After an hour, I begin to wonder if we are going somewhere or if she's simply waiting for me to say something. If so, she'll be waiting a long time. This is her idea, not mine. After another hour of silence, I wonder whether we're actually going toward Cambridge for a reason or if this highway simply going in that direction.

I find that I'm starting to get bored. Boredom is a great antidote for my seething emotions. The Jag really is a lovely car and Nettie drives it well, too fast perhaps, but with casual competency. I wonder if Willy has made any progress finding a decent MG TD for me to buy. Green maybe, or red. Any color but white.

We arrive in Cambridge and immediately get on north A10. Apparently Nettie is leaving town without stopping. It may be time to reconsider. She was always stubborn. I said I didn't want to talk so will she drive until I do? Maybe. All the way to Scotland if that's what it takes? Quite possibly. Would Claudette? Sure.

On the other hand Claudette had a habit of not explaining what she was doing or thinking unless asked. I suppose that puts the ball in my court but, damn it. This wasn't my idea. I have nothing to do for the next month so if we do end up in Scotland, it will be her problem, not mine.

It appears that she isn't interested in going to Scotland when she turns on Ely Road and starts back the way we came. I lean back and smile to myself. She's so predictably unpredictable. So what comes next?

I'm still asking myself that question when Nettie turns on a small road on the north edge of town. We're driving through a semi-rural area not far from the river. We pass a railway yard, a dump, and pockets of new residential houses going up. The narrow lane we're on runs along the river but after half a mile rapidly degenerates. Nettie must have a specific destination in mind. If this was a pulp-fiction thriller, it would be the site of my murder. I smile. Somehow I'm not worried.

When the road comes to a dead end, Nettie parks, gets out and opens the boot. Okay, I give up. She wins. I open my door and clear my throat.

"Nettie," I break down and ask, "Where the hell are we and what comes next?"

"I thought you'd never ask," she grins and hands me one of the torches she's holding.

"Watch your step. Once we get to the path you shouldn't have any difficulty."

That's not an answer but I begin to suspect what she has in mind. It takes a minute for my eyes to adjust to the dark, even in the moonlight. I know I'm right when we reach the walking trail along the Cam. It's a brilliant and creative apology. She may not be Claudette but I can't help liking Nettie.

"You used to be fond walking along rivers with Claudette," she says conversationally. "How do you feel about taking a walk with me?" She offers me her hand as if it were the most ordinary thing in the world.

"The pleasure is all mine," I say stuffing the torch in my pocket and taking her hand. We walk beside the dark river, hand in hand, Nettie unobtrusively matching her pace to my limp. Her hand feels small and familiar in mine. With a rush I realize how much I like the flesh-and-blood woman at my side.

A gentle breeze ruffles the reflection of the moon in the river. It's very quiet this late. Nettie switches off her torch and we stop and listen. The soft sound of the water is occasionally interrupted by small rustlings in the undergrowth and the faint barking of a distant dog. It would seem almost sacrilegious to shatter the peace with words.

Somewhere ahead a nightingale sings. I remember reading that only unpaired male nightingales sing regularly at night.

"Did you know that he's singing his nocturnal song to attract a mate?" Nettie whispers.

"I did," I whisper back. "His song is so lovely, let's hope she's out there listening."

The moon comes out from behind a cloud, illuminating the river ahead of us. I see a majestic weeping willow tree leaning out over the water. I look at Nettie and she laughs.

"I've come to rather like bearded thugs with broken noses," she says. "Here, take this, it's getting heavy and cane or not, it's your turn." She hands me the blanket I hadn't noticed her carrying over her shoulder.

I drop my cane on the ground and lay the blanket next to it.

"I thought you said you didn't mind rough ground," I say gathering her in my arms and giving her a tentative kiss.

"That was Claudette. It's considered bad manners to forget which woman you are with."

"Mam'selle Jeanette Eugenia Hicks, may I have the pleasure of your company under yon tree?"

"Most assuredly, Professor Henri Emil DuBois. My company and whatever else you have in mind."

A bit earlier Thursday night in the Cadigan garden
Anna

Meurig clears his throat, breaking the stunned silence following the sudden exit of Henri and Nettie.

"Perhaps it would be wise to get Mrs. Llewellyn before it gets any later, Angharad," he says and then turns to Alan and Andy. "Is it done?"

"Yes, Meurig," Alan replies. "We've made it almost twice as wide and a foot and a half deeper."

"Anna, we are going to lay the Llewellyn's cat to rest in the front garden," Angharad tells me. "I'm sure Mrs. Llewellyn will understand if thee wants to go inside until we finish."

"Of course, I want to stay." Gosh, I've been so lost in my memories of Snowball, I haven't even thought about someone else's cat being murdered last night. I feel just terrible. I want to say something but the words won't come. Grady leans over and slips his arm around me.

"I'll go get Mrs. Llewellyn," Meurig says quietly getting up. "Is Tomas ready, Angharad?"

She nods and disappears inside. A few minutes later Meurig reappears with an elderly lady clinging to his arm and carrying a bucket with a small rose bush. No one says a word as we gather by a large new hole in the front garden.

Meurig gets his Welsh pipes from the table and begins a haunting lament as Angharad comes out carrying a cloth-wrapped bundle. Mrs. Llewellyn manages to lay it in the hole with Angharad's help. Alan sets the rose bush on top and holds it in place as Andy begins filling the hole. When I see the one lovely white rose on the bush I break down. That's when I hear Mrs. Llewellyn begin to wail.

The sound of that wailing and piping is more than I can stand. I really can't imagine how people like Nettie and Henri manage to deal with their huge losses. Or my mother. Gosh. I suddenly realize I've never really grieved for the father I never knew. The handsome young man in a uniform was only a little older than I am now when he died. My heart feels like it will burst when I think that the stranger in the photo must have held me, loved me, played with me. I turn back toward the house, crying softly to myself. Angharad puts a gentle restraining hand on my arm.

"Wait. It is not just Tomas who Eilwen mourns for, Anna. She keens for all loses since the beginning of time. Let her keening ease thy pain. And listen to Meurig's pipes. They sing of loss but also love and renewal."

I sink down on the grass, close my eyes and lose myself in the sound.

When the keening and piping cease, I don't want to move. The grass under me smells so green. Paper-thin clouds scud across a nearly full moon in a starry sky. I slip into my cosmic sandwich and know that I am a great deal older than I was the last time I looked into infinity.

I haven't the faintest idea how long Grady has been quietly sitting nearby. When he sees me look his way, he slides over and lays down next to me looking into the sky. We lie there in a companionable silence for a time.

"A penny for your thoughts, Annie," he says softly. "You look ... I don't know ... deep and wise and ... ancient."

"Ancient? I better go in and put on some makeup," I laugh, a lame attempt to cover up the emotions I'm feeling. It may be a mistake but I suddenly find myself telling him all about my cosmic sandwich.

He silently goes on staring at the sky and I wish I'd kept my cosmic sandwich to myself. After a bit, he turns toward me and props himself up on one elbow.

"I like your cosmic sandwich, Annie," he solemnly tells me. "I get the same sort of feeling in the outback when I'm riding alone. There I am in the middle of a great expanse of nothingness. I don't know how to explain it, but it's like time and the land are the same. Like the ground and sky and today and tomorrow and yesterday are all right there together. It makes me feel very small and part of something very big at the same time. It's like your cosmic sandwich except that while it is deep and good, it is frightening, too. The outback is not a safe place. Neither is life."

Grady reaches over and takes my hand. I catch my breath. Geez, I'm very, very much afraid that I'm falling in love with him and that would be a complete absolute disaster.

"Annie," he says bringing my hand up to his lips. "Annie, I love you. Not 'the summer time romance' kind of 'I love you.' The 'I want to spend the rest of my life with you' kind of 'I love you.'"

I want to throw myself in his arms. I want to jump up and run away as fast as I can. What I really do is to burst into tears. I can't fall in love, I must not fall in love. I have to go to college. I want to have adventures. I sure don't want to live in Australia.

"Annie, please," he says and puts his arms around me. "Please, don't cry. It's all right. You can't help it if you don't love me. Oh, bugger. Sorry, I mean, oh, blast."

"Can't you see it's impossible, Grady? You can't fall in love with me. We aren't going be together long enough."

"It's too late, Annie. I already have and that isn't going to change. We can work it out if we want to."

"It's not just too late. It's too soon, Grady. Tell me, how old are you?"

"Twenty-three. I'm twenty-three and you're eighteen. That's a fairly ordinary age difference, Annie. All it means is that I'm in a position to take care of you, give you a good life."

"But you weren't when you were eighteen. I'm just starting college, Grady. I'm not even sure whether I want to be an artist or a teacher or a writer or a photographer. It's too soon to know what I want to do with the rest of my life or who I will spend it with. I want to have adventures."

"I can wait. I will wait. I can't find another Annie, but I can wait until the Annie I love is ready to be loved."

And then somehow I'm in his arms, letting him kiss me and hold me close. I tell myself this is a mistake, but it is too late. I'm not listening. I'm kissing him back, for pity's sake. An hour later when I push him away, I'm still a virgin, but it was a near thing.

Dawn Friday in the Cadigan's guest room
Nettie

Somewhere in the deep recesses of my mind, there must be a memory of feeling like this. I want to dance and sing and laugh all at once. And run for the nearest exit. It's wonderful and terrifying. It's a fricking disaster, that's what it is. Henri and I aren't the kids we were in Paris. There's no room for each other in the lives we have now. It's a cruel illusion to pretend otherwise.

I park on the street in front of the garage and slip through the back door of a sleeping house. The kitchen floor is full of sleeping Aussies, a painful reminder that when the sun rises I have to deal with the realities of life. I quietly step over the bodies and make my way upstairs to the guest room. I see Anna's silhouette sitting in the chair by the window. She obviously has been crying. Damn, and the sun hasn't even risen yet.

I sit on the edge of the bed and take off my shoes. Anna gives me a wan smile, leans over, and pulls a leaf out of my hair.

"Let me guess," she says wiping her eyes. "Wherever you'll been, you've been there with Henri and now you live happily ever after. Congratulations."

"Annie, that only happens in the movies. Now my life gets complicated and my heart gets broken all over again. Can you really see me as a faculty wife in North Carolina?"

That obviously was the wrong thing to say. Anna bursts into tears and throws herself on the bed. I forget how young she is and how hard things can be when you're young. I'll wager these tears have more to do with the Aussie downstairs than her dead cat. Oh, God help me, I'm the last person to give advice to the love-lorn.

Even eighteen-year-olds have a limited volume of tears. I stretch out next to her, prepared to wait and let her cry.

"Oh, Nettie," Anna finally whispers. "I'm in such trouble."

Not good. Where is her bloody mother when we need her?

"Life is full of troubles, honey," I tell her. "No matter how bad our troubles are, somehow we eventually get to the other side of them but they can make us pretty damn miserable on the way. Want to tell me about it?"

"It's Grady. I think I'm in love with him but he wants to marry me." The dam bursts and there's a new flood of tears. Oh great. I count up the days since she met the man and heave a sigh of relief. At least she isn't pregnant.

"That doesn't mean you have to marry him, honey," I tell her. "Not if you don't want to."

"I love him," she sobs, "but I don't love who he is. Or I love the inside but not the outside. I don't want to live in the Australian out-back. Even if I did, I don't want to get married now. There are too many things I still want to do."

"So tell him that. You owe him that much but no more. The longer you wait, the harder it will be. He won't like it, but he'll survive."

"You don't understand," she wails. "It's already too late. I do love him. I let him make love to me. I mean almost. I let him go farther than a nice girl is supposed to. That's as good as telling him yes. At least that's how he acts. He says he'll wait for me or I can go to college in Australia. His father would pay for it."

"Let Grady believe whatever he wants to, honey. For pity's sake don't marry him and start having babies because you don't want to hurt the guy's feelings."

It's damn good advice but it doesn't seem to help Anna much. She's weeping buckets of tears again.

"Annie," I try again. "The relationship between sex, love and marriage is impossibly confusing. They fit together in different ways for different people. The best advice I can give you tonight comes from Henri's grandfather, the one who taught him sword-making. Never grab ahold of something you can't let go of. It might be hot."

"Is that why you and Henri didn't get married?" she asks as if she seriously wants to know. Damn. Anything I tell her will be only half true so I don't say anything.

"I'm sorry, Nettie," she whispers. "It doesn't have anything to do with me. It's none of my business."

"Annie," I relent. "Henri and I were so in love I don't think it ever occurred to us that we wouldn't get married and live happily ever after but it's a good thing we didn't. Our best friends, Jean and Josette, were married and as deeply in love as we were. They got back together when Josette got out of prison but they were no longer the same people. Their heads were in such different places, they couldn't find each other again. Josette committed suicide last year."

"That was different. War changes people."

"It's not really so different. Have you really listened to what you just told me about you and Grady? Grady wants to wait for you to change into who you're going to be. Do you really think college is going to change you into someone who wants to give up on adventures and live in the Australian outback? Annie, there may be a happy ending to your love story but don't bet on it."

Anna is silent for a long time before she says anything. "What about the end of your story, Nettie? You and Henri go your separate ways and have sex every now and then? That won't ever work for either me or Grady. We're the kind of people who need to be together, to share our lives."

"So were Jean and Josette. If you try to hold on to things going in opposite directions, it will tear you apart."

Neither of us says anything for a time until Anna finally yawns and softly says, "You're right, Nettie. I hate it with all my heart, but you're right. I'll talk to Grady but not yet. Not until I figure out the right thing to say." She rolls over and I hear her quietly crying herself to sleep.

A nightingale breaks into song in the tree outside our window. I look out into the dark garden for a few minutes, then go to bed and quietly cry myself to sleep, too.

Part Six

Adventures in Wales

XXI

The Fifth Touring Day
Aftermath of the Chepstow Crime

Oxford

Friday morning in the Owl and Fox
Henri

Back in Oxford, I wake up to sunlight streaming in the window with a smile on my face and the smell of baking bread. I automatically look at the clock, then remember the time doesn't matter. No lectures, no appointments, and above all, no faculty meetings. There's no reason I can't stay in bed all day if I want to but I don't. I'm eager to get the day started.

Lured by the good kitchen smells, I start down the hall. When my bad knee buckles I have a pang of guilt. My preoccupation searching for Claudette and finding Nettie has made me negligent and my morning routine has suffered. A mistake and I'm noticing it. I return to my room and do my morning workout with renewed enthusiasm. If I'm going to keep up with Nettie and Anna on the proposed day hike in the Cotswolds, I need to get in the best shape I possibly can.

As could be expected, Molly is laying in wait for me when I go downstairs.

"Don't think you can get away with coming in at five in the morning, young Henri. You owe me a story, several in fact. What happened in Wales? Who is your lady love in the white Jag? Where did she take you? I don't suppose you were running from the Welsh police, were you? Come on, tell all."

"With regret, I must disappoint you, Molly. My precipitous exit when the Welsh police called yesterday proved to be nothing more dramatic than a case of vandalism."

Molly frowns and shakes her head. "You expect me to believe that? You don't own anything in Wales to get vandalized and I could hardly help hearing your side of the phone conversation yesterday. You want this breakfast I'm cooking for you, you'll have to do better than that."

"You are a hard woman, Molly. Very well, the lady in the white Jag is an old friend and the vandalism was pretty nasty. Someone killed a cat and spread its intestines all over her Jag."

"Very, very nasty," Molly says putting an amazing plate of sausages, eggs, beans, grilled tomatoes and black pudding in front of me. "That does not explain your late-night escapades, my boy."

"You are more inquisitive than my mother and I'm too old to have account for my doings. But if you must know, yes, the white Jag lady is a very good old friend I haven't seen in years. We went to Cambridge and took a sentimental walk along the Cam."

Molly smiles the kind of knowing smile that means she has a pretty good idea of what we were doing on our midnight walk.

"So what comes next? Are we going to need to look for a bigger flat?"

"Good Lord, no," I respond without thinking. "You listen to entirely too many of those radio soap operas."

I sigh. Sadly, Nettie and I both have commitments and complex lives. We live worlds apart in more ways than one. My intrepid Claudette has grown to be a globe-hopping ... what? Quaker activist saving the world one disaster at a time, I guess.

"I think a flat with a bit of garden, a touch more privacy, perhaps," Molly grins.

"If Mrs, Phillips is as nosey a landlady as you are, I may indeed look farther afield for a flat."

"It's not fair to call me nosey, Henri, not when you get calls from the Welsh police and foreign telegrams, not to mention racing off in the middle of the night. Haven't you ever heard of the landladies' bill of rights?"

"No, as a matter of fact I haven't. I don't believe there is such a thing," I laugh.

"Well, if there isn't, there should be."

"Molly, my dear, I believe you and the white Jag lady have a lot in common. Speaking of which, I need to make a few more trunk calls, if you don't mind, preferably without eavesdroppers."

"All right then, on the condition I get to meet this mysterious Jag lady if she keeps showing up in the middle of the night. I need to give Duncan a hand out front anyway."

I pour myself another cup of tea before calling Jean. He made a valid point yesterday. Nettie interprets the red braids and teddy bear as pointing to her ancient failed mission but it's hard to see someone with a grudge about that old, minor incident as the motivation for something of this nature. There's a political element to some of Nettie's work with refugees but a politically motivated attack would be simple and direct.

This nonsense with pornographic threats and dead cats smacks of personal obsession, of unrequited love gone out of control. Nettie vehemently rejects the suggestion but she may discount some minor encounter or incident that an unbalanced man took very much to heart.

After talking at length with Jean, I'm further inclined to doubt Nettie's interpretation. Only six people were involved in the funds transfer and they are all accounted for. Claude is working on a list of eleven others who could conceivably have been aware of it. However, Jean thinks we are on the wrong track and I agree. He takes the dead cat seriously and volunteers to come over and help me protect Nettie while we eliminate the threat. We work well together and his offer tempts me but I can't trust that his idea of eliminating the threat would be appropriate in 1954 England.

I vacillate between believing that we're making a mountain out of a molehill or that it is unconscionable not make Nettie's protection my top priority. Fortunately the visit to the Jacobsons comes at an opportune time. Getting Nettie and Anna safely off the road may give us the opportunity resolve this problem.

I return to my room and unpack the draft of this next chapter of my book I am working on, or maybe I should say not working on. It's impossible to concentrate. I am in an untenable position. I care entirely too much to simply ignore the fact that a possible killer is stalking Nettie but I can't risk jeopardizing our relationship by even suggesting that I follow them on their tour. She'd view such an offer as woefully inappropriate and intrusive.

I throw my manuscript down in frustration and decide to walk off some of the tension by taking a stroll around the university.

Chepstow

Friday mid-morning in the Cadigan's guest room
Nettie

At Angharad's gentle knock on the door I jerk awake. I can't believe I slept so long. It's almost ten and I see that Anna is already up and gone.

"Nettie dear, wake up," Angharad calls through the door. "The inspector is downstairs waiting to speak with thee."

Damn. I'm not in the mood for this. I truly hate that sick cat-killing son-of-a-bitch. He's out there somewhere planning his next nasty move and I'm still stuck dealing with the aftermath of the last one.

"Ply him with bara brith and tea," I tell her. "Have him talk to Anna while I pull on some clothes."

"He's already on his second cup. Anna and Grady are out on a walk. Alan and Andy have gone with Meurig to pick up some car parts."

"The bloody Aussies are supposed to be going on ahead to Cardiff to wait for us," I sigh. Apparently it's going to be harder than hell to get those characters to stick to a plan.

Inspector Jones is at the kitchen table drinking tea and eating Meurig's wonderful speckled bread. Jones is looking damn contented. Me, I'm longing for a cup of coffee but I want to get this over with. Hang the Aussies. Anna and I need to get on the road if we're going to see anything of Wales and get to Scarborough by the fourth.

"Ah, Miss Hicks," he says standing and holding out his hand. "I apologize for waking you. I know you were up late. When you left South Wales late last night the Assistant Chief Constable in Cardiff was considerably distressed. He made it clear that I was to make speaking to you before you continue your travels my top priority."

The damn cops have been spying on me. I am so angry I can hardly speak.

"I beg your pardon, inspector," I snarl. "I fail to see that my travels either last night or today are any concern of the Assistant Chief Constable in Cardiff or anyone else. I declare this interview over and done."

I surge out of my chair prepared to do battle. Disconcertingly, Inspector Jones bursts out laughing.

"Oh my, once again I demonstrate why I will never make chief inspector." He wipes his eyes and continues to laugh. "Miss Hicks, I assure you that your travels are of no interest to South Wales Constabulary but the evidence suggests that the same cannot be said for the man who vandalized your car so dramatically Wednesday night."

Angharad gently pushes me back down in the chair and pointedly pours me another cup of damn tea. "The inspector would have indeed looked the fool, Nettie," she says, "if had thy vandal returned last night and caught us all napping."

The inspector turns serious and puts down his tea. "Miss Hicks, from the very first it has been obvious to me that there is more to this than simple vandalism. The grisly display of the cat's carcass accompanied by death threats written in blood immediately caught Cardiff's attention as well. When I learned that this had been the fourth incident in as many days and you proved to be a wealthy foreign visitor, the Assistant Chief Constable himself took an interest in my handling of the situation.

"Once we learned that the car and the entire scene had been wiped clean of finger prints in quite a professional manner, South Wales Central has had their fingers in the pie. Of course I had your vehicle and the scene under observation last night," the inspector tells me. Then very softly under his breath adds, "and South Wales Central had this small town inspector under bloody close observation, too."

I suppose it was inevitable that the police would get involved as the bastard's harassment escalated, but it is a damn nuisance. Frankly there isn't a damn thing they can really do short of assigning police protection and from a practical, if not financial, point of view that is impossible. When Jones gives me a long look, I suspect he is thinking along similar lines.

"Miss Hicks," he says, "an individual or individuals have had the time and resources to follow you from one side of Britain to the other making increasingly open death threats for the better part of a week now. It is not unreasonable to believe that you are in some danger. We would have a responsibility to protect you even if you weren't a wealthy philanthropist with influential connections. To do that effectively will require your cooperation."

"Thus far I have fully cooperated with you, inspector. That cooperation does not extend to changing my travel plans."

The inspector leans back and morosely closes his eyes. "I am charged with encouraging you to break your tour here in Wales long enough for us apprehend this miscreant. After learning of your involvement with the Quaker disaster-relief efforts, I considered that the task might be a difficult one. I admire your courage greatly although in all probability you're going to get me demoted back to constable."

"Bloody hell," I growl. "I'm not the criminal you need to be investigating here. When did this become a bleeding police state?"

"Miss Hicks, the Assistant Chief Constable did not set out to investigate you but London was involved in the first incident and the Yard is now following this case. You must realize it would only have been a matter of time before we learned that you are well known in certain circles. It stretches credulity to believe that you are the random victim. The perpetrators of this harassment are acquainted with you either directly or indirectly. Being on the move makes it easier for them and impossible for us."

Shit. I don't know which is worse, being stalked by a madman or being a so-called case followed by Scotland Yard. In spite of that I can't help liking this Jones guy. I suspect he's very good at his job for the very reasons he won't make chief inspector and that's why I like him.

"Okay, Jones," I say. "Henri and I have reached a similar conclusion but an extended holiday in Chepstow or even Cardiff is simply not going to happen. You'll be relieved to learn that my intention is to move the problem to the Yorkshire Constabulary. I intend to be in Scarborough by Saturday night."

"I suppose it would be entirely inappropriate to say that I'm relieved," Jones grins at me. "It greatly reduces the likelihood of me being demoted and you will find a sojourn in Scarborough by the sea more entertaining than one in Chepstow."

The inspector consults his watch. "You will need to get started soon if you are to be in Scarborough tonight."

"As it happens, I don't," I tell him. "We intend to make our way north along the Welsh coast. Anna and the Aussies want to explore Cardiff then go exploring your quaint fishing villages. We'll spend the night in Harlech and drive to Scarborough tomorrow, then on to the Lake District the following week."

"So Wales gets another opportunity to play host to the cat-killing madman," the inspector sighs heavily. The effect is spoiled by the grin on his face. "I shall inform Cardiff of your itinerary and warn the Gwynedd Constabulary that you will be spending the night in their jurisdiction at Harlech."

Southwestern Wales

Friday midmorning on the highway to Cardiff
Anna

Geez. About now yesterday, Nettie and I were in the big kitchen in the Chepstow hostel finishing up a real Welsh breakfast arguing about calling the Professor for advice or going to Cardiff with the guys. Now here we are following the guys to Cardiff but every other blasted thing is different. The crazy creep is now the cat-killer and a whole lot crazier than we thought. The professor is Henri, the good guy and he and Nettie ... are very good friends. I refuse to ruin the day by thinking about me and Grady. It's so good it's really, really, really bad.

Nettie made such a darn fuss about the Aussies leaving first this morning that Grady was worried that she had something up her sleeve that didn't involve them riding shotgun. Nettie has an independent streak a mile wide but she's not sneaky and I told Grady so. When she spent a whole hour sitting around with the guys getting advice from Inspector Jones, he finally relaxed. She's all for the inspector's suggestions of how the guys could recognize followers and still be ready to protect us if anything happened.

Cardiff is the biggest city in Wales and traffic is heavy for most of the thirty-five miles there. I'm kind of excited about seeing the big castle but I was up almost all night so I sleep most of the way. When we get there, that castle is sure big. With its grounds, it takes up a huge chunk of the center of the city. I love it. We park about two blocks from the main entrance. Uh, oh, what's this? Nettie is going the wrong way.

"Hey, Nettie," I say. "Isn't the castle that way?"

"Don't worry, Annie, we'll get there," she says. "I just want a few quiet moments alone with you to think out what to do. We're going to stop off at the Rummer Tavern for a while."

"Darn it, that's not fair, Nettie. Grady will be worried sick. He'll be sure we've been waylaid or ditched him." Geez. What is she up to now?

"No, he and I have come to an understanding about several things including meeting him in ..." she looks at her watch. "In about an hour from now."

I take it back. Nettie is definitely sneaky. Blast and double blast. I don't even want to think what her other understandings with Grady might be but you can bet they involve me. I don't know whether to be angry or grateful. Oh, well.

I follow her into the tavern. It's the oldest one in Cardiff and very, very cool. Nettie gets us a table in a dark corner and something to drink.

"Okay," Nettie says putting down her glass. "First topic, the cat-killing creep. How serious do we take his threats? If we take them seriously, do we turn and run or try to catch him? I can lose him anytime I want to, Annie. I'll call in some favors and get us quietly to Calais or Rotterdam by tomorrow if you like. We could get another less noticeable car over there, one with left-hand drive and move your adventure to the continent."

Holy smoke. I never saw that coming. I don't know what to say. I'd really love to go over to France or Holland but that would be letting the darn, no, I mean damn, cat-killer creep win. It sure would take care of the Grady and Henri problems, but that's the wrong way to do it.

"Would we have to cancel the Fourth of July party?" I ask. "I was looking forward to seeing Scarborough and I wanted to go to the Lake District and paint a picture of Ambleside village."

"If we think the threats are serious enough that we should go, then we go right now. I make a few calls, we take a taxi to the train station where we catch the Express to London about 45 minutes from now. Your call."

"Leave without even saying goodbye? What about the Jag?"

"Grady and Henri can cope. I imagine the police will use the car as a decoy."

"Geez. You have this all planned out don't you?"

"Of course not. I just happen to have some resources that could make us disappear fast if we decide to. Then we'd make a plan together at our leisure once out of the cat-killer's reach."

"Do you think the threat is that serious?" Gosh, I guess that's the big question. Is it?

"Annie, if I knew that, I wouldn't be giving you any choice in the matter. This is your adventure."

Gee whiz. I believe this is a choice even Mrs. Wentworth would agree I don't have enough experience to make. "Nettie," I say, "I don't have the experience to go by and you do. How about helping me out?"

"Well, if someone seriously wanted me dead, I'd almost certainly be dead by now," she calmly says like it's no big deal. "All this riga-marole with drawings and cats smacks of mental illness. Madmen usually are more bark than bite. They can't get it together enough to go through with their threats. They don't even want you dead. It's all about having power over you."

"Then you don't think we're in that much real danger?" I ask and heave a sigh of relief.

"I didn't say that. Mr. Cat-killer is well enough put together to suc-cessfully follow or catch up with us from one side of Britain to the other. Not many people could pull that off. Every year a certain num-ber of women are stalked and killed by ex-husbands or even strangers. It could even be something left over from the war. There are still some of us running around with a bit of battle fatigue, sometimes a lot of it. I wouldn't have made the suggestion I did if I didn't think there was a chance that it's serious."

Now what? This is more darn adventure than I'm ready for. Osa and Martin, what would you do? Well, they stood their ground and faced angry cannibals and wounded wildebeests. I'm not a famous lion hunter, for crying out loud. Blast. No, I mean damn. I look at the clock. I have about five minutes to make up my mind. I don't have the faintest idea what to do. Nettie, darn her hide, just sits and smiles sym-pathetically. She's not going to decide this for me.

"Okay, Annie," she finally says. "Close your eyes, breathe deeply and make your head totally empty for a few minutes and see if you don't find the answer."

Great. Some help that is. I wonder if this is what Nettie means about trusting karma. Oh, well. I try it and time seems to stop for a while. When I open my eyes, I still don't have any idea what I'm going to decide. The clock chimes noon.

"It looks like it's time to go meet the others," I hear myself say. "What did you say topic two was?"

Nettie laughs and laughs and I join in. People turn and stare at us. I don't care. Nettie is rubbing off on me.

"Wales has more castles than any other place else on earth," Nettie grins. "It's full of quaint mountain villages where they still speak Welsh and the coast is dotted with picturesque fishing villages. It will take a good four or even five hours driving time to get to Harlech but it won't get dark for another nine hours. Topic two is how do we use those extra four hours?"

"We do our best to do it all." I look out at Cardiff castle. I could spend all four hours right here but I have three other castles on my list and then there are those fishing villages. Oh, well.

"It looks like we'll have to give up eating lunch," I moan. She just laughs.

Swansea, Wales

Friday afternoon coming into Port Talbot
Nettie

Given our timetable and the time we spent in Cardiff at the castle, we all agree to get through the flatlands of southern Wales as quickly as possible. Anna largely sleeps through it and doesn't miss much. Grady is a good driver and the Humber Super Snipe has the horsepower to almost keep up with the Jag but I've out-distanced him.

I slow down as we approach Swansea. Mercifully the highway largely bypasses the city to the northeast and we agreed to rendezvous at the pub at Port Talbot for lunch.

"Where are we?" Anna yawns and looks at her watch. "It's almost one-thirty and I'm starving."

"Swansea. Don't I remember a certain adventurer saying something about going without lunch?"

"Yeah, and I remember a certain eccentric aunt bragging about castles and fishing villages. We haven't see anything worth staying awake for since Castle Coch just outside Cardiff."

"Well, look alive. That's Port Talbot ahead. It may not be quaint or picturesque but it's a village and has a pub and a castle." I sigh. "And industry and coal and freight trains and docks and smoke stacks and now a steel mill."

"Enough, enough for pity's sake. I get the picture," Anna says impatiently. "As long as it has food and a water closet I won't complain ... much."

I park in front of the Lamb and Flag. The place is almost empty. It's late for lunch but I smell something good cooking. Team Aussie bursts in. Grady looks tired and I tell him so.

"I've been playing tag with that bloody blue Rily hard top we saw in the Cardiff car park but it was a waste of time," he complains. "After all that, he turned off on the road to Candleston Castle."

"Worse luck. If you're tired you might let someone else drive for a bit."

"I'm okay. The Humber is not mine, you know. MacFarland Exports lined it up for me to use while I'm here. If anything happens to it, the Guv will take it out on my hide and God help me if it turned out that I'd let someone else drive."

"Exports, too? And Glasgow woolen mills? You bloody MacFarlands must have your fingers into every blinking pie over here," Andy says shaking his head. "Isn't owning the biggest sheep station in New South Wales enough for you blokes?"

"Don't blame me if my Guv's da was One-eye Edward and clever at investing his ill-gotten gains. Periodically I get stuck running errands over here like now, but our Queensland station is where my heart and energy live."

"Oh, get on with you. Your grandda was never One-eye."

"Shut up, you guys, and eat," Anna pipes up, "It's still an hour till we get to Cardigan and start seeing the things we came to see."

"So what do we find in Cardigan?" Alan asks around a mouthful of lamb stew. "Besides ladies' sweaters, that is."

"I can't swear to the sweaters," I tell him. "but we'll have our first quaint village, the sea, boats, beaches and even the ruins of a small castle. Oh, yeah, and the Black Lion on High Street. That's where we'll meet next. From then on things will get a lot more interesting."

By two fifteen, we are all fed, rested, in a better mood and back on the road. We make damn good time across Carmarthenshire. The road runs along a valley next to the river Afon Teifi, not exactly dramatic but very Welsh. The Aussies' suspicious blue Rily appears behind us again at one point but otherwise the next hour is uneventful. I haven't seen either the Humber or the Rily for a while as we approach Cardigan an hour later.

The Afon Teifi widens considerably as we enter the village. The ruins of the castle sit at the end of the old bridge that spans it. Not exactly a fishing village, but quaint and old and full of life on a Friday afternoon. Anna is enchanted.

We find the Black Lion easily enough. As I park, the Super Snipe pulls up and Grady opens his window. "What's up?" I jog over and ask.

"You know the blue Rily? We're pretty sure it's him after all. You want us to stay with him?"

I think for a minute. If the Aussies are right, this is good news. We've got him.

"No," I say. "If you're right, he'll stop up ahead and wait for us. Assuming you have the number of his plate, the Welsh police will catch him now in any case. Come in and tell me what's been going on."

"Of course we have his number. We aren't complete idiots and unless he is, he knows we're with you by now and that I'm keeping track of him. He may have escape on his mind and try to shake us, ditch the Rily and disappear."

"You give yourself too much credit, Grady. He's got reason to fear the police, not a car full of boys."

"Then he doesn't know much about us blooming Aussies, does he?"

"Just come in, Grady. Take a break and tell me why you're so sure it's him."

Much to Anna's delight, the handful of customers in the Black Lion are all speaking Welsh.

"I imagine about half the people in Cardigan speak Welsh," I tell her. "It will be closer to a hundred percent in the small towns as we get farther north. There are enough holiday makers that there's usually someone around who speaks English, at least near the beaches."

There's only one table big enough for all five of us and it's smack-dab in the middle of the room, not exactly ideal for talking. Alan and Andy are bursting with excitement and I have to hush them. The Welsh-speaking waitress claims to speak English but I have my doubts. Somehow we all end up with some wonderful looking Welsh rarebit in front of us we didn't mean to order.

"Okay, Grady," I say. "Talk fast and low. The rest of you shut up."

"You probably noticed that the blue Rily we lost between Cardiff and Swansea showed up again and he stuck to you like glue. When we knew a choice point was coming up, we overtook him like Jones suggested, then gradually slowed down letting you get farther and farther ahead to see what he'd do. He was willing to take some chances to get around us and keep you in sight to see which road you'd take.

"I believe I'd have done the same thing if I'd been behind you, Grady. No one wants to be stuck behind someone going slow," I point out.

"The real test was earlier when we all stopped for petrol, Nettie. Remember, we spent a long time there. He should have gotten a long way ahead of us if that was all that was going on."

"Yes, I remember," I grin. "It was all I could do to drag you away from that Vincent Motorcycle."

"It was the first Black Lightning I've seen, Nettie. They just came out and it was a beaut. That bike has a top speed of one hundred and fifty miles an hour. I'd give my ... anything to have one."

"A hundred and fifty? I'll have to see that to believe it, Andy. Now fermez ta bouche." *(Shut your mouth.)*

"I love it when you talk dirty," Andy grins.

"Shut up, finish your Welsh rarebit and let Grady get on with it. I'd like to get to Aberystwth in time do some exploring before dinner."

"We weren't even half a mile past the petrol station when the Rily appeared from nowhere," Grady says. "He pulled out behind you and he's stayed there ever since."

"Not conclusive, but very suggestive. Good work, guys. The next test will be whether he turns up after this much longer break," I tell them. "Now let's get back on the road. What about exploring the coast a little and maybe doing some beach-combing at Aberaeron, then having dinner in Aberystwth. I imagine the Ship and Castle is still there.

Welsh Coast

Friday afternoon at Aberaeron harbor
Anna

I love it. I simply love it. This was definitely worth waiting for. Quaint village, dozens of fishing boats and fabulous beaches on both sides of the river and we pretty much have them to ourselves. The villagers and fishermen are pleasant enough but not what I'd call friendly and if anyone speaks English I haven't heard it. What I can't understand is where the guys are.

Oh well, who needs them? Nettie and I take a long walk along the beach. I find lots of pretty pebbles, beach glass, some small shells and finally a starfish. We are just about to turn back when I make the big find, a glass ball the size of a baseball. Wow. Nettie tells me it's a float from the net of a Japanese fisherman and it's rare to find one on the Atlantic. Double wow. What a souvenir.

I'm sure that we'll see the guys or at least the Humber when we get back. We don't. That's not good. Nettie and I drive down every darn lane in the village looking for them. They aren't here. Really, really not good.

"Nettie, Aberaeron is only a half an hour from Cardigan," I finally say. "We've been messing around for an hour since we got here. Aren't we supposed to call Cadigan's if we get separated? It's been an hour-and-a-half. I'd call that separated."

"Yeah, that's separated all right," she agrees. "Finding a phone may be an issue, though."

I get the feeling that Nettie is a whole lot more worried than she lets on but doesn't want to worry me. Not good. I'm eighteen years old, for crying out loud. Mrs. Wentworth was off in New Caledonia preaching to cannibals when she was eighteen. I'd say something to Nettie if I could think of what to say but I can't.

We go straight to the shops around the village square. I have longer legs than Nettie but I can't begin to keep up with her. She goes in to the butcher and comes out before I can get to the door.

"No phone?" I ask.

"No English, let's try the tea shop."

Blast and double blast. We even try sign language and charades but can't make anyone understand what we say. The market is the fifth place we try. The grocer there tries hard to help but the word for phone must sound like the word for ginger beer. At least that's what he's holding up now. Nettie shrugs her shoulders, pays for the ginger beer and some chocolate digestive biscuits and we leave.

"This is a waste of time," Nettie growls. "Come on, let's get out of here. It's less than twenty miles to Aberystwyth."

Nettie takes the narrow coast road fast even for her but I'm getting immune to her driving style. We race though hamlets that make Aberaeron look big and sight Aberystwyth in twenty minutes flat. The town may be unpronounceable but it's big, even bigger than Cardigan – in other words, pretty darn small. The Ship and Castle is easy to find. It's right on Castle Street near, of course, the castle but this is one castle no one has lived in for a long, long time.

The pub is cool even as pubs go. Yay, and double yay, the publican speaks English. He and Nettie go off somewhere to put through a call to the Cadigans while I drink a cider I don't much want and wait. And wait. And wait. Gosh, it's a bad sign that it's taking so long. Even sipping really slow, I've finished the blasted cider long before Nettie gets back.

"They're okay," Nettie tells me, "but they won't be catching up with us tonight. Come on, let's order some dinner. I'll tell you what's going on, then we'll push on to Harlech."

Not good. Something's gotta be wrong.

"What do you mean, when you say that they're okay? What happened? Where are they?"

"At the jail in Cardigan," she says over her shoulder, already halfway to the lounge.

"Jail. What do you mean jail? Nettie, don't do this to me." Geez, I just hate it when people leave something hanging like that.

We go over to a table by the fireplace. Before she can even answer my questions the waitress is putting plates down in front of us. I guess ordering is not part of the deal here. Oh well. We're late and they must be in a hurry.

"Does this mean they caught the guy?" I ask Nettie. The waitress gives me a curious look. I don't care. We haven't done anything wrong.

"No, Annie," Nettie says lowering her voice and pointedly waiting for the waitress to leave. "They're the ones who got arrested. Damn it. Sit back down, girl, they're out of jail now but there's going to be a God-awful rigamarole before they can leave. They'll meet us at the Lion Hotel in Harlech as soon as they can but it may be late."

"What on earth happened?" I ask lowering my voice almost to a whisper.

"That blue Rily fell in behind us again just the other side of Cardigan. The boys gave chase. It turned off on one little side road after another. The Rily is smaller and more maneuverable but Grady managed to keep up with it. After a wild chase all over rural Wales, the Rily pulled over and stopped in front of the Constabulary in Cardigan."

"The police station? I don't get it. Why did he do that?" I asked, giving the hovering waitress a dirty look.

"Not him, them," Nettie says, all but whispering. "It was a terrified young couple from Bristol on holiday with their kids. They noticed the Humber seemed to be following them. It was full of young men and that made the mother nervous so they tried to lose them around Swansea. I think you can guess the rest of the story."

"So who did they think was really in the Rily?" the waitress asks, then quickly puts her hand over her month.

"For us to know and you to wonder, my dear. What's for dessert?"

XXII
Roses are Red

Harlech

Dawn Saturday, at the Lion Hotel
on the sixth day of the tour
Nettie

I stand by the window looking down at the village as the sun comes up. It wasn't that long after midnight when Team Aussie wandered in looking a bit sheepish, but I haven't been able to sleep. Anna has been tossing and turning, too. I'm not surprised. This is where we all part company. The boys go climbing in Snowdon and Grady goes on to Glasgow. I hate to admit it, but I'm going to miss all of them. Poor Anna.

It's only two hundred and fifty miles to Scarborough so I guess we can take our time saying our goodbyes. Anna and I spent several hours exploring Harlech yesterday evening but I promised we'd go again with guys. The castle is worth a second look. It has a raw power that the tamer castles lack. You can imagine soldiers fighting for their lives here but not people actually living ordinary lives. Somehow I'm not surprised Anna liked it the best of the ones we've seen so far. I predict that she'll make a better adventurer than housewife.

Anna must hear me thinking about her. She gets up and stands next to me at the window. We listen to the faint sound of a dog barking and a distant motorcycle. A farm truck pulls up. It turns out to be delivering milk.

"You know Grady wants me to go to Glasgow with him, don't you," Anna quietly tells me.

"You don't want to go, do you?" I ask.

"Sure, I want to go. I just don't want to go, even more. I wish he could magically just be gone without having to say goodbye to him. I don't suppose I could talk you into sneaking out right now?"

"I'm not sure my Quaker conscience would let me get away with it, Annie. Grady is one of the good ones. He doesn't deserve that. Frankly, my dear, you don't deserve to try living with the memory of being that cowardly and cruel either."

"Can I at least be a little bit cowardly and skip breakfast? Maybe we could say we changed our minds about going back to the castle with them and keep the goodbyes short. We could say we need to get on the road early after all."

"Actually it may not be that bad an idea. If that's the way you want to play it, I'll cooperate."

The Lion does a good breakfast but the Aussies seem somehow deflated and I guess I feel the same. I think we are all a bit relieved when Anna finally shows up. I note she's wearing the new dress she bought in Oxford. She sits across from Grady and quietly orders tea and toast. God, this is painful. How do any of us survive adolescence?

Breakfast seems to last a very long time, but eventually Andy and Alan shoulder our backpacks for us. Grady and Anna quietly follow them to the car hand-in-hand. Alan is the first there.

"Hey, I can't believe you didn't lock the car, Nettie," he says opening the door.

"I did lock ..." I start to say as he jerks back bumping into me.

I hold my breath and look over his shoulder. The ornate silver handle of a huge knife protrudes from the back of the passenger's seat pining a piece of notebook paper there. A stain on the curved blade looks like blood. Grady pushes me aside.

"Wait, Nettie. Don't touch anything. We need to get the police."

I know he's right but balk at the idea. First Chepstow, now Harlech? There's no new news here. There won't be any prints and if he's hiding somewhere watching us we'll never know.

"Okay, people, try to look normal and not attract attention while we think about what to do," I tell everyone. Grady looks at the others silently supporting me.

"You don't want to call the police, do you?" he quietly asks.

"I don't know," I honestly say. "I had more than one motive for moving the investigation to Yorkshire. Harlech is even smaller than Chepstow. I doubt that there are a hundred thousand people in all of Gwynedd. At least Chepstow was next to Cardiff."

"Aren't we going to read the note?" Anna asks. "It doesn't look like a drawing this time."

No one seems to notice the thing most on my mind. Why the damn passenger's seat? I'm the one they're after aren't I? Or am I? Who would want to hurt Anna?

"Not if we're going to call the police," I say hesitantly.

"Are we?" Grady gets right to the point and gives me a questioning look.

Should I call the local cops or not? The desire to avoid being trapped in rural Wales obviously clouds my judgement. If it were just me, I'd head to Yorkshire without a second thought but there's Anna. My God. I don't even want to consider she may be the real target. That alone is reason enough to call for help. I suppose I could phone Henri. Not fair and not particularly useful, either. The weight of being responsible for our safety would cloud his judgment as much as wanting to escape Gwynedd clouds mine.

"Me, I say trust karma," Anna pipes up. "I say we go to Yorkshire. Give me that note."

So be it. I reach around Grady and wrench the knife loose. Several long blonde hairs are stuck to the stains on the blade. I surreptitiously palm them, a mistake if we intend to call the police. I'm certainly not going to let Anna see those blonde hairs here with the Aussies looking on.

The notebook paper falls to the seat and I pick it up. It's definitely not a drawing. I start to read, then sigh and hand it to Anna. After all the choice was hers. Watching her face as she reads the neat block letters, I immediately regret my decision.

"Your blood runs red,
Your face turns blue,
You die screaming,
I'm laughing at you," she reads.

Grady clenches his teeth and looks at me. "You want to rethink going to the police?" he asks.

At the same time Saturday, at the Lion Hotel
Anna

This is not good. This is really, really not good. That is my seat, not Nettie's that got stabbed. Damn, not darn. Damn, damn and double damn, we've been wrong all along. It's me, not Nettie the cat-killer is after. I'm really scared now, I look over at Nettie. I can see she's thinking the same thing and she's scared, too. She wasn't scared before, but she is now.

I slip out from under Grady's arm and go over to my side of the car and run my finger over the slit in the leather. It's gotta be a good two inches long but it's so thin you can hardly see it. That awful knife sure must be sharp. So was the one that killed Snowball, I mean Tomas. I've been telling myself that a suspicion lurking in my mind since Chepstow is irrational. It doesn't seems so far-fetched now. I feel sick.

'You die screaming, I'm laughing at you.' It's me, not Nettie he's laughing at. I can see Craig Dawson saying something like that. There's a fear in the pit of my stomach I've never felt before. I just know Crazy Craig was itching to do something like that to me or one of us girls before he was sent back east.

Grady squeezes my hand and slips his arm from around my shoulders. Using his handkerchief, he takes the knife from Nettie.

"Whether you call the police now or this afternoon when you get to Yorkshire, we need to do something with the knife," he says. "It's the first real clue we have. Look at it. It's got to be a collector's item."

It has a deadly beauty. It's old and it's foreign. There's fancy filigree on the hilt and the big blade gently curves up at the tip. It looks Arab. Geez, I bet it's stabbed more than car seats in its past. I shiver and look away. A rich man could buy one like that and the Dawsons are rich.

Nettie gets her purple scarf out of her backpack and hands it to Grady. He carefully wraps the knife up and sends Andy to the Humber to look for something heavier and some twine if he can find it.

Andy comes back with a towel and hands it to Grady. Grady raises his eyebrows. "Property of the Southside Rugby Club? You sure you want the police to see this, Andy?" They both laugh but they aren't smiling. Grady wraps up the purple bundle, ties it with some twine and hands it to me. I feel sick.

"You now have custody of Exhibit One," he says. "What comes next, ladies?" He puts his arm back around me and pulls me close. He looks at Nettie. Nettie looks at me. I look at Exhibit One.

"The real question is where will we be at dinnertime," Nettie slowly says. "At the constabulary in York or at the one here."

"What I want to know is how many cops do they have in Harlech they can assign to protect us from whatever comes next," I say, looking down at the bundle I'm holding. "I don't see that we'll be any safer here than on the road."

"Annie has a point," Nettie agrees. "Dealing with this problem is likely to take over our lives until this guy gets caught. Leaving it to the Gwynedd Constabulary doesn't seem wise to me. Unless Anna objects, I say we push on to Scarborough."

Grady sighs. "I don't like it, but I agree. I'd go with you and watch your back if there was any way I could put off going to Glasgow for another day."

"I'm not worried about our backs, Grady," I say, hoping that I'm right and that my voice won't shake. "Nothing ever happens until we get where we're going. He's done his deed for the day and is off planning his next move. Meanwhile it's time for Nettie and me to pack up and hit the road."

Nettie gives me one of those long looks that as good as says she knows there's something I'm not saying. She's right. I don't want to talk about Craig Dawson here in front of the Aussies. I could just see

Grady canceling his trip to Glasgow and losing his father's trust for no reason. Nettie nods and I figure she understands.

"I think I'll give Henri a call in Oxford first," Nettie says. "He and I always made a good team when things got hairy. I imagine I can persuade him to join us in Scarborough."

"Anything to put off saying goodbye," Grady groans. "Actually I think it's a bloody good idea. I'll come to Yorkshire myself when I can, probably sometime late Monday night or Tuesday. If not, I will definitely catch up with you in the Lake District. I'll give you a Glasgow number where you can at least leave me a message if you need me ... or even if you just miss me." He holds me close and lightly kisses my cheek.

It's a long time before Nettie comes back out of the hotel, but she's smiling.

"Henri is meeting us half way. We'll be having lunch with him in Sheffield if I can ever pry you two lovebirds apart. It sounds like you'll be seeing each other in a few days anyway, for God sake."

Yeah, she's probably right at that.

Sheffield, England

Saturday early afternoon on the way
to the Nailmaker's Arms
Henri

Sheffield is large and industrial, not the easiest place to meet but it's on the way to Scarborough and about an equal distance from Harlech and Oxford. The Nailmaker's Arms is the oldest pub in the city and the only one Molly can put a name to so that's where we agree to meet.

I suspect I may have broken the land speed record for a 1939 Morris Mark V and get to Sheffield just after one o'clock. I stop for petrol and to get directions. The pub is somewhere around the Norton Oakes Cricket Ground on Blackmoor Road, I'm told. Too bad I don't know how to find Blackmore Road.

I finally stumble on the Nailmaker's Arms. No sign of the Jag yet. I've made better time than Nettie? I would never have predicted that. I order a Bass and strive to avoid imagining all the unpleasant things that could delay them. I agree with Nettie. The stabbing of Anna's seat implies that she's the target. It's difficult to imagine the motive but even harder to accept that it is coincidental. Anna will doubtlessly be thinking along the similar lines. It wouldn't surprise me if she will have some idea about who might be behind this.

Saturday is a busy day, I look up each time someone new comes in. When the women finally arrive, I make something of a spectacle of myself, sweeping Nettie off her feet in a bear hug. Anna giggles. Nettie grins. I blush.

"I'm looking forward to seeing the dagger and the note," I tell them.

"No, not here," Anna says. "Exhibit One is in my custody. It doesn't get opened up until we get to the hotel in Scarborough."

Nettie lowers her voice and turns her back toward the room. "'*Your blood runs red, your face turns blue, you die screaming, I'm laughing at you'*,'" she softly quotes.

Nettie already quoted the message over the phone but it still hits me hard. The little rhyme calls up images as vivid as his drawings. Whoever this pervert is, I'm coming to hate him passionately.

"Annie, do you have your sketch book with you?" Nettie asks.

"Gee, Nettie, that's a silly question. I guess you want me to draw the knife," she smiles. "Grady calls it our first real clue. It's very distinctive." She gets out her sketch pad.

"I can help some," Nettie offers. "I have the shape of the blade and hilt down pat. I tried to memorize the fancy work on the hilt but the details are getting fuzzier by the minute."

"It sounds like a dagger of some sort," I tell them. "I'll have to actually see it to know how good a clue it is but a drawing might prove useful. I'm more interested in any insights you have into who could be behind these threats, Anna.

"I do have an idea but it may be a bit far-fetched," she says, lowering her voice.

"Annie and I talked about it on the way here," Nettie tells me. "The very idea that someone is a threat to Annie seems far fetched. We can expect that significant clues are likely to be so as well."

"You know about the cat at the Cadigan's," Anna says, her eyes cast down at the closed sketch book in her lap.

"Yes, I remember you were upset. You had a cat at home that was killed a similar way."

"It happened when I was in seventh grade. Snowball was white, too, and her insides were spread out in fancy patterns on the porch floor just like Tomas's and I know who did it. I can't prove it, but I know it was Craig Dawson. Snowball wasn't his first victim. He liked hurting things."

"I never heard that detail about the patterns," I tell her. "This is definitely a coincidence that needs further examination."

"There's a lot more, Henri," Anna groans. "Craig Stewart Dawson, the third, was a nasty, emotionally disturbed kid even in elementary school. By high school I honestly believe that he was dangerously mentally ill. We were all afraid of him, even the boys, but it was us girls he really harassed."

"Tell Henri about the notes and the stalking, Annie," Nettie says and gives me a meaningful look.

"The notes started way back in fifth grade. Really dirty notes got left in our desks. I guess the boys got threatening messages, not dirty ones. The teacher caught Craig doing it, but he didn't get expelled or even suspended. He is untouchable. His family is rich as all get out and his father is a big wheel in state politics."

"And that may explain some of Anna's story," Nettie tells me. "Tell him about the stalking and Karen's window, Annie."

"I guess you would call it stalking. He followed us around all the time, especially me and Karen. It got so bad none of us girls would go out alone even in the daytime. He must have been peeking in windows, too. Anyway, Karen woke up in the middle of the night and he was outside her window. She screamed and he ran away. Her father discovered that he'd pulled the screen loose so he called the cops. Nothing came of it because his parents gave Craig a cast-iron alibi. That was right near the end. His parents pulled him out of school in the middle of the next semester and sent him off to some fancy school out east. They never said which school but we all thought they'd put him in a mental hospital."

"That was almost three years ago," Nettie adds. "None of the kids ever saw him again, not even in the summer or at Christmas."

At this point, Anna is clearly shaken and actually pale. Enough is enough. We need to switch to something else and give her time to regroup.

I shake my head and whistle. "That is quite a story, Anna. If we can put him here on this side of the Atlantic, we may have our culprit. Now how about working on that drawing for me?"

Anna looks relieved and opens up her sketch pad. She and Nettie get to work. I sip the last of the Bass and stare at the ploughman's lunch in front of me. Right now I couldn't eat to save my soul. Hard as it is to believe, I'm sure Anna is the target, not Nettie.

When Anna finishes her drawing, she hands it to me. I immediately recognize the type of dagger.

"It's an Arab janbiya." I tell them. "It isn't something you can pick up at Sears Roebuck but janbiyas are easy to come by. They're Arab symbols of social status. Men over the age of 14 wear them these days as much as clothing accessories as weapons. They're a dime a dozen in much of the Middle East. On the other hand, vintage janbiyas with well-forged blades can be quite valuable. Antiques with rhino horn pommels or Damascus steel blades can cost a small fortune. I'll be able to tell you more after I see it."

"Somehow I don't think it was an Arab wielding this one," Nettie sighs.

"No, either do I. Janbiyas are readily available in London," I agree. "There are a good number of inexpensive replicas on the market, too."

"There's something else," Anna says hesitantly. "It's just a rumor so it probably isn't true but if it is, it makes this a whole lot scarier."

"Then this is a rumor I want to hear," Nettie growls.

She took the words right out of my mouth.

"There was a serial killer in Des Moines four or five years ago. I don't remember but he killed a couple of street walkers. Then they found some more bodies buried in some vacant land out by Camp Dodge. I think there were at least three more and some of them had been there a while. That was before Craig left town."

"What kind of camp is it?" I ask. "Boy Scout, Girl Scout, YMCA?"

"It isn't any kind of camp now but it belonged to the army during the war. It's deserted and the buildings are gone but the paved streets are still there. That's where Mom gave me driving lessons. There's a big swimming pool that is open to the public out there, too."

"Ah, yes. That would make a good place to bury bodies," Nettie nods. "I think I can guess what the rumor was."

"Craig was sent back east about then. When the murders stopped after he left, we all thought that maybe his parents figured out that he was the murderer and quietly had him committed as far away as possible. We knew it was probably a coincidence but you know kids, we found the idea exciting."

No one says anything for several minutes. Then Nettie stands up. "Order dessert and some coffee if they have any. I'm going to call Maureen Jacobson, tell her what's going on, and make plans for tomorrow."

When she comes back, Nettie's beaming. "I think we can stop worrying about what the cat-killer may have planned for tonight," she says. "Maureen's folks have moved back to Stoneyfield House, the Evers family home. It's very secluded near a small village on the edge of Scarborough and they have bedrooms to spare. Better yet, there several outbuildings where we can hide the Jag. And get this," she lowers her voice and whispers. "Colonel Evers, aka, Dad, was a chief inspector at Scotland Yard until he retired."

If something is too good to be true it usually isn't but if there's a catch somewhere I can't see it. I heave a sigh of relief. Actually it's worked out so I am traveling with Anna and Nettie after all.

"My appetite just came back," I laugh. "I think I'll have a piece of that apple tart."

Friday afternoon on the road to Scarborough
Anna

It's another hundred miles to Scarborough. After getting lost three times in Sheffield trying to find the Nailmaker's pub, I kind of doubt we'll find Stoneyfield House as easily as Nettie thinks. It's only one mile from Scarborough just off Racecourse Road. Great. So where is Racecourse Road? I am so tired of being scared, I can't wait to get there. I hope it has real stone walls and they are really, really thick.

I keep yawning. I shouldn't be sleepy but being scared wears me out. I keep thinking about Crazy Craig. One minute I'm certain it's him and I'm scared to death. The next minute I think that we're a long, long way from Iowa. Maybe Nettie really is the target and the cat-killer creep is just playing with us.

A few miles out of Sheffield, Nettie clears her throat. "Annie," she says. "I wish I had paid more attention to what you said about Snow-

Gail Meglitsch

ball. If I hadn't been so bloody obsessed with Henri, things might have gone differently in Wales. I'm used to taking risks myself but I'm horrified that I've been putting you at risk. Where are Jack and your mother this week?"

Not good. Very, very not good. "Nettie, I thought you had at least a bit of respect for me. I don't have your experience but I'm not a child," I work to keep my voice steady and not act like one. "Calling Mom is a bad, bad idea."

"Annie, she trusts me. She's your mother and would want to know."

"I trust you and I don't want her involved, at least at this point. It sure would add to our problems."

Neither of us say anything for a while. I hate this.

"Geez, I can deal with this," I finally tell Nettie. "I have a right deal with this. Mom herself was married and pregnant at eighteen. For an awful lot of girls it's out of high school, up the aisle and into the maternity ward. Hells bells, I have it more together than Mom ever did or will. She hears about this and she'll go crazy and we're already dealing with one crazy too many. I can just see her calling Craig's mother and inviting the two of them to dinner so she can talk sense into them. You simply have to trust my judgement on this."

We're coming into a village and Nettie slows down. She's let us get too far ahead of Henri so she stops by an old parish church for a few minutes.

"Annie," she says. "We go through life acquiring a lot of scars and calluses. We learn as we go and get better at things. There is an old saying, however, that one person may get twenty years of experience while another person is getting one year of experience twenty times over. The depth of those calluses and scars says a lot about how long a person has lived but not how capable they are or how good their judgement is. I just made a common mistake. I saw your lack of scars and calluses as a measure of how good your judgement is and how capable you are. I apologize."

Henri shows up while we are talking, stops and comes over.

"Annie, I accept your judgement that calling your mother would be a mistake," Nettie quickly says as she opens her window. "I also accept your mother's right to be mad as hell at me for not telling her but that's not your problem. Hello, Henri."

Gee whiz. What am I supposed to say to that? I can't think of anything brilliant. Thank you, I'll try to not to let my lack of scars and calluses get in our way? Oh, well.

"It feels good to stretch my legs for a minute," Henri says leaning his elbow on the edge of the open window. "This is Driffield so we must be getting in range. Give me Maureen's instructions again in case we get separated." He leans in and gives Nettie a kiss on the cheek. I look on, wishing Grady were here and being very, very glad he isn't.

"We've got roughly twenty miles to go and this is a choice point," Nettie tells him. "We can stay on the main highway to Scarborough and find East Ayton from there but it's more direct to get to East Ayton going north from here on B1249. When we get there, we simply turn left on Main Street and take the first right onto Castlegate Road. Stoneyfield House will be on our right after the village peters out."

"It sounded fine until you got to the part of looking for Main Street," Henri groans. "Just how big is this village?"

"About a thousand. Of course we can look for Racecourse Road when we get to Scarborough if you prefer. I believe it's got a population of fifty thousand or so."

"What I prefer is for you to slow down so I can mindlessly follow you."

"Yeah, I seem to remember that you couldn't find your way around anything but a chessboard."

"Geez, stop arguing you, two," I complain. "Even I'm smart enough to figure out that since old cat-killer isn't following us, he's hanging out with his binoculars trained on the main highway. I say we take the back road to East Ayton and leave him twiddling his thumbs." They smile and I know they had already thought of that a long time ago. Oh, well.

"Okay, Anna has convinced me," Henri grins. "Let's get a move on. I seem to remember that it's a country house tradition to offer visitors brandy or the like when they arrive."

I'm not interested in any darn brandy. What I want is a good strong place to hide with lots of friends around.

The road north isn't nearly as wide as the one we were on but it's straight and flat, nothing like the narrow things they called roads in Wales. Of course Nettie drives too fast but I make her stop in every village for Henri to catch up. Oh, wow. This next village is called Foxhole. Only in England. I love it or I would if somebody wasn't planning on laughing while I die screaming. Blast and double blast.

Part Seven

A Sojourn in Yorkshire

XXIII
Stoneyfield House

Near Scarborough

Late afternoon Saturday in the village of East Ayton
Anna

Okay, East Ayton has to be my favorite village of all time even if I am scared to death. Unlike Foxhole, it really does have a Main Street with shops and everything. The houses are older and bigger than most of the places we've been and that's saying a lot. I've also learned that these Englishmen do not believe in street signs, just arrows on every corner pointing to other villages too small to even be on the map. We might never have found Castlegate Road but I see a little hand painted sign on a stone wall by the lane between houses. It looks like a driveway but turns out to be Castlegate Road.

I suppose they call them cottages and they do have wonderful cottage gardens but the old houses on Castlegate Road are all really big and made of stone. Good. I like the sound of that. I see the ruins of a tower on the hill behind them. That will be the castle of Castlegate, I bet. And now there are no houses at all, just woods and a river.

I don't know about Henri and Nettie but I am getting a bit worried before we finally come to a high stone wall. Hiding behind that wall and trees is Stoneyfield House. Wow. It's big and it's old and it's stone and it's wonderful. I can easily believe it has six bedrooms. It may not be a castle or fancy manor house but it sure looks like it can keep Crazy Craig or maybe even an army out. I love it. We pull into the drive and three dogs come up barking and wagging.

Moira and Ted ride up on horseback. Horses. Wow. I bet Teddy has stopped complaining about visiting his boring English grandparents now. With luck, maybe I'll even get a chance to do some riding between dodging the bad guys.

The man that comes out smiling must be Colonel Evers. If I was casting a play, I'd sure hire him to play someone called Colonel Evers. He leads us around the back of the house to the stable block and some picturesque stone outbuildings. Wow. I bet it looks exactly the same as it did a hundred years ago, maybe more. There's plenty of room to hide both cars. For once I feel confident Mr. Cat-killer will have a tough time finding us here and if he did, he couldn't get to us. I hope he spends a miserable night in Scarborough watching for us to arrive.

Friday evening in the Stoneyfield House kitchen
Nettie

I follow Maureen in to the big kitchen and watch her put the kettle on the old Aga. I look at the big battered oak table and the bunches of drying herbs hanging from the ancient beams and realize that I may never have felt as safe as I feel at this moment, at least not since I was very, very young. It's an unfamiliar feeling. I feel like crying and realize how deeply tired I am.

Maureen turns and smiles. "I love this old kitchen," she says "When I followed Mother Evers in here as a new bride I had such a sense of ... sanctuary, that this spot has been the heart and haven for Evers women for four-hundred years. If there are ghosts here, the ghosts are comfortable and content and simply too deeply at home to leave."

I do like Maureen. For no reason I could explain, I recognized her as a kindred spirit the first time I saw her. I like to think she's the kind of woman I might have been if I'd never been touched by the evil of Ravensbruck. I am overwhelmed by a sudden hatred for the evil mind who pinned the sick poem to Anna's seat. Oh, God, please let all her cherished adventures be carefree and light-hearted ones.

Maureen takes the whistling kettle off the hob, sets the tea to steep and sits down next to me at the table. "In its way, Stoneyfield House is mightier than the fortified ruins on the hill behind us," she says as if reading my mind. "It just as old and still standing. This is one place the madman who's been harassing you can never, ever penetrate."

"Your stalwart and contented ghosts would never allow it," I grin. "Seriously, Maureen, I am grateful. Ghosts not withstanding, we have brought trouble to your door. I'm afraid those troubles will put a damper on the girls' party tomorrow."

"With the load of fireworks Dad and Randy bought? Not a chance. Remember Stoneyfield House has stout doors built with Scottish raiders in mind. Frankly Dad Evers relishes a challenge. Judging from his reaction to my confused description, I'd say your problems are going to make his day ... days. I think it gets in their blood. Once a cop, always a cop."

"He doesn't seem that old. How long has he been retired?"

"Around five years, and no, he isn't that old. I guess he was sick of London."

"Sick of the Yard's bureaucracy, you mean," Mrs. Evers says appearing at the door, muddy, in her stocking feet and carrying a basket of carrots. "Grahame never suffered fools gladly, my dear. He came out of army intelligence after the war totally unwilling to pretend. I was not a bit surprised when he left the Yard in the lurch."

Mrs. Evers sees me and introduces herself. She's very British and very nice.

The terrible twins troop in after her, along with a red-headed kid a couple of inches taller than them. They all have sticky faces and baskets not exactly full of strawberries.

"Okay, out with you, laddies. Go help your dad in the stables," Mrs. Evers says and shoos them back out the door, then excuses herself to change out of the gardening clothes.

"I suppose we'll have to talk to the police but I hope we can put it off until Monday," I tell Maureen. "The Welsh police said they were alerting them to the problem but we're the only ones who know about the knife and note we found this morning."

"If I don't miss my guess your Henri is holed up with Dad Evers dealing with that sort of thing right now," she smiles. "I do like your big Frenchman, Nettie. But you misled me. He doesn't look at all like a thug. The scars are sexy and the beard makes him look distinguished. He is a very attractive man."

I smile. Maureen should have seen him ten years ago. I never thought I'd see him again with or without the scars. It makes my heart glad but God only knows how I'm going to survive it. How I'm going to survive the fireworks tomorrow is an even bigger question. I don't deal with firecrackers at all well.

"What's the plan for tomorrow?" I ask to change the subject. "Do we need to make potato salad and cole slaw tonight? I'd enjoy doing something, anything to get the bad taste of this week out of my mouth."

At the same time Friday on the grounds of Stoneyfield House
Henri

I estimate that Stoneyfield House is close to the same age as the ruins up on the hill behind it. It is not dissimilar from the DuBois Inn in Lisieux. The onetime smithy by the stable brings a lump to my throat. I believe we may have at least temporarily chanced upon a safe harbor. I pull into the old tithe barn as directed and park.

Nettie introduces me to Colonel Evers. He's an impressive gentleman and unless I miss my guess, very bright indeed. Anna has wasted no time and is off to the stable with Moira and Ted. Nettie notices me watching her and grins.

"Moira is saddling up Queenie for Anna. The kids are going to for a quick ride up to the ruins up on the hill," she tells me.

I predict Nettie's mighty girl adventurer is going to enjoy that.

"Moira and Ted had their first riding lessons on Queenie earlier this week," the colonel tells us. "From what Anna says, we are going to have to find a more spirited mount for her tomorrow."

"Yes, I've rather gotten the impression that Anna is an accomplished rider," Nettie tells him.

"Are these backpacks all your luggage, Miss Hicks?"

"That's it for the luggage but we should put the knife and note in a safe place," she says.

I retrieve the towel-wrapped bundle from the Jag boot and follow Nettie and the Colonel into the big old house. Maureen gives Nettie a hug and the two of them disappear with the backpacks, talking nonstop.

"I take it that bundle you're holding is the evidence," the Colonel says. "We'll take it to the library for safe keeping. Can I offer you a brandy, professor?"

"I definitely would not say no to a brandy, sir. Anna and Nettie made a pretty fair sketch but I have as yet to see this knife myself."

"I'm Grahame to my friends and I'm confident you fit in that category," he says, putting two brandy snifters on the table.

"And I am professor to my students, Henri to everyone who counts." When he puts the bottle on the table, I'm impressed.

"Courvoisier XO. You have good taste, Grahame. A professor's salary rarely runs Courvoisier of any age, XO never."

"Consider it a bribe. I'd like to take a look at the Jag stabber you've got. What do you say to unwrapping it and taking a look?"

Grahame hands me a pair of surgical gloves from the desk drawer. "I know a number of people have touched this and the wielder will have wiped it for prints but it pays to be careful."

We lay the bundle on the library desk and carefully unwrap it.

"Ah, a janbiya, I see." Grahame gingerly picks up the knife and examines it. "Late nineteenth century, I'd guess."

"Omani, wood handle, mediocre blade. Fairly easy to come by and not terrible expensive. It tells us something about our man but may not prove traceable. A bit disappointing but hardly surprising."

"You are obviously knowledgeable about knives, Henri."

"Roman Britain may be my area of interest but I teach military history. More significantly my grandfather was a master swordmaker and so was his father and his father's father. I dabble a bit myself."

"Not much in the way of Roman sites to interest you here, I'm afraid. This area was Viking. The ruins on our hill are not of a castle but a tower-manor with traces of a barmekin, agricultural terraces and fish ponds, nothing that would interest you, but I digress. Let's have a look at the note, then I'd like to hear a quick overview of the events, if you're willing. I'd like to question young Anna about your potential suspect but tomorrow will be soon enough. Anything you can tell me in the meantime will be most welcome."

I'm grateful to see Grahame has the bit between his teeth already. My next hour is spent being debriefed by a past master. We go over and over my version of Anna's story about Crazy Craig.

We've put a significant dent in the bottle of Courvoisier by the time Maureen and Nettie come looking for us. Grahame gives me a long, serious look. "If you don't mind me poking into this a bit, Henri, I think I'll make a few calls tonight and talk to Anna tomorrow. Regrettably, she will have to come with me to the police headquarters in York on Monday."

"We'd deeply appreciate your help, sir," I say, seriously understating my feelings.

Later when Nettie and I prepare to say goodnight, Grahame takes me aside.

"I have started two things quietly and unofficially in motion," he tells me. "Sometime tomorrow we will know whether Craig Dawson has been issued a visa and if he is in this country. If so, we might conceivably have an address."

"That's fast work, Grahame. I see it pays to have friends in high places, thank you."

"I hope also to have a verbal summary of the police reports on the Des Moines serial killings. If they are of interest, Scotland Yard will send for them. We'll have copies in a day or so. We are going to have to tread lightly to avoid stepping on toes, I'm afraid. I'm sure the North Yorkshire Police will get around to calling in Scotland Yard but at this moment not even our East Riding Watch have been notified."

XXIV

The First Day at Stoneyfield House

The Fourth of July

Sunday morning, in a bedroom in Stoneyfield
Anna

Darn it, someone is pounding on the bedroom door. "Go away," I mumble and put the pillow over my head.

"Annie, baby, wake up, damn it. We're supposed to be riding up to explore the castle before the old folks get up and put us to work baby-sitting. Come on. Get a move on."

Oh, for crying out loud. Yesterday I woke up dreading saying goodbye to Grady one minute and reading Craig Dawson's description of laughing while he kills me the next. Now here I am twenty-four hours later waking up in a country house right out of an Agatha Christie mystery with the world's most gorgeous, charming, smooth-talking, self-centered, egotistical, irritating, spoiled, would-be ... seducer pounding at my door.

"Go away, Teddy. I never said I would go with you. You know I've got strict instructions to stay close to the house from now on."

"Nonsense. There's no one within five miles to see. Come on."

Blast and double blast. Maybe if I ignore him he'll get sore knuckles and go away. Good. Moira and her cousin, Linda are yelling down the hall at Teddy to shut up and go away. Jeepers, he's rattling my door knob. What the heck? The idiot is kicking the door now. Gosh, and to think I felt dumb for propping the chair against the door when I went to bed. He finally stomps down the stairs but I'm wide awake now. I stretch, look around the room and smile. It is so cool and ... ancient, I guess. Just maybe this is going to be a good day for a change.

One thing for sure. This is going to be a Fourth of July for the books. I slip on the frilly borrowed robe, peek out the door and sneak down to Moira and Linda's room.

Linda opens the door. "Oh, good," she says. "Come in here and let's make a plan. The Donaldsons and Moira's heartthrob won't be here until three."

"Heartthrob? Linsey may make my heart throb but he hasn't exactly come courting, Linda."

"Don't be so sure of that, Moira. Our English boys aren't quite as forward as your brother. I don't know how he managed it but Teddy has something going with the girl at the pub already."

"Teddy is in a class of his own. Don't forget he's your cousin, too. If we can't go into Scarborough and we can't go riding, what can we do to keep Anna out of his clutches?"

I can't help laughing. "Yeah, keeping out of Teddy's clutches is number one on my list," I say. I really do like Linda. She and Moira are a lot alike even if she is English.

"Well, I know something you two foreigners don't," Linda giggles. "There are three attics above us with all manner of fascinating things to discover and somewhere there's supposed to be an escape tunnel that no one can find. Mom and Auntie Ellen looked for years but we're smarter than they are."

Our plans fall apart a little later when the Colonel comes to the breakfast room and asks me to join him in the library. I guess I knew this was coming but it was lovely just to pretend life was more or less normal. Well, as normal as it can be on an adventure. Geez, I wish this adventure was just a little bit less adventurous.

The colonel asks me a lot about the dirty drawings we gave to the cops in London and Wales. I finally just give up and make some quick sketches showing the general idea. He really seems interested in the way the women had been stabbed in the throat. Golly, I never thought about it before but I guess throats get slit and hearts get stabbed.

The colonel makes me go over and over everything I can remember about Crazy Craig all the way back to kindergarten. Just when I think I've told him everything, he asks some sneaky question and I end up telling him things I had completely forgotten.

It's almost noon when I finally escape the library. The big tables are already set up under the trees in the back garden and the older cousins are all making the red, white and blue decorations. I paint an American flag on a big piece of butcher paper and Mr. Jacobson puts up a makeshift pole out by the clothes line where he hangs it up next to the Union Jack.

Henri comes up and watches us for a while and then quietly asks me to follow him over to the far corner of the kitchen garden.

"Okay, what's up?" I ask him.

He takes his time answering me. "It's the fireworks, Anna. Nettie has not spoken of it, but she's clearly concerned. Frankly, I'm not entirely sure she's going to be able to tolerate the display."

"The fireworks? Golly, fireworks aren't dangerous if you know what you're doing and you can bet Colonel Evers does."

"You don't understand, Anna and I'm not sure this something I want you to ever be able to understand," he says, giving me a dark look. "You know by now Nettie and I were both in the French Underground during the war. Did you know Nettie spent the last years of the war as a prisoner of the Nazis?"

"She kind of hinted something like that in Tewkesbury," I catch my breath. "I wondered if her fingers might have been wounded in the war. Wow. Prison. Nettie was actually in prison. Gosh."

"Her fingers? Oh, them. The SS interrogation would be responsible for that. She was lucky there. Evidently they decided she wasn't worth it after only two and a half fingers. No, the problem is Ravensbruck. She would have been a victim of the Hyena's infamous roll calls."

"Hyena? I heard you guys refer to Ravensbruck a couple of times. What is it? Or was it? It must have been bad if they had hyenas there."

"It was a Nazi slave-labor prison camp for women including Resistance workers designated as enemies of the State. It was as bad as the Jewish concentration camps, only smaller. The prison was built to hold only fifteen thousand but housed many times more. Thousands were tortured, executed or died of overcrowding, starvation and exposure. In spite of the Geneva Convention the weakest political prisoners were routinely shot to make room for newer, healthier ones able to work harder. A lot of the medical experiments were done there as well. Perhaps as many as a hundred thousand women and children died there. Thousands more died on the death-marches just before liberation. At the end only a few thousand of those too weak to walk were still in Ravensbruck to be liberated."

How awful. Poor Nettie. I can hardly believe it. How could things like that be allowed to happen? War. I hate war.

"Nettie was once a crack shot, but she came out of the prison camps with a crippling phobia of guns. The guards, particularly a woman they called the Hyena, taunted the prisoners. At the morning roll call, the Hyena would take her time randomly executing an unpredictable number of them, sadistically tormenting them, sometimes giving them a choice to be shot or choose two or three other women to die their place. A hideous mixture of suspense, fear and guilt designed to cause trouble between the prisoners and break their spirit."

Oh, my God. I stare at Henri with my mouth hanging open. It's too terrible to believe. It can't be true. It just can't. I try to say something but the words stick in my throat.

"Gosh. The fireworks must sound sort of like gunshots, at least enough to upset Nettie."

"More than upset her but she refuses to tell anyone. We need to unobtrusively stay with her. If we can't get her to remain inside, then we need to quietly get her away from everyone, possibly to watch in private from the hill back by the tower."

I blink back a tear and look over at Moira and Linda laughing as they help the younger cousins making the decorations. I'm beginning to understand that I'll never be the same girl that boarded the SS Liberté two weeks ago.

Sunday night, in a bedroom at Stoneyfield
Nettie

I am such a fool. Bless Anna and Henri. Thank goodness everyone is laughing and roasting marshmallows now in classic American tradition. Henri practically carries me back down the hill and into the house. I lie in his arms on the great four-post bed mindlessly staring at the ancient beams overhead. I'm still lying there when Colonel Evers taps on our door just before midnight. Henri opens the door a crack and then invites him in.

"I got a call back from ... let just say I have some new information. Craig Dawson was issued a student visa three years ago and extended it twice. His address is listed as the Parker Manor Residential Academy in Coventry."

So Anna was right. I'm too numb at the moment to even think about our next move.

"That puts him right here in England." Henri says. "I will be shocked if we don't learn that he's been playing truant."

"AWOL might be a better description. For several hundred years the Parker Manor Academy has been a very discrete nursing home for the mentally compromised offspring of rich, powerful and even noble parents. The West Midlands Police will be interviewing an Academy representative tomorrow."

"Thank you, Colonel," Henri says giving me a long worried look. "That certainly fits, doesn't it?"

I can't help blinking back a tear. "I'll never forgive myself if anything happens to Anna," I whisper.

"Rest assured, we will see that nothing does," the Colonel smiles. "We are seven hours ahead of the American Midwest, but we should hear something back from the police in Des Moines by tomorrow morning. I'm going ask the East Riding Constabulary to refer us to the police in York. Tomorrow I'll make an appointment to see the Chief Inspector there. We'll need to give them the knife and note. I can set it up for the afternoon if you don't feel up to it in the morning."

Henri takes my hand and I say though clenched teeth. "I promise I'll be up to it, Colonel and so will Anna. Thank you."

Colonel Evers leaves, quietly closing the door behind him. I'm exhausted but there's a fifty-fifty chance I'll still be lying awake in the morning when it's time to go.

XXV
Second Day at Stoneyfield House

York

Monday morning at the Fulford Road Police Station in York
Anna

The drive to the York Constabulary takes a little over an hour and I enjoy the heck out of it. For once I don't feel like I have to look over my shoulder all the time. York is definitely cool. It even has medieval city walls. So what I want to know is, where are the knights in shining armor and the damsels in distress? Golly gee, that would be me. I am definitely a damsel in distress. Oh, my.

This is the first time I've ever been in a police station and it's exciting but intimidating. The deal is that the Colonel has an appointment with Chief Inspector Hammond and Nettie and I are along as exhibits A, B and C. That's fine by me. More than fine. The chief inspector is an unfriendly man with a red face and what Mom would call a disapproving mouth. It doesn't seem to help a bit that he trained under Colonel Evers. Maybe it makes it worse. One thing for sure, I don't like him. Oh, well.

The Colonel introduces us as his guests visiting from the United States. I'm kind of surprised when he just says that we have had a spot of trouble being followed and harassed for the past week. Is that what he calls it? He goes on to explain that Miss Hicks has not as yet re-

307

ported the most recent incident in Harlech on Saturday and wishes to do so now and transfer custody of the evidence to him. I can see the chief inspector is struggling to hide a yawn. I sure hope the Colonel knows what he's doing.

Nettie puts the box with the knife and note on his desk without a word. The big knife is wrapped in plastic now and so is the note. Chief Inspector Hammond does a double take when he looks in the box. He turns the knife over in his hand and squints at the blade. "Blood?" he raises his eyebrows.

"Presumably. Possibly cat's blood from a prior incident." The Colonel doesn't elaborate. I think I'm starting to get the idea. The Colonel is smart. Instead of trying to convince the inspector to take this seriously he's letting him come to that conclusion himself.

Chief Inspector Hammond reads the note over several times, then coldly looks up at Nettie. "Very well, Miss Hicks. Describe the circumstances connected with finding these items, please."

Nettie follows the Colonel's lead and lets the details of all our misadventures emerge one bit at a time. Ha. When the Colonel tells him about me being stalked in America by a disturbed classmate three years ago and that the stalker is currently a resident at the Parker Manor Residential Academy the inspector really sits up and takes notice. We mention that the Des Moines serial killings abruptly stopped after Craig was sent away. Hammond's face actually turns pale.

Boy, oh boy. The chief inspector sure doesn't want to touch the very discrete Parker Manor with a ten-foot pole. He suggests calling in Scotland Yard even before the Colonel points out that the incidents happened in three different jurisdictions. The way the Colonel smiles I have a feeling he knows exactly who the Yard will send and that they are already on the way.

The rest of the morning is boring. Between going over the ugly details, signing statements and such, I start thinking about Grady. Dollars to donuts, he'll be starting for Scarborough this evening. Not good. We aren't at the hotel where we told him we'd be. This is going to be awkward for sure. Wrong. It is going to be impossible. It would have been bad if we were all staying at the same hotel or even different hotels but now we're hiding out at Stoneyfield. If we asked her to, I bet Mrs. Evers would invite him to stay here but Stoneyfield House must be running out of bedrooms with all the cousins and us here, too. Then there's the small issue that he and Ted don't exactly get along. Oh, well. It's something to worry about that isn't me screaming while my face turns blue.

When we get back to Stoneyfield, I'm not feeling very sociable so I hole up with good old Martin Johnson and his cannibals. Before long, Nettie comes and tells me the news. Whatever they learned from Des Moines was interesting enough that Des Moines is airmailing copies of the files to Scotland Yard. Wow. I wonder if that means we kids weren't the only ones who suspected Crazy Craig. Blast, blast and double blast. If that's true, he isn't just fooling round trying to scare me. Thinking about that, I feel really scared for the first time since we got to this house.

In the late afternoon, the Scotland Yard inspector himself arrives at the door. Chief Inspector Sanders and the Colonel are obviously old friends. He's not at all like the chief inspector in York. He and Henri hit off right away. I like him myself even though I know he'll end up questioning me and Nettie. Oh, well. At least for now he isn't pressing the matter.

What the Scotland Yard chief inspector does do is give us news, good or bad news depending on how you look at it. Me, I call it bad, real bad. The West Midland police interviewed the people at Parker Manor. Craig has been missing all week but the doctors didn't realize it until Friday. Blast and double blast. They notified his parents Saturday and hired a private security company to find him. Now he's officially listed as a missing person by the police. Worse than bad. It's all true. Craig Dawson is right here in England. Geez. He must be the one out there chasing me.

Nettie is as angry as I've ever seen her. "I can't believe it," she snaps. "How in the hell can he go missing on Monday and they don't notice until Friday?"

Chief Inspector Sanders sighs. "I'm afraid it's all fairly understandable, Miss Hicks. Mr. Dawson's high intelligence is an unfortunate complication. Apparently he has been doing so well at

Parker Manor that for the past year the doctors have had him on a program aimed at eventually reintegrating him into society."

"Then he's been pulling the wool over their eyes," Nettie say grimly. "The man who made those drawings and wrote his little rhyme is mentally ill."

"I told you he's smart and he's no longer an inexperienced kid of fifteen. He came up with a clever plan on the fly when he spotted Miss Ambleside at the museum. Apparently he was on a routine monthly outing on Sunday last. Not long after they left the British Museum, he claimed to have seen a news article about Wimbledon or at least that's what he told them. Art Lawson, a somewhat colorful American whom he greatly admires, was playing last week. Dawson requested and got permission to stay in London for three days to watch him compete. The doctors have been encouraging him to take an interest in sports, so they approved his request."

"But what he really was doing was chasing Nettie and Anna around England," Henri groans.

So the Dawson's really did stick Craig in a mental hospital, one all the way over here. Geez. Now he's seen me and he's after me. What rotten luck. If I'm not careful, I'm going to embarrass myself and start bawling.

"Dawson failed to return Thursday but called in from a cottage hospital in Birmingham," the chief inspector continues. "He claimed that he had time to go see the Pre-Raphaelite paintings at the Art Museum there and still get back on to Parker Manor on time. He fell on the platform at the train station, hit his head and was taken to a nearby cottage hospital where he was admitted for observation."

"I suppose that he checked in and right back out immediately after the hospital talked to his doctor at Parker Manor," the Colonel groans. "Very clever."

"Another thing emerged just an hour ago. It seems that in the past year he's been granted permission to take several solo day trips to London. He's been taking advantage of the trips to meet with a solicitor and banker. When he turned eighteen he came into an inheritance from a grandmother and has been quietly accessing it without calling it to anyone's attention. The bank has now frozen his funds but he withdrew two hundred pounds on Monday morning and another five hundred on Wednesday morning. That is a great deal of money."

Great, just great. Wouldn't you know it. As usual the rich weirdo's got the money to do whatever he wants and he wants to kill me. I'm safe here for the moment but we can't stay here forever. Boy, we better hope they catch him real soon.

At least one worry is taken care of even if it isn't about keeping me alive. I talked to Nettie about Grady and she has it under control. He left his Glasgow number with her and she called him. Mrs. Evers herself even got on the phone and invited him to stay here. They know better than to put him in with Ted so he'll get my room and I'll move in with Linda and Moira in a big room up on the top floor. As if that will solve the problem. Unless Teddy has changed his spots, putting Grady and him in the same house has the makings of a disaster. Blast and darn.

Linda and Moira and I spend what's left of the day in the garden. Moira brought a bunch of movie magazines with her and they're poring over them. I'm working on a watercolor of the house and trying not to worry about things. The house, the garden, the trees, the stable and even the girls under the big oak have great possibilities but I can't concentrate. My mind keeps wandering back and forth between Grady and Crazy Craig.

Teddy tries to make a nuisance of himself but Moira and Linda run him off. Would you believe he's been flirting outrageously with Linsey's little sister? And she's barely fifteen. Men. They're the root of all my problems, Craig, Grady, Ted. Heck, it's even their fault that it matters whether I've gained two pounds or not. I haven't got a thing to show for my efforts when I finally pack up for the day.

When I yawn for the second time after dinner, Henri volunteers to stay up until Grady gets here and introduce him to our hosts. That makes him a hero in my book.

Knowing how jealous Teddy gets, I figure things will go better if I'm not around. I make it a point to go to bed early and Moira and Linda do, too. Up in the top-floor bedroom we see the car lights when Grady arrives. Linda has never seen him so she and Moira sneak out and peek at him from the top of the stairs. I smile to myself, but don't join them.

Monday night in the Stoneyfield House library
Henri

Grady's arrival just after midnight finds the household gone to bed with the notable exception of the Colonel and myself. I introduce the Aussie to the Colonel and the three of us proceed to the library to acquaint Grady with the situation and the Colonel with Grady. Grahame is a man who calls things as he sees them and is impressed by Grady's polite but unvarnished description of his relationship with Ted. I take it Ted's conflicting story is that he and Grady are the best of friends.

I sense that Grahame already has the measure of his grandson. I venture a guess that he'll be taking the boy in hand. Ted is not a bad kid, just spoiled ... and vain ... and jealous.... I guess someone does need to take him in hand, at that.

"I consider myself fairly warned, Mr. MacFarland," Grahame tells Grady with a warm smile. "The idea of you getting a room at the pub is preposterous. I won't hear another word of it. Can I offer you some brandy?"

"Thank you, no. I'm a simple grog man, myself," Grady smiles. "A drink of anything stronger than ginger beer tonight and I'll fair fall asleep. It's good to know that there's been no more incidents but I want to catch up on what's happened since I parted with Nettie and Anna in Harlech."

"Our situation would be tenuous indeed were it not for Colonel Evers help and the protection of Stoneyfield House," I tell him. "Anna and Moira's Fourth of July celebration has coincidentally saved the day."

"As they say, hindsight is 20-20, sir," Grady smiles. "Unfortunately the five of us sat around in pubs any number of times cheerfully sharing our planned itineraries with each other and evidently with the cat-killer at the same time. He must know about the Scarborough plan and is lurking out there somewhere. In fact, I figure he must know my car so I went to some lengths to be sure no one followed me here. I avoided the village altogether by coming across the North York Moors. I only got lost the once around Cow Wraith Bank."

Grahame burst out laughing, "Good man," he grinned. "Not many would have thought to take that precaution and few strangers would have made it here through the moorlands."

"Is there anyway he could have heard you were coming to Stoneyfield?" the Colonel asks.

"An apt question," I nod. "Nettie called Maureen from Sheffield. When she returned to the table she told us about of the change in plans. I believe she may have mentioned Stoneyfield by name. Is there any way Dawson might have been in Sheffield?"

"Of course," Grahame points out. "He could have followed Nettie from Harlech."

"It is a possibility but Nettie would have been on the alert for that."

"He knew," Grady groans. "He definitely knew, professor. After Nettie called you from the hotel in Harlech, she came out to tell us that she was meeting you in some Sheffield pub."

"Forewarned is forearmed," Grahame points out. "It's a situation that we can address. I think he'll find Stoneyfield a hard nut to crack."

"Speaking of nut, Grady, we believe that can put a name to your cat-killer," I tell him. "Craig Dawson, formerly of Des Moines, Iowa."

"Des Moines, Iowa. The United States? What is he doing here, I mean other than chasing Anna and Nettie?"

"Conning his way out of a mental hospital. Remember your visit to the British Museum? You know, the one where you sneaked Anna down the freight elevator?" I innocently ask.

"Some rules were meant to taken with a grain of salt, sir," Grady says with a sheepish look. "I suppose Anna must have told you."

I shake my head in denial. I can't help enjoying his discomfort just a little bit.

"No, but I've used that elevator myself from time to time," I smile. "The significant point is that we were both there that day and so were Anna and this deranged old classmate of hers. I have yet to see a photo of Craig Dawson but there is no doubt in my mind that he's the guy the guard and I noticed mesmerized by Arab daggers. He must have spotted you and Anna at the same time I did. Ironically, I lost you two, but he didn't."

"The next day, Nettie made it easy for him," the Colonel sighs, "buying an attention-getting car like the Jag. The unusual white color made it even easier to spot. His good luck, our bad luck."

"Our task now is to reverse that," I say. "Stoneyfield is remarkably good luck for us and he's sloppiness has cost him. Leaving clues recognizable by Anna was a serious error. But for those, he might have escaped our attention indefinitely."

"The two questions we must consider are what will he do now, and how immediate is the danger to Anna?" the Colonel says thoughtfully. "In his place I'd go to ground until this case made its way lower in the queue of police headaches. On the other hand, he's been successfully outwitting his doctors for some time and may be over-confident."

"I suppose the answer to both questions depends on the extent of his fixation on Anna," Grady says. "If it's overpowering he could be very dangerous and will bloody well strike again. He must be aware that Anna is only here in Britain for a limited time. If he doesn't know just how limited he'll have to act as quickly as he can. Are the doors locked, sir?"

"We are a bit lax about such things here, but yes, they are all locked with Yale locks, the Colonel sighs. "The old bars are still in place and can be used as added security if we like. I doubt anyone

could come in through the upper-floor windows but we should certainly latch the ground-floor ones."

"I shall help with the project," I yawn. "Now on that note I propose
we reconvene in the morning. We have a lot of talking and thinking
ahead of us."

"An excellent suggestion, Henri. Grady?"

"Call it unanimous. I would like a minute in the morning to talk to
Anna though."

"Come on, Romeo," I tease him. "I'll show you to your room."

XXVI
The Third Day at Stoneyfield House

East Ayton Village

Tuesday Morning in a bedroom
at the top of Stoneyfield House
Anna

I wake up confused, then I remember. I'm now sharing a bedroom of medieval splendor with Moira and Linda. The big third-floor bedroom, or I guess that would be called the second-floor over here... anyway, it hasn't been used much in the last hundred years or so. The canopies over the great carved beds have seen better days but the room is still wonderful, like something out of Ivanhoe. We needed a ladder to climb into the beds. I love it.

I lie here not wanting to get up. Moira and Linda are already up and gone but they don't have two giant worries on their minds like me. One man who loves me and wants to marry me and another who hates me and wants to kill me. Geez.

I give up and get up. I look through the little wavy glass panes of the big window. The front garden is full of flowers. The two guys I see walking the dogs over by the wall turn out to be Grady and Mrs. Jacobson's husband, Randy. Back to earth, Annie. I bet they are doing guard duty. Oh, well. Maybe it will keep Grady busy enough that I can avoid having to deal with him until I ... What? I figure out how to tell him I'm not going to Australia and marrying him either now or later? Geez. Maybe I should go back to bed after all.

Instead, I sneak down to the kitchen. Breakfast has come and gone. I smell bread baking and I'm suddenly ravenous. I rob the cookie jar of a handful of chocolate-chip cookies, yes, cookies, not biscuits. Moira's lovely all-American mom baked them.

I don't feel like seeing anyone. I go back and get "Martin Johnson, Lion Hunter" from upstairs and take it over to a big chair in the far corner of the music room where no one makes music anymore. It turns out not to be the best plan I've ever had. I haven't read ten pages before Grady comes in and worse yet, I am really happy to see him. Blast it. I hate Australia.

"Good morning, Annie. I've missed you." He comes over and sits on the floor by my chair and looks up. He really does have amazing blue eyes.

"Grady, it's only been two days," I tell him. He shrugs his shoulders.

"By my count it's been closer to two days and five hours, love."

Not Good. Nettie is right. I have to deal with this now. "Oh, Grady. don't make this any harder." I gently tell him. "Nothing has changed. I told you that I'm not ready to make promises and won't be for a long time. I don't know what I want to do with my life. Much as I love you, I don't think it's going to be being an Australian housewife."

Neither of us says anything for the next few awkward minutes. Finally Grady looks at my book, starts to says something, shakes his head and stands up.

"I've got something you out in the car, Annie," he says. "I'll be right back." He's up and out the door before I can protest.

Geez, this could be awkward. I sure hope it's something small and cheap. I hold my breath when he comes in with something hidden behind his back. He grins and brings out a book and hands it to me. I can't believe my eyes. "I Married Adventure" by Osa Johnson, Martin Johnson's wife.

I clutch it to my chest with my mouth hanging open. I stutter, then open and close my mouth a couple of times like a beached fish and, of all things, I sneeze.

Grady bursts out laughing. "That book isn't anything to sneeze at, dear one. You won't believe what it took to find it."

"I'm sorry, Grady. I don't know what to say ..."

"Then sneeze instead, love. Your sneezes are just as beautiful as the rest of you. I love your sneezes. Sneeze away and I'll tell you something else that I think will please you."

"Oh, Grady, thank you," I stammer.

"Hey, I haven't told you the something else yet," he laughs. "I went to the Kevingrove Art Gallery and spent three hours in the French gallery trying to understand what you see in these impressionist blokes. I liked all the colors straight off but to my eye the pictures just looked messy. After an hour they started to look better. Then I found this painting by a woman named Mary Cassatt and I really liked it. There were some paintings of aborigines by a man called Gaugin that were even better. By the time I left even the messy ones were looking pretty good. I'm an idiot, Annie, but I won't stay one, not if I can help it. I bought some books on art and I'm going to read them cover to cover. You can hardly be expected to marry an idiot."

Now what do I do? Please God, keep me from ending up on an Australian sheep ranch or I guess it's cows up in Queensland. I'm saved by the bell and the noisy arrival of Chief Inspector Sanders.

Just when it seems things are as bad as they can get, the Chief Inspector drops his bombshell. I can't help it, I burst into tears and run for the bedroom or try to. They make me come back. Darn, darn, darn.

Tuesday afternoon at Stoneyfield House library
Nettie

I'm wandering around at loose ends this morning still unsettled by last night's fireworks. I'm not sure what Annie is up to, but Henri, Grady and Colonel Evers have been taking turns walking the dogs around the house and gardens. I watch Maureen's husband, Randy join. I'm not sure it's necessary but it's comforting and gives them something to do. Dawson will not find it so easy to play his tricks now.

Mid-afternoon, Inspector Sanders arrives with a driver and his sergeant. One look at his face and I know something is up and it isn't good.

He leaves his men outside and assembles all of us, including a reluctant Annie, in the library.

"There are details about the 1951 serial killings in Des Moines the police never made public," he announces once we are settled. "I have them now. Anna, I'm afraid that you must be put in protective custody immediately."

"In effect, Charles, she already is," Colonel Evers quietly points out. "I take it the details are suggestive shall we say?"

"Extremely so," he tells us. "The previous victims were all stabbed in the throat. Nursery rhymes were pinned to the throats of the last three. Do you wish to hear the rhymes?"

"Need you ask?" the colonel answers for all of us.

Chief Inspector Sanders gets out his reading glasses and clears his throat.

"The first one said," and he reads,

> *"Mary, Mary quite contrary, how does your red blood flow?"*

"The next one said:

> *"Me, me, the big man's son,*
> *Killed the girl and away I run."*

"And finally,

*"The owl and the pussy cat went to sea. The owl stabbed
her in the throat*
*Her blood got runny, he thought it was funny and hurried
on home to gloat."*

Oh, dear God. That's more than suggestive. I feel sick. The danger
facing Anna just became horrifyingly graphic and deeply frightening.
A stunned silence settles over the entire room.

The inspector folds up his notes and puts them back in his briefcase. He looks around at our shocked faces, then turns to Colonel
Evers. "You are right, Grahame. Stoneyfield House is as safe a place
as any and would be decidedly more comfortable for Miss Amberside.
It would mean stationing a constable here around the clock though,
and that would mean overtime."

"The truth is that we have been patrolling the grounds with the
dogs ourselves," the colonel tells him. "Maureen's husband was a U.S.
pilot in World War II. Henri was one of the French maquisards and I'll
warrant Grady is used to taking care of himself. If our Yankee serial
killer is out there, he hasn't found us unprepared."

Saunders looks over at Anna. She's looking simply awful, as white
as a sheet and shivering.

"I suppose we can manage the overtime for a few days," he tells
Anna. "You'd have to agree to stay indoors and away from windows at

all times, young lady. Promise that under no circumstances, will you put so much a toe out the door."

"I won't. Believe me, I won't," Anna whispers. "Please don't lock me away somewhere." She bursts into tears and runs from the room with Grady close on her heels.

Ted watches them, looking like a volcano about to erupt. Maureen pushes him back in his chair and all but sits on him. Alas for unrequited love or maybe just lust in Teddy's case. I should have read the fine print about being a step-auntie. What an awful situation. Poor Anna.

Chief Inspector Sanders leaves his sergeant behind on temporary guard duty. There will be three shifts. At 3 p.m., the first constable will arrive to relieve the man the Chief Inspector leaves behind now. The evening shift will end at eleven and some unfortunate guy will be on night duty until seven in the morning.

The Stoneyfield men remain in a huddle in the library, discussing strategy, I imagine. Grady comes downstairs without Anna and joins them. I probably should sit in, but Anna comes first. I go up to the big attic bedroom. She's asleep on the bed and nothing could be better for her right now. I pull a blanket off one of the other beds, tuck it around her, and tiptoe out of the room.

Downstairs I pass the library door without stopping and join the rest of family in the drawing room. Maureen and Mrs. Evers have their hands full. The kids all know something is wrong and are upset.

Moira and Linda rise to the occasion and organize the tribe of Evers descendants, including Teddy, in a game of charades. Mrs. Evers takes the two youngest upstairs for a nap and Maureen goes to the kitchen to make popcorn. Things begin to settle back to something approaching normal. I take refuge behind a book I don't actually read and idly watch the kids playing charades.

Poor Ted. I don't know if it's an oversight on the part of the men or not but he's been left out. In effect he's been lumped in with the women and children and he doesn't like it. At nineteen, I wouldn't either. He is obviously going through a rough patch. He's just discovering that being handsome and having the top high-school batting average doesn't necessarily make you top dog in college. He'll come to terms with it eventually but right now he is a liability even to himself and this isn't a game we're playing here with Crazy Craig.

I guess both Anna and I are going through our own rough patches. I've had some tough times since the war. God knows I've struggled with the ghosts of Ravensbruck but finding Henri opens new wounds and Crazy Craig reopens old ones. For Anna's sake, I must not give in to any of it.

Craig Dawson may be another Nazi sadist in modern dress, but there's only one of him. The forgotten years in Paris with Henri and the Resistance have resurfaced but those years weren't all bad. I can deal with this. I'm not going let anything happen to that precious niece of mine.

The rest of the day, news dribbles in a little bit at a time. Dawson owns a white Vespa. On Wednesday he used five hundred pounds of the money he withdrew to buy a new Vincent Black Lightning motorcycle. When there wasn't one instantly available in London, he took the train up to Stevenage where they make them. That tells me something about him. I sigh. I automatically file the bits of information somewhere in the recesses of my brain, a habit leftover from working with Jean. Survival training sticks with you, including the target practice I do my level best to forget.

I actually did see a white Vespa that first day in Canterbury. Apparently it didn't take him long to discover that the Vespa wasn't powerful enough to keep up with my Jag. The big Vincent made the perfect thing to tail us with. It all fits, God help us. We're on to him now but that's not the same as catching him.

Tuesday late afternoon in the girls' bedroom on the top floor of Stoneyfield
Anna

Geez. I didn't know I was asleep until I wake up. I must have been really tired to take such a long nap. Wrong. I was upset, not tired. I am still upset. I swear I dreamed bad dreams the whole time. Oh, well. At least it's still daytime. The clock seems to think it's only an hour until dinner. I kind of doubt that I'll ever be hungry again. I sure don't feel like getting up and seeing everybody downstairs.

You know, there are times when a person really, really wants to be wrong. I was right, it was Crazy Craig harassing us and killing poor Tomas. Us kids were wrong about being wrong in Des Moines. That made us right, we just didn't know it. There really and truly is a madman out there and he wants to kill me, wants stab me in the neck and laugh.

It's almost like a movie or book or something. I wonder if Craig wrote another nursery rhyme to use when he does the deed ... if he does the deed. Boy, oh, boy. This is one time when I don't mind being grounded, I'm overjoyed to be grounded, in fact. At least if I have to be stuck indoors, this is the house for it.

Oh, well. I sit up, brush my hair and promise myself to stop acting like a baby. I peek over the bannister and don't see anybody in the hall. The library door is closed. They're probably still in there talking about all this. There's a lot of noise coming from the drawing room. Kids. It sounds like the parents must have banished all the cousins in there. I ought to go and help Moira and Linda.

Parents and kids get me thinking again. I wonder how Craig's parents found out. The cops never made the nursery rhymes public. Gosh, if I was his mother and found drafts of something like them around, I'd be pretty darn suspicious. He must have gotten blood on him, too. Even without seeing any blood, they might have just guessed but they had to figure it out when the killings stopped. Dollars to donuts, they never told the Parker Manor doctors about that. Darn, darn and double darn. Please, please, let them catch him quick.

I go back to the bedroom for Martin Johnson. I see the new book and fall apart again. I look at the photograph of Martin and Osa on the dust jacket. She was so beautiful. So was he, for that matter. They have on helmets and goggles, like old-fashioned pilots used to wear. They were real people who had real-life adventures. I start to cry and giggle at the same time. Stop being hysterical, Annie. After all, this is a king-sized adventure you're on.

Oh, blast. I can't seem to stop crying. Maybe adventures are more fun in theory than practice. I don't care. I refuse to be an Australian housewife knee deep in smelly cows and sheep.

When I wake up again, it's full dark. Dinner was over hours ago. This time I wash my face, put on some makeup and a clean dress. Good. I'm back in control. It sounds like everyone is in the drawing room listening to the radio. They're laughing. It must be a comedy but I don't recognize the voices. They probably listen to different shows here. I'm not feeling sociable enough to deal with it.

I've been itching to draw the wonderful palm-looking thing out in the room they call the conservatory. I get my watercolors and watercolor pad and quietly sneak down the back stairs and slip through the kitchen. The moon is so bright it really isn't dark in there. Gosh, I wonder if turning on the lights would be a mistake with the glass roof and all the windows. Oh, well. I leave the lights off and go sit on the big wicker couch in the corner enjoying the quiet and the indoor jungle. I hear the door open behind me and sigh.

"Waiting for lover boy?" Ted sneers and stands over me. "Bad timing. Your cowboy is holed up in the library with the other big heroes."

"You sure are in an ugly mood tonight, Teddy," I tell him. "Why don't you go bother someone else? I'm not in the mood for your bad temper."

"Why? Aren't I good enough for you? You only spread your legs for guys who are rich?"

I gasp. I can't believe I heard him right. I must have misheard him. "What did you say?" I ask him in surprise.

"You heard me, little Miss Hot Pants." He leans over, grabs my face, and kisses me hard.

I can't believe this is happening. I pull loose, roll away and struggle to my feet. He slaps his hand over my mouth, backs me against the wall and pulls at my dress with the other hand. He tears the buttons off and gets his hand in my bra. I can't believe this is Ted. It must be someone else who looks like him or maybe I'm asleep and having a nightmare. No, I smell alcohol on his breath. He must be drunk.

I struggle and try to bite his hand. I fail. Blast.

"What's the matter, slut? Grady tells me you like it rough."

He's lying. Grady would never say something like that, but I cry harder. I try to scream but the only sound I can manage through his hand is a muffled moan that no one will hear.

"He says you squeal like a pig when he puts it to you. Let's see if he's right, Miss Round Heels."

He tries to push me down but I grab the back of a chair. It bumps the lamp next to it, which falls with a crash. With my other hand I frantically grope for something, anything. I touch something cold and small. It's the spout of the big watering can on the table. I grab it. The can is heavy, hard to lift this way but I swing it up with all my might and hit him in the side of his head with a glancing blow.

He snarls and loosens his grip for the second I need to pull away and try to run. He grabs the hem of my dress, stopping me. I pull harder and hear something tear.

Suddenly he grunts and lets go. I look back and see Nettie with her arm half around this neck. She jerks him back hard but he wrenches loose and turns on her. She looks tiny next to him but she has a grim smile on her face. She knees him in the groin and he doubles over, half falling. She slugs him in the jaw so hard that it straightens him up and he falls over backwards. She casually puts her small foot lightly on his big throat. He stops struggling and begins to cry.

She looks down at him with a contemptuous smile.

"Are you okay, Annie?" she asks.

"Don't tell Grady, please don't tell him." I frantically grab Nettie's arm. "He'll kill Ted and they'll put him in jail."

"Don't worry, I'll kill Ted myself. Get back upstairs and change that dress, for God's sake. I'll be there in a minute."

Tuesday night in the Stoneyfield House library
Henri

An English colonel, a French historian, an Aussie cowboy and an American football coach; for all intents and purposes strangers. we make an unusual but exceptional team. We bat around ideas for a while. A while, hell. We've been at it since dinnertime.

Dawson is out there somewhere but he's only one man and we are four. He must eat and sleep occasionally though he may be sleeping rough. Randy Jacobson proposes that we systematically search the woods. If he has the Vincent with him in these woods along the river, finding him wouldn't be difficult.

The colonel argues against it on the grounds that we'd just drive him into the adjacent North York moors. I can't help pointing out that with all their men and resources the Nazis had a hell of a time finding us maquisards in much tamer territory. Grady points out that the man could just as well be holed up in Scarborough or even London, for that matter.

On and on. Around and around. The grandfather clock in the front hall chimes one.

The Colonel clears his throat and quietly assumes command, summarizing our position "The police presence here at Stoneyfield is valuable but we judge their resources to be inadequate to the task of protecting Anna. Our prime objective is to see that Anna remains safe. We are largely operating independently. It would do my heart good to catch the bastard but that has to come second. Is this an accurate reflection of your attitudes?"

What is there to say? Naturally, we all nod in agreement.

"Our unspoken assumption has been that we have more manpower than the police guard assigned here. Not true. A fresh constable comes on duty every eight hours. They are three, not one and the four of us have to take time off to sleep. Our opponent is nondescript, smart and has significant resources, we don't know how extensive. The police aren't likely to apprehend him quickly. It's been a long night already and there will be more of them. I for one, am tired. Let's get on with it."

"Well put, Grahame," I say. "We can't be everywhere at once but neither can he. What we lack in manpower we must make up for with brainpower. This Dawson character is clever but sloppy. We need to out-think him. He'll be trying to get to Anna someplace where we aren't. We'll be predicting where he'll make his try and be there waiting. If we are to block his attempts, we must think like he thinks. Anna is going to have to stay under cover until we do."

"Okay, mates," Grady laughs. "If I've got this right, in order to defend Anna and maybe even catch this bloke, you want us to think like he does. But, Henri, he's bleeding insane. You want us to think like a certified madman?"

"Right," Randy chips in. "I say think football, instead. What's his next play gonna be?"

"That's not football, that's American gridiron," Grady teases him, "But you're spot on."

"It's a matter of anticipating what he'll try and of deploying our forces, human and otherwise, to foil his attempt," the Colonel says. "We have the house and the perimeter with Anna in the center. We have the walls, doors, locks. We have dogs and we have us. As we sit here talking, we have locked doors and one constable wandering around out there. How many of our resources do we use to beef that up? And for how long? Or even how useful is it to beef up that defense. Is offense the best defense?"

"In my not so humble opinion, we need less talk right now and more action," I mutter impatiently. "As you point out, it's late."

The Colonel clears his throat again. "Randy and Grady, for now you are responsible for the perimeter. Figure out what to do and do it. You have the dogs. We can get more if you want more. Let me know if there's something else you need. In extremity, we may have some archaic tools around here we can resort to. Henri and I will develop an overall battle plan. Now let's go to bed."

Part Eight

A New Strategy

XXVII
A Battle Plan is Hatched

East Ayton Village

Tuesday night in the girls' bedroom in Stoneyfield House
Nettie

"Okay, that's it. We're out of here, Anna," I say nursing my bruised fist. "You and I are leaving for Norway tomorrow. No good-byes to anyone except Grady so think about what you want to say to him. Treat this as classified information."

"But Nettie, we can't," Anna sobs. "What about Craig? What about the police? Aren't I in protective custody or something?"

"I don't have time to argue. I'm leaving now to make the arrangements. Quit crying and pack anything you can't part with. We'll buy what we need when we get there. Whatever you do, don't say anything to anyone. Get yourself down to my room as soon as you're ready. I'll join you in about an hour."

I leave quickly before she can argue. I know I can trust her to be ready, whether she agrees or not.

Downstairs, Grady and Randy are coming out of the library deep in conversation. I wait until they disappear around the corner, then go in without knocking. Henri and the Colonel give me a startled look.

"Anna and I are going to be on the Newcastle ferry to Norway to-morrow afternoon," I baldly state. "It would be a mistake to try to stop us and a great deal easier if you help."

"Whoa, there," Henri calmly responds. "I, for one, am on your side one hundred percent but obviously there's a first chapter behind this decision of yours that we have yet to hear. Sit down and fill us in."

I slump down in a chair and fight off the tears I have no intention of shedding. I realize I'm behaving like a hysterical old maid. I've been so busy running scenarios of how to safely get Anna out of the country that I ignored the step of enlisting my allies. Damn.

I take a couple of deep breaths and the glass of brandy Henri holds out to me.

"The first chapter is unimportant," I tell them. "Let's just say a new straw turned up that broke this camel's back. We'll have to leave that chapter on a need-to-know basis for now." I look from one man to the other and hear no objections but I see Henri eying my bruised right hand. I quickly tuck it out of sight. This is not the time to deal the issue of Ted.

"Chapter two has been in the back of my mind ever since Sanders read us those perverted nursery rhymes," I say. "Okay, so we've iden-tified the culprit, so what? Damn it all, the Nazi SS never managed to catch Jacque Le Ru or countless others of us on their "most wanted" lists. Unlike Scotland Yard, the Nazis weren't hampered by rules or morals and had plenty of manpower and they still failed."

"Henri has been saying the same thing for ..." the Colonel starts to interrupt me. I'm not ready to be interrupted. I ignore him.

"You don't need to convince me that your friend, Chief Inspector Saunders, is a good man, Colonel," I continue. "Eventually he will catch this Craig Dawson but it's not going to happen overnight. Dawson's good, he's smart, he has money and no ties. He could be anywhere or nowhere. He won't be easy to catch. The one thing he can't do without a passport is border-hop. I'm getting Anna out of the country now. It's not up for debate."

Henri and the colonel exchange a look. "We're with you. Nettie," the Colonel smiles. "Let's hear your plan and see how we can help."

"Thank you. I actually reached my decision less than an hour ago. I freely admit my plan could use a bit of refinement. Ferries routinely leave Newcastle for Norway every afternoon. We will be on one tomorrow afternoon. Anna and I will slip out of Stoneyfield a few hours from now, possibly with some help distracting the constable, then make our way north by back roads."

"I support the general outline," Henri smiles. "It could certainly do with some refinement. Dawson is still out there waiting for you to show yourself, Nettie. What's to prevent him from following you again? After you successfully sneak out of the house, what's to prevent your police watchdogs from realizing you're gone and intercepting you before you safely board the ferry?"

"Maybe we can say we have the flu. Maybe we can disguise ourselves. We might fool Craig and the constable at the same time."

"That's some big maybe's, Nettie, but it is doable," Colonel Evers smiles at me encouragingly. "We've been kicking around similar ideas ourselves. The idea of putting you and Anna safely out of reach somewhere in Europe is appealing. Sending the two you off to Newcastle without a plan and someone to watch your back is unacceptable."

"I'm not sure it's that risky, Colonel. I've been trying to imagine being in Dawson's shoes. I think he intended to make his big move at Harlech. He had the knife and note in hand. I think he intended to lure Anna out of the hotel, probably on the pretext of meeting Grady. Grady got held up in Cardigan and didn't show up as expected, so his plan fell through. Dawson stabbed Anna's seat in pure rage and frustration. Sure, he's out there. Yes, he might follow us but he has to get Anna alone somehow and that simply isn't going to happen in the time it takes to get to the ferry."

"You and Henri think a lot alike," the Colonel chuckles. "However he and I remain in agreement that you must have secondary support and I want you to carry my service revolver as well."

"No, Colonel, I won't do that." I panic even at the thought of it. "Guns and I do not get along. I wouldn't use one if I had it so you can keep your bloody gun."

"Ah, yes, the Colonel says. "You are a Quaker, aren't you. We will have to work around that."

Let the Colonel think what he wants to but I learned two things in Ravensbruck. Killing people is the ultimate evil but so is passively allowing to happen. Unfortunately I also came away unable to bear even the sight of a gun.

Henri immediately intercedes. "Anna can carry it, Grahame. I'll give her a quick lesson in the basics and have her practice firing it empty. In the unlikely case she needs it, it will be short range."

"But if push came to shove, could she pull the trigger?" the Colonel asks dubiously.

"I'll talk to her. If she's scared and angry enough I believe she can rise to the occasion." Henri and the Colonel exchange a long look and the Colonel backs down.

I don't like it. I very much don't like it. I can believe Anna would shoot the man who murdered her Snowball but I'm not sure that I can tolerate just knowing there's a gun in the car. I'll argue the issue with Henri later. This isn't the time.

After the Ted incident, I was geared up to fight the world. It's oddly disconcerting to realize I didn't have to talk anyone into my plan. Colonel Evers, Henri and for all I know, Grady, were already discussing it. I don't like brandy but I finish off the drink Henri gave me, sigh and prepare to get down to work.

"There's no chance that Scotland Yard will go along with this, is there?" I ask hopefully.

"Not a chance," the Colonel sighs. "Saunders couldn't permit it even if he thought it was the best idea. No, getting you out of here and away unseen will be a greater challenge than getting you out of the country. Whether Dawson is sitting there with his binoculars or not, we'll have to smuggle you out."

"Vehicles are an issue," Henri adds. "Using your Jag is out of the question. We believe both Grady and his car are potential assets. I propose we wake him up and get him in here. Anna should be here, too."

"No," I tell them. "Not Anna. We do need Grady, but I insist we leave Anna out of this until we have a firm plan. I've alerted her. She doesn't have to be in on the planning to do her part when the time comes. At least one of us ought to get some sleep."

Henri and the Colonel are both damn smart. I see in their eyes that they know the first chapter involves Anna and it isn't good. I hope they just think that she's breaking down under the stress without wondering why now. It will not be helpful if Grady learns about Ted.

It only takes a moment before Henri returns with Grady. The first thing out of his mouth tells me that he's on my side.

"Seven o'clock is shift change for the constable. Dawn is the best time to do something unnoticed," Grady says without preamble. "We ought to shoot for getting Anna and Nettie on the road by 5 a.m., two hours before the constable on night shift goes off duty. He'll be tired and bored by then."

He looks over at the grandfather clock standing in the corner. "Our work is cut out for us. There's no time to waste, let's get on with it."

XXVIII

Out of Hiding

East Ayton Village

Wednesday, 5 a.m. by the Stoneyfield tithe barn
Nettie

"Okay, Annie. There goes Grady and here comes Henri. Unfortunately Constable Billingsley still looks bright-eyed and bushy-tailed."

"Jeepers, Nettie. I'd feel a lot better about this if it was a bit darker," Anna complains. "It's only five in the morning but it's already light."

"It won't be when you're under the blanket. It's summertime, stop complaining."

"Here, let me pull that stocking farther down over your hair in the back. Your red hair is trying to escape. Be sure to hold on to Grady's hat when you run, Nettie. It would be a disaster if it falls off."

"There goes Grady waving goodbye. Henri and the constable have started over to the dog run." I take a deep breath. "This is it, Annie, pray and run like hell."

We make it to the Humber and duck down on the far side. "It looks like Grady made it back in the house," Anna whispers. "Time for us to get him in the car."

Anna lays down in the back seat, I get in the driver's seat, straighten Grady's much too large jacket and pull his hat down low. Damn it.

Trouble. Sitting on this pillow, I can barely touch the pedals. I'm not going to be able to operate the Humber's clutch. I have to do better than touch it with my toe if I'm going to start the damn car.

I tip over to the left, stretch as far as I can and turn the key. The Humber starts but I'm not sitting tall enough now to pass for Grady. I put the Humber in first, hold my breath, let off the clutch and sit back up. We creep out on to Castlegate still in first and turn right. Once we are on the other side of the wall, I pull the pillow out from under me and cautiously put the Humber into second. We've done it! We're out. If anyone is watching us, Grady is now on his way back to Scotland taking a shortcut across the moors.

Wednesday, 5 a.m. behind Stoneyfield House
Henri

"Well, I'm off to Edinburgh," Grady tells us. "If I don't see you again constable, it's been a pleasure. Henri, I hope to see you in a week or so in the Lake District." Grady scratches Duchess behind the ear and walks toward the car as quickly as he can without calling attention to himself. He looks over his shoulder. I divert Bilingsley's attention to an imaginary tick on Sampson's chest while Grady darts around the corner of the house.

The Humber starts up just as Bilingsley gives Sampson a clean bill of health. I have my fingers crossed as we go back around the house.

The women are in the car. Grady is not in evidence. I conclude that he safely made it around to the side door and heave a sigh of relief.

From where Constable Bilingsley and I stand, Nettie makes a surprisingly convincing Grady. I'm pleased that she's remembering not to take off like she's Stirling Moss in the Grande Prix.

I yawn and stretch. "Well, constable, since I'm up, I may as well get started, too. You said the shortest way to Scarborough Castle is also across the moor, I believe? I have a notoriously poor sense of direction. If it's not too much trouble, could you go over the instructions again?"

"It will cut your time in half and is easy enough as long as you don't get lost," he says. "About a mile up Castlegate Road you come to a Y. Low Road goes off to the right. It will put you right in Scalby in about four miles. You'll see the castle on the headland straight in front of you on the other side of the village."

"It's the Roman signal tower I wish to see. Do you know where it is relative to the castle, perchance?"

The constable scratches his head. "I'm not sure but I think it's by the ruins of St. Mary's Chapel right out on the edge of the cliff."

"Romans typically chose such a site for their signal towers. I thank you, constable. You've been a great help."

I estimate Anna and Nettie are safely out of sight by now. Most excellent. Things are going as planned. I climb into the Morris, fire it up and wave goodbye to the constable.

I overtake Anna and Nettie on Low Road a mile beyond the Y. Nettie has shrunk. I conclude that she's readjusted the seat to her size but Grady's hat is still in place. Anna remains out of sight in the back. Should Mr. Dawson be nearby with his binoculars that will be sufficient. He'll see both Grady and me leaving the area.

I follow the Humber out onto the moors. The only other vehicles on the moorland roads at this hour are farm vehicles. We encounter our first car when we cross A171 in Scalby. We neither see nor hear any motorcycles. If there are binoculars trained on the cross roads, they'll reveal Grady and me driving into the Scarborough suburb.

As we pass through Scallby and out of Scarborough, I drop back a bit making it less obvious that we are together. By six thirty we reach the coast near Whitby. The lightly traveled coastal back roads and lanes should now get us to Newcastle before noon.

North Riding Coast

Wednesday, 7 a.m. on the coastal road
Henri

The drive along the northeast coast is exceedingly pleasant. On the outskirts of Whitby our road literally runs along the edge of the sea. On weekends the beach at Sandsend will doubtlessly be crowded with holiday makers but this early on a Wednesday, it is all but deserted. I briefly lose sight of the Humber while I slowly drive along watching the tide roll in.

Our road curves away from the beach, going through an area of low, heavily wooded cliffs, then passes through a tiny village of a dozen houses or so. I come around a hill. Some distance ahead, the damn Humber is sitting at a rakish angle in the ditch. It had to happen sooner or later considering the speed that woman drives but unquestionably this is an inconvenient time.

Anna climbs out waving and shouting. Good. They aren't hurt.

A tall, slim figure steps out into the roadway between me and the Humber. It can't be Dawson or can it? Mon Dieu! It is him and he's got a rifle. I failed to foresee that. Ce ils de pute *(the bastard)* has out maneuvered us.

He raises a rifle taking aim at Anna. Jesus, no! Not here. Not in England, not now. I lean on the horn and stomp on the accelerator. Startled, Dawson turns and fires in my direction. I feel the impact as the Morris's right headlamp shatters but keep coming at him. Dieu merci, Anna is still standing.

I urge the Morris toward the bastard with all the speed it can muster. He darts back into the trees. Despite a frantic need to get to Nettie and Anna, I slam on the brakes at the point where he disappeared. Nettie may be injured, but the sniper has to take priority or he'll simply pick us off. The car offers at least some protection, but Anna is a sitting duck.

Keeping my head low, I slip out of the car. Giving the Colonel's service revolver to Anna proved to be a major blunder. My sword cane is useless as a distance weapon. I duck behind the fender and scan the stand of trees for movement. A gun or even a crossbow would be exceedingly handy right now. A motorcycle roars to life somewhere off to the left. I turn just in time to see a big motorcycle exiting a rough track twenty yards or so behind me. Kicking up loose gravel, it pulls on to the highway and disappears around the next curve.

Rage all but blinds me. I fight down an overwhelming urge to give chase, mow the bastard down, and kill him with my bare hands. I grit my teeth and jump back in the Morris. Bah! As if the bloody Morris could overtake a motorcycle!

Up ahead Anna is running back to the Humber. Getting her and Nettie to safety is far more urgent than vainly chasing motorcycles. The bloody Morris picks this moment to die. I pray the shot hasn't done more than knock out the headlamp. Cursing, I hit the starter and the Morris coughs back to life.

There is an ominous stillness about the accident scene. A disheveled Anna hides behind the car but where's Nettie?

"Nettie?" I croak, as I throw open my door.

"She's conscious and I can't see anything wrong but she won't say anything," Anna stammers and bursts into tears.

"And you? What about you?" I manage to ask, barely controlling my rising panic.

"I'm okay," she says smothering a sob. "I hurt like hell and twisted my ankle but I don't think it's broken."

I limp away toward the Humber in a pathetic attempt at running, screaming Nettie's name.

"Is anyone hurt? Can I help?" a gruff voice startles me. I failed to notice the big workman who's pulled up in an elderly Bedford lorry.

"I'm about to find out," I say, wrenching the passenger's door open.

Nettie is huddled against the driver's door, her eyes blankly look through me. Please God don't let her neck be broken. Or her back. I lean in and gently touch her cheek. My hand is trembling.

"Nettie, are you hurt?" I can hardly choke out the words. I reach out and stroke her tangled hair. "Claudette, Claudette. Je t'aime plus la vie elle-meme," I whisper. (*I love you more than life itself*)

I choke back tears and touch her lips with my fingers. Her eyes fly open. Wild-eyed, she chokes and whispers, "Ravensbruck ... the Hyena," and struggles to sit up.

"Ravensbruck. Oh, ma petite, what did they do to you there?" I mutter. The bloody ghosts of Ravensbruck still lurk in her head always ready and waiting to ambush her. "You are safe here with me in England, ma cherie. You haven't been shot but are you hurt?"

Her eyes focus, meet my eyes and blink back shut. "Henri? Henri ..." she shakes her head as if to clear it. "I'm okay, it just ... I'm sorry," she softly stutters.

She grasps my hand with surprising strength and with my help clambers out of the car. She staggers a few feet in the direction of the stranger. He reaches out a hand to steady her a moment too late. She collapses at his feet, a tiny trickle of blood running down her cheek.

"Where are you hurt, girl?" he asks in alarm. When she doesn't respond, he looks at me. "I'm Tom Woodruff. I live just up the road," he says. "We need to get this woman to a doctor."

"I don't think she's injured, Mr. Woodruff, at least not badly, but she's in shock." My real concern is getting her under cover in case the sniper comes back.

"I have a couple of lap rugs in the lorry," Tom offers. "Wait here, I'll get them. Ducking, he runs back to his truck.

Under cover... Mon Dieu, I've forgotten about Anna.

"Anna, run, get behind the Morris. He may come back," I call. "I'm bringing Nettie." Pale-faced and shivering, Anna limps over and leans against the Morris.

My left leg may not be worth a damn but I have the shoulders of an amateur blacksmith. I pick up Nettie, carry her over and gently maneuver her into the passenger's seat. Unresisting, she numbly stares into space.

Woodruff returns with a relatively clean lap rug and I tuck it around her.

"What about, you young lady?" Woodruff asks Anna in a surprisingly gentle voice. "Are you hurt, too?"

"No, sir. I'm just banged about a bit and bruised, I think. I'm worried about Nettie."

"It's going to be all right, Miss. I'm Tom, Tom Woodruff. You are?"

"Anna Ambleside."

"Ambleside? From over by Windermere? But you're a Yankee, aren't you Miss Ambleside?" he asks. "Don't you fret. We'll get your friend Nettie to town and Doc Stanley will patch her up in no time."

He beckons me to join him over by the Humber.

"You aren't a Yankee, too, are you?" he asks. "You sound like a Frenchy. You traveling with these ladies?"

"I'm Henry Dubois, a Yank for the past seven years or so. Nettie and Anna are old friends. We're doing a bit of sightseeing together." A Yank? In America I'd have said I am French. I realize how close I am to hysteria and suppress a rueful smile.

"Well, Mr. Dubois, I think you ought to take a look at this." He points at a couple of bullet holes in the front fender of the Humber. I nod and groan. Once the shooter took off on the bike, I keep dismissing him from my mind. I'd never have made a mistake like that ten years ago but apparently I've gotten away with it thus far. We're all still standing, but that rifle changes everything.

I nod. "Yeah, I came around the hill there just in time to interrupt a man in the road with a rifle. He took a pot shot at me, broke the Morris's headlamp and got away on a motorcycle."

"Whoa. That's ... that's terrible. That kind of thing just doesn't happen around here. Look, you passed the Lythe pub about a mile back. We should take these ladies back there, get ahold of the watch constable and get Doc Stanley here from Whitby. Is the Morris drivable?"

"Probably," I tell him, "but the sniper could be up there waiting in ambush."

"A big black motorcycle damn near ran me off the road up at the junction with the A171. I bet it was him. The next thing I saw was your smash-up."

"That must have been him. Which way did he go?

"Toward Middlesborough like he had the devil on his tail. He's long gone by now. Our chief worry is taking care of the women and reporting this to the watch."

"You are probably right," I say. "We'd have heard the motorcycle if he'd backtracked."

"I'll wait here with the cars while you take the ladies to the pub. You can call Doc Stanley and the watch constable from there. Tell him that we've had a smash-up in that wooded spot just west of the old Normanby gate house. And best tell him it wasn't an accident. There appears to have been some skullduggery with a rifle going on. I imagine he'll need to get help from Scarborough."

I sincerely hope Tom is right about Dawson but if he does circle back and find us gone, would he take his revenge by shooting Tom? We are vulnerable here. We technically should stay at the scene until the police arrive but the damn rifle changes everything and the pub is only a mile away.

"It's a good suggestion,Tom, but you could be at risk if the sniper does come back."

"Not to worry. I'll take cover if I hear him coming. Get along with you, now. Time is awasting.

Part Nine

The Final Chapter

XXIX
North Riding Coast

Wednesday 8 a.m. in the pub at the hamlet of Lythe
Anna

Jeepers, I sure wish Henri wasn't calling the cops. Now we'll never get to the darned ferry. One look at Nettie and I see that it's hopeless anyway. Even the Fourth of July fireworks knocked her for a loop. It's no surprise real guns shooting at us has laid her so darn low. Geez, I'm scared to death, too. Now we got guns instead of binoculars aimed at us. I sure do wish we were back at Stoneyfield House.

Henri comes back from making his call with Ellie, the pub keeper's wife. Naturally she has a pot of tea for us whether we want it or not.

"The watch constable is on his way to the scene of the crime," Henri tells us. "The doctor has his hands full delivering a baby. I told his wife that ours was a case of better to be safe than sorry. It probably wasn't important that we see him. You know, Ellie, for once that tea looks good, thank you."

Ellie smiles and pours us each a cup.

"I put a tray of scones in the oven with the loaves of bread for the lunches," she tells us. "There's nothing going on until we open at eleven. If you need to lie down, Miss Hicks, please use the bedroom at the top of the stairs as our guest. That's the least we can do."

Nettie struggles to pull herself together. "Thank you, ma'am. I'll be okay in a few minutes. I'm more upset than anything else." She sure doesn't sound okay.

"And who wouldn't be? I can't believe it," Ellie says indignantly. "I saw your headlamp. Someone actually shot both your cars on purpose?"

"I thought people didn't much use guns over here," I can't help saying.

"I suppose that's true. Not many of us own hand guns like you Americans do," she tells me.

"But that was a hunting rifle," Mr. Woodruff adds coming through the door. I really like him but golly, he sure has some accent.

"Nothing like this has ever happened here," he says angrily. "At least not since we got shelled by the German battle ship in 1914. I guess the citizens of North Riding owe you people an apology."

"Hello, Mr. Woodruff," I say. "I was really scared. Thanks a lot for helping us."

"You were very brave, young Anna. I didn't actually do anything. The gunman ran off before I ever got there. Do you have any idea who it might have been, Henry?"

I look over at Henri and wonder what he'll say. I guess he's wondering, too, because he sure takes his time answering.

"The citizens of North Riding don't have anything to do with this, Tom," he finally says. "Ellie, I'm afraid we unwittingly brought trouble to your door. There's nothing we can do about that but we at least owe you an explanation. A week ago, a serial killer walked away from a mental hospital in Coventry. He's made several attempts to make Anna his next victim. We were on our way to the ferry in Newcastle to get her safely out of his reach. We failed. Now we'll just have to depend on the watch to protect her and pray they're up to it."

Ellie and Mr. Woodruff are giving each other a funny look. "Potter and Burnside?" Ellie frowns.

"Potter radioed Scarborough. They're sending someone up to sort things out, Ellie," Tom mutters. "Don't forget, there's young Arthur."

Great, just great. They don't seem to have much faith in their small-town cops. I kind of want to say something about calling Scotland Yard but since Henri doesn't bring it up, neither do I. It's probably just as well. Chief Inspector Sanders is going to be real unhappy with us when he hears about this.

"I need to get the scones out of the oven," Ellie says. Mr. Woodruff follows her out to the kitchen.

I watch them leave. "Geez, I hate to say it, but this isn't good," I say to Henri. "What on earth are we going to do now, for pity's sake?"

Nettie suddenly comes back alive. "We sure as hell aren't going to be safe in Whitby and I'll be damned if I'll go back to Stoneyfield. We only have to keep out of Dawson's way for another six or seven hours. He must have been somewhere he could see over the high wall and watch us pull our trick on Constable Billingsly but he can't know we're going to Newcastle. This is exactly the route we would take if we were trying to get to the A66 to the Lake District from East Ayton without being seen."

"That might be useful if Dawson was still figuring out where we're going and getting there first," Henri says. "He doesn't care where we're going, now that he has armed himself with a rifle. He knows where we are. All he has to do is get to a place with a good view a mile ahead of us and ambush us again."

"Yeah, but what if we're in a car he's never seen before?" I say. "Then we could drive right by him and he would never know."

"And if wishes were horses beggars might ride," Henri points out the obvious. Oh, well.

"Maybe Nettie could buy one?" I suggest. "Gee whiz. There must be something we can do."

"At which of the handy car lots in Lythe, population one hundred and forty two, would that be, Anna?"

Ellie comes back with hot scones and a new pot of tea. Mr. Woodruff's right behind her already munching on one, a big grin on his face.

"Currants," he says. "A pity you people don't come more often. Nellie's baked currants into them."

"They're still hot," Ellie smiles holding out the plate. "Don't burn your fingers."

"What are your plans now, Henry?" Mr. Woodruff asks. "I ought to get on to the ironmongers but I'm not in such a hurry I can't lend a hand if there's anything I can do."

"I'm afraid all our choices are bad ones, Tom," Henri says, standing up and offering his hand.

Choices. It makes me think of Mrs. Wentworth. If I had Craig in front of me right this minute, I know what I'd choose to do. I'd get the Colonel's blasted revolver, pull the trigger and get my choices back. Bang. Bang. Crazy Craig, you're dead. I watch Mr. Woodruff walk over to the big truck out front and want to cry.

"Wait, Mr. Woodruff, come back," Nettie shouts and runs after him. "Will you sell me your lorry for a hundred pounds?"

Wednesday 9 a.m. in the pub at Lithe
Henri

I choke on a mouthful of tea. Buy the Bedford? Nettie drags Tom back to the table. A crazy idea, but there might just be an outside chance we could get away with it. I need to give this some thought.

"I don't know," Tom mutters. "I suppose I could sell it to you but not for a hundred pounds. I'm not a bank robber. Anyway, I doubt that the Bedford could outrun a serial killer even on foot, let alone one on a motor bike."

"Sit down, Tom, and let's try to think this through together," I say, looking over at Nettie. Lord, she needs for me to make this work if I can just find a way.

"For crying out loud, it doesn't have to outrun Crazy Craig," Anna blurts out, her color better than it's been since the crash. "Not if he doesn't know we're in it."

"It doesn't do any good to get safely to Newcastle if he shoots you when you step out of the truck," I tell her. "Anna, all he has to do is go to the ferry in Newcastle and wait for us to appear."

"Geez, Henri. He has no reason to think that we're going to Newcastle," Anna argues. "We never said we were going to Newcastle. We said we were going to Ambleside when we left Scarborough."

"He'd believe we are going to Newcastle for the same reason we are going to Newcastle," I say, bursting her bubble. "Under the circumstances it's the logical move."

We fall silent and Ellie goes back for new pot of tea.

"Henri," Nettie says. "What do you suppose Dawson thinks our circumstances are? We think he overheard us talking at the Nailmaker's Arms in Sheffield but he hasn't had another opportunity since then. All he knows is what he can figure out from watching us through his damn binoculars."

"Nettie's right," Anna bursts out. "He can only know what he sees, Henri. We said we were going to call the cops when we got here. We did. He's seen them come to the house and maybe us going to the cop shop in York. He can see that they have a constable posted but he doesn't know one other thing. Don't you get it? He can't know that we figured out who he is or anything else. Why would he think we are scared enough to skip the country, for pity's sake?"

"Because he saw us go to great lengths to sneak away from Stoneyfield without being seen, that's why," I point out.

"Sure, he saw us sneaking away from the cops but I say that was just to keep them from spoiling our trip. He saw us more or less pull the same trick in Chepstow and Harlech." Gosh, I already talked myself into believing it. "The cops aren't doing us any good anyway, so we decided not to let them go on spoiling our fun. I can see it plain as day. Fourth of July is over and done so we headed on to Ambleside just like we said we would. I can see it really working, by gosh, by golly."

Tom hasn't said anything but he's been avidly following the conversation. He runs his fingers through his thinning hair and clears his throat. "This is all a bit complicated but if I understand what you're saying, this killer has been chasing you all over the country. You have reason to believe that our police aren't able to protect young Anna, so you were trying to smuggle her out of the country when the killer waylaid you. Is that about it?"

"In a nutshell, Tom," I say. "Never mind about the lorry. We had no business getting you involved. I apologize. We were just grasping at straws."

"Well, hold on there, Henry. If young Anna is right, it sounds like it might work. He wouldn't think to look for the girl in the lorry, not even when you got to the ferry. The problem is what do we tell the watch when they come to the pub looking for you?"

He's right, of course. It's only a matter of time before the police get around to us.

"A fatal flaw, I'm afraid," I sigh. "I wouldn't ask you to lie to cover for us even if you were willing."

No one says anything. Tom looks at the stairs and over at the clock on the wall. "What time is Murray getting up, Ellie?" he asks.

"I don't know. It was after two when he came to bed. He usually sets the alarm for ten to have some time to himself before we open at eleven."

"Henry, suppose that when the police come back to talk to you there's no one here but Murray." Tom gives me a sly look. "Ellie leaves Murray a note and the two of us go off to Whitby before he gets up. As long as we stay out of the way until you are safely on the way to Norway at five, no one lies to anyone. When we get back, I tell them I sold you the lorry and that's the last we saw of you. It will be the truth."

"I'll just go change my clothes and write a quick note," Ellie says. "I'll tell Murray that I went to do some secret shopping for his birthday next week."

"I'll help you pack a quick lunch for them so they don't have to stop except for petrol. It's got close to half a tank, Henry. I bought petrol last week. The Bedford gets a hundred miles or so on a tank."

You have to like these North Riding people. I look over at Nettie, who is eagerly undoing her concealed money belt. I don't dare turn down their help. Nettie would never forgive me.

"Tom, Ellie, I don't know what to say ..." I stammer. "It's a hell of a lot to ask of you two."

"Say you'll drive carefully and get these ladies safely on the ferry to Bergen," Tom grins. "Be quick Ellie, we need to get out of here before Murray wakes up."

"We can't take the Bedford with us on the ferry, Tom. You can have it back. We'll leave it for you in the long-stay car park with the keys under the seat. Consider the hundred pounds rent."

Middlesborough

Wednesday 10 a.m. on the way to the Newcastle Ferry
Nettie

There is something ironic about an enormous truck having such a small seat. My left leg is going to sleep. I shift my weight a bit but it doesn't help. Poor Anna. It has to be even worse for her with her long legs; still it's a small price to pay.

Just outside of Middlesborough we stop for petrol. I'm tempted to take the opportunity to get out and stretch until I hear Henri asking the guy pumping our petrol if he's seen a Vincent Motorcycle go by recently. He hasn't, but I change my mind anyway.

I dig out my map. The three of us do the best we can to unfold it across our laps. We're only seventy miles from Newcastle. Even rattling along at a snail's pace in this big heap we'll be there before two o'clock. The ferries leave sometime around five. Check-in time will start ninety minutes before that. We're going to have an hour or so to kill. I hate that, but there's not much we can do about it.

We debate stopping at a pub for a while but Henri talks us out of it. He wants to get the lay of the land before deciding how, when and where to leave the truck. He plans to play it by ear once we get to the ferry terminal, look around and buy our tickets. If worst comes to worst, we can park in the shade and hang out with the truck until we can check in.

When we rumble into Newcastle, we are all stiff and sore. The ferry terminal is easy to find on the Tyne estuary in South Shields. It's still hours until check-in but there are rows of cars already lined up to get on. We stop by a car at the end of one of the first rows. Henri gets out to ask if the driver knows where the long-stay car park is.

"I talked with a nice chap from Canada," he tells us when he comes back. "The long-stay car park is just ahead across from the passenger terminal and to the right of these boarding queues. The Canadian says that there's a pub somewhere within walking distance but unfortunately he couldn't remember the name or which direction."

The car park is enormous. The area designated for lorries is near some weedy-looking trees in the far back behind some stacks of construction materials and it's very nearly empty. It's uncomfortably warm, with acres of concrete around us but the trees do give us at least a bit of shade. Anna and I wait while Henri hikes over to the passenger terminal for tickets. Predictably Anna gets out her sketch pad and wanders over to the water's edge while I hunt for something to read.

Wednesday 1 p.m. in the Newcastle Ferry car park
Anna

This place is really cool for a parking lot. The waterfront here is shabby and disorganized; it will make an interesting picture while we wait for Henri to get back with the tickets. I'm really lost in what I'm doing when a shadow falls across the page. I look up and my heart stops beating.

God, no! Craig stands there grinning down at me, much, much taller than I remember. I wildly look at the empty car park behind him. There's nobody around to hear me but I scream anyway, or try to. Craig grabs me by the hair, tips my head back and stuffs a rag in my mouth. A nightmare deep terror sweeps through me. The cold look in his eyes freezes my soul.

"You guys think you're so smart, don't you?" he sneers. "I hate to break it to you but I'm a great deal smarter. I knew your whole plan the minute the old rattle-trap truck drove away and the truck driver got in the pub keeper's car five minutes later."

Desperate, I look around for someone, anyone. The lorry is too far away, much too far. I can see Nettie sitting on the running board but she's looking down, reading something. The rows of cars over there waiting to board might as well be on a different planet. I'm going to die. Time seems to stop. I'm going to die right here, on this dirty piece of concrete.

Craig pushes me down and kneels on my arms. It hurts. He wants it to hurt. I am totally helpless. With my mouth full of rag, I can barely breathe. Great sobs silently wrack my body. I'm at his mercy but know that he has none.

He gently fingers my hair. "Poor Annie. I'm afraid your beautiful blonde tresses are going to get very sticky."

Oh, God. He really is going to stab me in the throat and laugh.

"I was heartbroken when I thought I'd have to just shoot you, Annie A. But no, this moment was fated, written in the stars seven years ago when you looked right through me as though I didn't exist. How I'm going to love watching the light go out of those bright blue eyes of yours now."

Please, God, this can't be happening. Can't anyone see what's going on back here?

"Want to hear your new rhyme? Sure you do, darling. Listen to this."

I choke and giggle at the same. I was right, he was writing a new rhyme for the deed and now he's actually doing it. I'm about to be dead. My whole life is only another few seconds long.

A long, long knife appears from somewhere, piece of paper jammed up by the hilt. He waves it in front of me and chants the rhyme that must be written there.

"Little Craig Porner, sat in a corner,

Thinking how Anna will die,

He stuck in his knife,

Pulled out her life,

And said what a good boy am I."

I can't breathe, my vision dims and I feel as if my heart is going to explode.

"This isn't the place I would have picked, Anna, my love. It's a goddamned shame I have to let you die a virgin."

I squeeze my eyes shut and offer a wordless prayer as he raises the knife.

"I hate to kill and run, sweetheart, but time's up. Bye bye, Anna A. See you in Hell."

There is a loud echoing in my ears and I feel a great weight as if something heavy is pushing down on my chest. Darkness closes in. It's over. I'm dead.

Wednesday 1 p.m. in the Newcastle Ferry car park
Nettie

I hate sitting here waiting. Sometimes I envy Anna her art. I'm not sure she even understands the concept of waiting. Out comes her sketch pad and she can sit there all day. I stand up, stretch and look over her way. I barely stifle a scream.

There's a tall slim man standing toe-to-toe with her. Good God in heaven, it's Dawson. He has her. I look over and don't see Henri. It doesn't matter, he couldn't get to them in time. Neither can I.

God, no, the bastard has Anna on the ground. I stare at the Colonel's revolver lying on top of Anna's pack. If Henri were here, he'd pick up the gun and blow the bastard to kingdom come. Me. It's me. My God. I have to do it or Annie is dead. I have to pick up that bloody gun and shoot him before it's too late. I can't. I can't. I can't. I'm crying so hard I can hardly see. I pick up the gun but I'm shaking too hard to hold it up, let alone take aim. He's going to kill Anna and it's my fault. He raises his knife. I dimly hear myself scream.

Unconsciously, a deep, forgotten part of me raises the Colonel's Welby. I automatically inhale, hold it and squeeze the trigger. I hear the report and feel recoil as my knees buckle. Dawson's down. Is he still moving? Yes, he is.

Oh, God. I missed. My head's spinning, my sight is dimming, I'm going to black out.

Wednesday 1 p.m. at the Newcastle Ferry car park
Henri

Tickets in hand I start back to the truck. The Canadian flags me down. "My wife remembered the name of the pub," he says, jogging over to me. I turn back to wait for him and the row of parked motorcycles catches my eye. There's a damn Vincent parked at the far end now. Mon Dieu, non. He's here.

I swear like a sailor and push past the Canadian. I point at the motorcycles. "Call the cops," I shout. "Call the bloody cops."

I dodge between the rows of cars and race across the parking lot as fast as I can, faster than I can. The Canadian is right on my heels. Nettie is standing like a statue between the lorry and ... Mon Dieu, no! He's got Anna down. He's raising the knife. I'm not going to make it in time. I screech Anna's name in a voice that isn't even human.

A shot rings out and he falls. Nettie screams and falls, too. Craig is moving. Anna isn't. With his two good legs, the Canadian beats me to them. He yanks Dawson off Anna, hurls him over on his back and puts an unsympathetic foot on his bloody chest. The knife slips out of Dawson's fingers and clatters to the pavement.

Anna is covered with blood and isn't moving. Sobbing unabashedly, I gather her in my arms. Her eyes flutter open. "Am I alive?" she whispers.

"Oh, thank God." I can barely choke the words out.

"What about Nettie?" Anna gasps. "Did he get her, too?"

Epilogue

London

Tuesday, July 13 at the Penn Club
Anna

Golly, what a week this has been. Mom was hell-bent on taking me back home. I don't know why. For crying out loud, everything is over now. Nettie saw Mr. and Mrs. Dawson at the embassy. If Craig doesn't die, they'll put him straight into Broadmoor and he won't be getting out of there on good behavior. I don't know if the U.S. courts will extradite him to stand trial for the Des Moines killings, but whatever happens, he's not going to be stabbing anyone or chasing them around, either.

At any rate, Mom and Jack have given up on the idea of taking me home and have stayed put in Rome. The summer is only half over. Our trip barely got started before Craig spoiled it all. I'm going to love not having to look over our shoulders when we get to Ambleside. Nettie says that Lake District is so beautiful that it inspired famous writers and artists. With any luck, maybe A. Ambleside's painting of Ambleside with be inspired, too.

And how about this. Henri picks up his new MG Friday. When he finishes what he's doing over at Cambridge, he's going to Inverness to see a friend of his. We're going to meet him there when we explore the Highland. Better yet, he says his Scottish friend up there breeds horses.

Do you suppose that I'll get to explore the highlands on horse back? Now that would be an adventure.

I know that we sail for home at the end of August but I have a feeling that Henri is going to get a lot of help from Nettie house hunting. Sooner or later, her work will bring her back here and I'm betting on sooner.

As for me, neither Craig nor Grady are going to make me give up on adventures. There are a lot more summers in my future. I'll be back, or for sure I'll be somewhere exciting. Not just summers, either. I don't know how but somehow I am going to really travel. Before I die of old age, I'm going to go around the world.

There's a tap on the door. I open it a crack. It's Mrs. Burton.

"There's a young gentleman in the lobby asking for thee, Anna," she tells me.

Uh, oh. Why do I think this gentleman will have an Australian accent?

"Thanks, Mrs. Burton," I say. "Tell him I'll be down in a minute." Gosh, I sure wish I weren't wearing this stupid green dress.

"Take thy time, dear. I believe Mrs. Wentworth has taken it upon herself to entertain him."

Holy smoke, forget changing clothes. I better get down there quick or no telling what might happen. That wonderfully unpredictable old lady might just turn our ill-fated romance upside down and inside out.